"Elkjer's first book boasts realistic characters and an exotic yet plausible mystery."

—*Booklist*

"Elkjer's fluid prose camouflages a nicely convoluted plot and a deceptively mild-mannered protagonist.... A solid and entertaining first novel."

—*Library Journal*

"*Hook, Line and Murder* isn't just a good 'first' mystery, it is a very good book, with the capacity to involve a variety of readers."

—*The Snooper*

"...fairly crackles with realism as we get to know the small town and its characters."

—*Mostly Murder*

"The outcome...is stunningly different."

—*Eclectic Book Reviews*

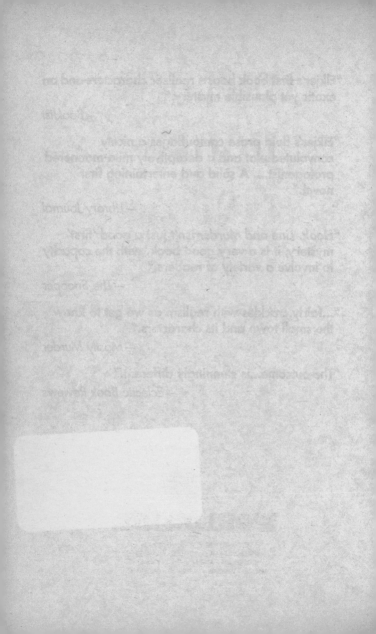

# THOM ELKJER

# HOOK, LINE AND MURDER

## WORLDWIDE.

TORONTO • NEW YORK • LONDON
AMSTERDAM • PARIS • SYDNEY • HAMBURG
STOCKHOLM • ATHENS • TOKYO • MILAN
MADRID • WARSAW • BUDAPEST • AUCKLAND

*For Bessie Stuart and Jim Williams,*
*wherever they are*

**HOOK, LINE AND MURDER**

A Worldwide Mystery/October 1999

First published by Write Way Publishing, Inc.

ISBN 0-373-26323-6

Visit us at www.worldwidemystery.com

**Printed in U.S.A.**

# Acknowledgments

The author would like to thank Joyce Schowengerdt and Harriet Pecot, for illustrative hospitality; Keith Arthur and Kevin Lewis, for the original spark; Amy Kossow, for believing; and Jackie Dennis, for everything.

# ONE

THE COAST ROAD that winds from San Francisco to the Pacific coast bluffs of Sonoma, Mendocino and beyond, is one of California's most beautiful. It takes you into another world, one that seems much farther from the city than a three-hour drive. That world is even stranger when you enter it for the first time as I did: late at night, during a winter storm that lashed the coast with wind and waves for a week. The two-lane highway was a continuous tangle of hairpins, plunges, and steep climbs, and there were few other cars going in either direction.

My destination was the little town of Pomo Bluff, where the Pomo River meets the Pacific Ocean. There I was to research my first assignment as a magazine writer. Unfortunately, it was not as glamorous as it sounds. I needed this assignment badly, and I just drove myself into it—literally. In fact I had not reserved a hotel or anything. There was evidently an old turn-of-the-century hotel on the edge of town, and I would take my chances there. It was, after all, the middle of winter.

At last the trees opened out, the road descended around a hill, and I was crossing a bridge. There was nothing but inky darkness on either side, and I guessed that the bridge spanned a river. I peered through the rain toward the lights ahead, and was soon rewarded with the sight of a rustic, Western-style structure that shown white as a ghost in the rain-blackened night. A hand-painted sign above a covered porch read "Pomo Bluff Hotel."

The narrow strip in front of the hotel was lined with

cars, trucks, and campers, so I pulled around the side of the hotel and parked in a gravel lot. It was still pouring rain, and the wind howled indignantly at the buildings that stood in its way. I walked quickly to the clapboard porch of the hotel, and looked around a moment before going inside. There was not another living soul outside, and not much of a town for a soul to be outside in: a gas station and post office up the road, a diner, a drugstore, and a few shops across the highway. I could tell from the featureless darkness to the west that the ocean was not far off. With a shiver I turned around, pulled open the first door I came to, and stepped inside.

The contrast was deafening. Jukebox music and people shouting to be heard over it, the smoke of cigarettes and cheap cigars, and pairs of eyes narrowed in frank appraisal. "I'm looking for the hotel," I said to a stringy guy in a leather vest.

"You're in it," he said over his shoulder, and turned back to his companions. As my eyes adjusted to the dim light, I noticed a swinging door with a sign that said "Lobby." The door did in fact connect the bar with the lobby of the hotel, but it was the smallest, plainest hotel lobby I ever saw. It was also deserted, except for a small desk with a hand-written sign. The sign directed prospective guests to see the bartender.

Determined to make a better impression on my second visit to the bar at the Pomo Bluff Hotel, I strode for the door and pushed through it manfully. This time the noise, the smoke, and the turning heads were not a surprise. I saw, though, that everyone in the place was dressed like a construction worker, a fisherman, or a drunk. In my creased chinos and Shakespeare sweatshirt, I must have looked like a real city slicker. Which, of course, I am.

A wall of male bodies blocked my view behind the

bar, but there had to be a bartender back there somewhere. Otherwise all these guys had brought their own beer and were making their own drinks. Heads turned to look at me as I walked along the bar, looking for the bartender. One ruddy face peered around at me through a haze of smoke. "Nice night," I said brightly. For some reason this penetrating insight met with a blank stare.

At last, behind the far end of the bar, I found a stout woman with lively eyes. She was wiping her hands on a rag, keeping up her end of at least two conversations, and nodding at someone hollering for more beer.

"Excuse me," I said, raising my voice above the din. "I'd like a room?"

"All full up," the woman replied.

"You sure?"

The woman shrugged, not unkindly but not encouraging either. "You want a room," she said, "you'll either have to get one of the boys to share or go on up the highway."

"The boys?" I asked.

She waved her arm out at the crowd. "Most everybody stayin' here tonight is probably in this room."

I took a look around at the denizens of the bar. The boys. I turned back to the woman. "How far up the highway?"

She looked at my clothes. "About five miles up there's a place on the right, got a big Italian kind of roof on it," she said. "That's probably what you're lookin' for."

I remembered reading about the place, renowned for its cuisine as well as its architecture. "Is that the place with the restaurant?" I asked.

"We got a restaurant here, too," the woman said, pouring whiskey with both hands. "But people don't hear about it."

"I meant—"

"I know what you meant," the woman said. "That's the place. Saint Horace."

I had never heard of this particular holy man, but perhaps he was the patron saint of those requiring rooms without a reservation. I left the bar, got back in the car, and headed on up the highway in the pouring rain. Then, in a fortuitous flash of lightning, the dark forest along the road suddenly included a red tile roof. Such roofs were common in San Francisco, with its Mediterranean climate, but I'd never seen one set in a forest on the north coast. Then again, I had never been on the north coast before.

As I turned into the driveway, my heart fell. The lights were mostly out, the building nearly dark. I steered around the building and into the gravel parking lot. There were plenty of cars, just as at the Pomo Bluff Hotel. This time, though, I understood what that was likely to mean. But I had to ask anyway. It was getting late and I was tired. Once again I opened the car door and stepped out into the rainy night.

This time I was not alone. I heard a car door close, and quickly walked in the direction of the sound. I found the car I was looking for and tapped on the top of the trunk. Then I peered inside to see if the driver had heard me. A moment later the car door opened and the person inside the car stepped out into the night. A wide-brimmed hat blocked its owner's face.

"Good evening," I said into the wind. "Do you work here?"

The brim of the hat lifted. It was a woman, I realized, one who seemed unafraid of the dark, the rain, and a strange man dripping with both. "I'm the innkeeper," she said. "Does that qualify?"

"Absolutely," I said. "Especially if you have a room for a lonely traveler."

"We're full," the woman said. "I just closed up for the night." A gust of wind and rain whipped her coat around her legs.

"Damn," I said. "Now what?"

"Everybody's full," the woman informed me.

"Great," I groaned.

"How far have you come?"

"San Francisco. Drove it straight through. I'm just about shot now and I have to get up first thing tomorrow." In my mind's eye, I imagined sleeping in the back seat of my subcompact sedan: not really conducive to a good night's sleep. I let a more plaintive note come into my voice, the one I used with editors when I needed more time to finish a story. "I just need someplace to dry off and lay down."

The woman looked up at the storm blowing around us. "It's pretty wet," she said. "And it'll get cold now. You don't want to sleep in your car tonight."

"No kidding. Any ideas?"

The woman was silent as she studied my face. With nothing to lose, I studied back. I couldn't see the color of her eyes, but I could see her freckled complexion and straw-gold hair tucked into her hat. The rain ran around the brim of her hat and dripped down past her face, posed in concentration. That was when I realized that water was running down my neck and under my collar.

"You're getting soaked," the woman pointed out. "You should come with me."

"Where is that?"

"I've got a garage on my property," she said. "You can stay there if you like. You have to walk in a ways, but it's warm and dry."

"I'll take it," I said. "How much?"

"You don't have to pay me anything," the woman said. "Follow me and park next to me when we get there."

With that she turned back to her car and pulled out her keys. "Who am I following?" I called out.

"The innkeeper," she called back, and got into her car.

I FOLLOWED HER up the highway, then up a road into the hills, then a half mile down a muddy dirt driveway. When I got out of the car, the woman was waiting by a wooden gate. The rain had stopped, at least for the moment. We walked without speaking as the wind whooshed down from the tree tops. A break in the clouds overhead showed a sprinkling of gleaming stars. "Nice night," I said, meaning it.

Soon we came to a dark structure that looked more like a small barn than a large garage. The woman walked up to a door, flipped on a light switch, and entered the building. Following her inside, I saw that the "garage" was done up as a cozy cottage. Paintings hung on the walls between paned windows spattered with rain. Rugs were scattered on the floor and comfortable furniture was arrayed around the room. There was a small kitchen at one end of the room, an alcove with a New England four-poster bed on another wall, and a door that led into a small bathroom. Through that door I could see a claw-foot tub that I could not help imagining full of hot water and my exhausted body.

"Will this do?" the woman asked, standing in the middle of the room with a brief smile. I pulled my gaze up from her wide mouth to her eyes, which were clear and gray.

"Nah," I said, "I'll just go lay down outside."

"Suit yourself," she smiled, and went to the kitchen to light the fire under a copper pot on the stove.

"Seriously," I said, "this is wonderful. You keep this for company?"

"I live here," the woman said over her shoulder. "You want some tea?"

"Wait a minute," I said. "You said you had a garage."

"I've been working on the permits to build a house ever since I got here," she said. "I might as well try to fly to the moon."

"This is nicer," I pointed out. "Much nicer. But I still don't—"

"You'll have to sleep on the couch," she said, taking off her hat and shaking her hair loose. "I've been told it's not bad for one night."

"I didn't want to impose on you," I began, but she put up her hand.

"I'm an innkeeper," she said. "I take care of people. And you obviously need some taking care of tonight. Now did you want tea or not?"

"Tea."

"Hot bath?" Without meaning to, I cut a glance into the bathroom. "I'll assume that's a yes," she said, and walked into the bathroom. I watched her prepare the bath, until I felt awkward again and forced my eyes away. There was a painting nearby, and it occurred to me that she might have painted it. The scrawled signature in the corner of the canvas told me nothing, and I cast my eye on a nearby desk for a scrap of mail, a business card, anything that might tell me her name.

"My name is Sarah," the woman said, standing in the door of the bathroom. "Sarah Gordon."

I looked at her. "Am I talking out loud, or can you read people's minds?"

"Some things are obvious," she said, and went to the stove.

"I'm Rigel," I said. "Rye for short. This is really kind of you."

"Thanks. What brings you to Pomo Bluff, Rigel?"

"An assignment. A magazine story."

"You're a writer."

"Well, I'm a reporter. But I don't have a newspaper at the moment, so I guess I'm a writer for the time being."

"This is not the season for travel writers up here," Sarah ventured, "so you must be writing something else."

"To tell you the truth," I said, "I got an assignment to do a piece about flyfishing for steelhead—"

"And you just found out that the fish don't run except when a storm blows open the sandbars at the mouths of the rivers."

"That's about it," I admitted. "I got the job because I was available—the first guy they assigned had to cancel for some reason. Then it started raining and a buddy of mine told me I better get up here fast. I borrowed some gear from him, tossed it in the car, and headed up. I should have called around first, but I just assumed there'd be rooms everywhere in the middle of winter."

"Assumptions are dangerous," Sarah pointed out, and handed me a mug of tea.

"This is delicious," I said, sipping the steaming tea gingerly.

"It's ginger tea," she told me. "Would you like to get into your bath?"

I nodded and went into the small bathroom. Candles

flickered on windows sprayed with rain. The scented bath had steamed the mirror, but not before I got a sight of my hair slicked down my forehead and my eyes shot red. I unbuttoned my shirt, then considered shutting the door. But there was quiet music in the other room and Sarah was not in sight, so I left the door open as I undressed and stepped into the water. It was heavenly. I thought briefly of the crowd at the bar in the Pomo Bluff Hotel. "I got the best of you this time, boys," I murmured, and closed my eyes.

When I opened them again, Sarah was standing in the doorway, wrapped demurely in an oversized robe of thick cotton.

"Better?" she asked.

"Words fail me."

"If you're going fishing tomorrow, you should get to sleep pretty soon."

"Was I dozing?"

"About ten minutes. I think you're probably cooked."

I sat up in the tub, but Sarah didn't move to leave. I wanted to thank her, say something meaningful, but it had been a while since I was hot and naked this close to a woman in a bathrobe.

"Listen," I said, "do you have a towel?" She handed me an oversized towel and glided from the room. When I emerged wrapped in the towel, I realized that I had not brought anything to sleep in.

"You can borrow something of mine, or we can make a fire and just warm the room," Sarah offered. "There are plenty of blankets too."

I said "a fire," fell into a nearby chair, and watched Sarah put a match to wood laid in the grate of a cast-iron stove. As the fire began to crackle, I felt my eyelids grow heavy. My mind, though, was full of memories of my college days, when wet winter nights sometimes included attractive women I had only just met.

Sarah stood up and pulled her robe closer around her. "Shall I get you up around seven?" she asked.

"Seven is fine," I mumbled, and watched her walk away into the bathroom. With an effort I pulled myself up from the chair and went to the couch. It was made up with soft flannel sheets and a couple handmade quilts. I looked up from the couch toward the bed across the room. There I noticed something I had not seen before: a stuffed buffalo head hanging on the wall, gazing down protectively over the bed.

"That's Jacob," Sarah said, coming up behind me. "I found him when I was driving out here from the east coast. I just couldn't stand to part with him."

"He's big, he's hairy…"

"And he's handsome," Sarah finished for me. "Although smooth skin is nice, too."

I was suddenly conscious of my own hairless skin, only half covered by a damp towel. I looked around for my clothes, but Sarah had already hung them up near the fire to dry. "Do you need anything else?" she asked me.

"Someone to pinch me so I'll know I'm awake."

"You're awake," Sarah said, pulling back the covers of her bed. "But you won't be long."

I got comfortable on the couch, lying on my back and listening to the rain drum on the roof. I thought again that I should say something meaningful, and closed my eyes to concentrate on just the right phrase…

I WOKE FROM a dream to the smell of bacon frying nearby. I had been on a bridge, in the rain. The dream faded quickly as I remembered the night before, how this woman had taken me home, how I had slept in the same room with her.

"Good morning," she called from the stove. It was barely light outside, but the rain had stopped. "Coffee or tea?"

We ate breakfast sitting at a small table. I kept quiet and watched the morning slowly grow light. When her back was turned, I watched Sarah. The way she moved was intensely pleasing in way I could not quite describe.

"You know," she said, "When a storm blows the mouth of the river open, it also clouds the water for several days afterward. You may not be able to see a thing."

It took me a moment to remember what she was talking about. Then I remembered I was here to go fishing. I snapped fully awake. I had to fish, write about it, and resuscitate a career that was gasping for breath. I took a deep breath and blew it out. "What the hell," I said. "I don't have a choice. I've got to deliver a story one way or another."

"I know a stream a couple miles from here that flows to the ocean," Sarah said. "It clears pretty quick and there's usually a few fish in it most years."

"Do I walk or drive?"

"There's a trail. It's a little rugged, but I think you can make it."

"Just point me in the right direction," I said. "I'll do the rest."

Fifteen minutes later I was standing outside the cabin with a rod case in my hand and a fly pouch on my belt. My hiking boots were still in good shape, mostly because I rarely left the city. My old down vest was snug around my middle now, so I sucked in my gut a bit. The sky was cloudy, but I had put on some sunglasses and my Giants baseball cap. In the photos in the flyfishing magazine I had picked up the day before, every single guy was wearing shades and a hat. I figured if I was going to be a fisherman, even for a day, it wouldn't hurt to look like one.

Sarah led me out to the back of her property to a clearing wet with the passing rain. There she pointed down the ridge and described the path. At last I headed off, turning once to wave. Sarah waved back and then she was gone.

Three hours later I stood by the stream and fought my temper. I had found the stream easily enough, and managed to prepare the rod as well. This progress was due mostly to my friend Doug, who had loaned me his rod and reel and showed me how to set it up. I had also managed to tie the little lure, called a fly, to the end of the long transparent leader. The knot was not as clean as the knots Doug tied, but it held tight when I tugged on it.

The infuriating thing was making the fly, with this impossibly small hook in it, actually *fly*.

My last fishing experience, twenty years before, had been sitting in a boat in a Wisconsin lake and hanging a worm over the side. Sure, I had cast lures a few times, but they were the big wooden ones set with half a dozen huge hooks, the kind that sailed through the air like stones when you brought the rod forward. The tiny weightless thing on the end of this line fluttered helplessly the first time I tried to make it fly, and then hung itself up on my own hat.

I worked it free, got it ready again, and drew the rod back. This time I snagged the hook in a tree. For such a damn small hook, I thought, it sure caught on anything handy. And since the line attached to it was nearly transparent, it took forever to unwind it from the tree branch.

Finally I figured out that I had to focus my eyes not on the tree, but on the air spaces between the twigs. That was where the line was wrapped.

The moment I succeeded in freeing the hook and stepped away from the tree, the line slid back down through the hoops on the rod and tangled itself into a pile at my feet. No amount of cursing made the line thread itself back up the rod, so I had to repeat the process myself.

While I did it I thought about the flyfishing magazine. Maybe there was a little "how-to" feature somewhere inside it, a few simple rules I could follow. Doug, of course, had tried to explain these things to me, but I had waved him off. If men were meant to fish, which obviously they were, then they would have some chromosomes or something to do it with. Having another man explain how to do it was either redundant or insulting.

Finally I was ready again. My anger had subsided and I was mostly feeling defeated. I looked behind me to make sure there were no hook-catching trees waiting to gobble up my line. Just as I was turning back around to look at the stream, I caught sight of someone coming down toward me. Just by the way she moved, I could tell it was Sarah. My heart leaped, but I turned around quickly so that she wouldn't know I had seen her. I could already picture the gleaming fish leaping above the water as Sarah shouted her approval. Clenching my jaw in concentration, I carefully drew back the rod and snapped it forward. The next sensation was a sharp bite into my backside, painful enough to make me curse out loud. The rod jerked to a stop in front of me. I had set the hook into my own bottom.

Sarah shouted, all right. "You caught a big one!" she called, and then laughed infectiously.

"You should have seen the one that got away," I called back. She laughed again, and came down beside me. The sun was just breaking through the clouds and the tree tops high above on the ridge. Sarah was flushed with cool air and the long walk, and the high color in her cheeks offset the cool gray of her eyes and golden lights in her hair. The frustration of the morning ebbed as I looked at her, and I carefully worked the hook out of my jeans. When Sarah got a look at the fly, her face changed.

"You're fishing an elk hair caddis?" she asked, surprised.

"What's a caddis?" I asked.

"This," she said, pointing at the brown, austere fly, "is made for trout fishing. Steelhead chase big, bright things with silver eyes."

I opened the plastic box of flies in the pouch on my belt. Sarah peered into it. "Here they are," she said.

"But this one *looks* like a fly," I said, holding up the wet caddis.

"It doesn't matter what looks like a fly to you," Sarah said. "You're not the fish. If you want to catch anything, you've got to look at the fly from the fish's perspective. That's why it's called presenting the fly—you have to present it so that the fish sees fish food, not just some brown thing designed to capture him." With quick glances, she looked up and down the stream. "And I don't think a steelhead is going to hang around in this part of the stream, either. We've got to move up or down."

I listened quietly. Evidently, among the rest of her considerable charms, she was also an experienced fisherman. Or fisherwoman. When she paused to look at me, I cleared my throat.

"So nice to see you again," I said drily.

She smiled at me and folded her arms. "I'm sorry," she said. "I should leave you alone to catch some more big ones."

I laughed and looked down at the rod in my hand. "This is harder than it looks, you know?"

Sarah looked at me, then folder her arms. "You mean you've never done this before?"

I was about to launch into a glib riposte when I remembered how this woman had taken me in and rescued me the night before. I still wanted to impress her, but I no longer wanted to lie. "This is the first time," I admitted.

"I thought you said you were doing a story about flyfishing."

"I am," I said. "If this wasn't a last-minute fill-in, I'd have had some time to practice first. But what the hell, fishing is fishing, isn't it?"

"How can you write about something you've never done?"

"Well, in the first place," I explained, "writers write all the time about stuff they don't know about. It's called reporting. In the second place, that's why I'm here: to actually do it, at least once. And I've got to do it today and tomorrow, because the story's due next week."

"Fly fishing is a little different from spinning rods," Sarah pointed out.

"So I've noticed."

"Well then," she said, "I guess I'd better hike up home and leave you to your work." She turned to go, but I quickly put a hand on her arm.

"Do you have to go?"

"The only thing worse than having trouble flyfishing,"

she said, "is having trouble with someone watching you. I'd just be in the way."

"Not necessarily," I said. An intriguing idea had invaded my mind. No one was around to see us, and she was mighty attractive besides. I would not force her to go along, either. She could say no if she wanted. But if I didn't ask, how could she say yes? "What did you have in mind?" she asked.

"Well," I began slowly, "we could..."

"We could what?"

I swallowed hard. "You could teach me how."

"How to fish flies?"

"Yeah. Just show me 'til I get the hang of it."

Sarah's mouth blossomed into a smile of pure delight. It was the kind of smile women use when men do something uncharacteristically sweet or unbelievably stupid. What could I do? I smiled back.

"Well," she said, "I could show you a few things. If you're willing to learn."

"I'm willing to learn if you think you can teach me."

"We'll find out," she said. "First we go upstream." I gathered up my gear and followed Sarah along the stream, noticing how slowly and quietly she moved as we neared a smooth-flowing pond with a soft bank.

When we reached the spot, Sarah stood still a long time. I became impatient and opened my mouth to speak. At that moment she put a hand on my arm and pointed toward the water with her other hand. I looked quickly, but saw nothing except flowing water. I shrugged silently. She held her hands more than a foot apart. I looked down at the water again, wondering how I had missed seeing a fish that large.

Now Sarah motioned for me to give her the end of the line with the fly on it. Without making a sound, she opened the fly box. She selected a bright green fly with a long body, tied it onto the transparent end of the fishing line with practiced fingers, and bit off the end of the knot. Then she knelt down and held the fly under water. When it was well soaked, she stood, played out some line, checked behind her, and raised the rod. With a series of short casts she played out more line, the fly snapping back and forth in the air above her, each time reaching farther out over the water.

With her last cast the line arched out and floated down toward the surface of the pond. The fly landed first, settling down onto the water just above where the stream flowed into the pond. The transparent leader floated down afterward, making almost no impression on the surface, and the rest of the bright neon green line laid down on the water in a soft S. I looked at Sarah in amazement, but she did not notice. She was watching the fly intently, her lower lip curled softly under her front teeth.

I turned back to the water and watched as the fly flowed gently along just beneath the surface of the water. Suddenly the leader disappeared beneath the surface and the green neon line straightened out. Sarah pulled the rod back firmly, and I shouted aloud when I caught sight of a silvery flash of color roil the surface of the water. Sarah held the taut line in her hand, slowing the pace and then holding the line tight in her hand. Finally she began taking in the line a little a time, her eyes never straying from the water.

A moment later she laid the rod gently on the bank and took the line in both hands. She played it in hand over hand until the fish was clearly visible, thrashing back and forth in the shallows like a bolt of shining mercury. Sarah leaned over the water and held the fish in one hand while freeing the hook from its mouth with the other. I felt both joy and longing when she released the fish and it shot away and disappeared in the depths of the pond.

"That was amazing!" I exclaimed, but Sarah shook her head.

"A small one," she said. "It'll be harder now." She handed me the rod and shook the fly out loose into the water. "Your turn," she said, and I took my position. She moved over next to me and put a hand on my arm. I fought to concentrate on the rod, not on her touch.

"Start here," she said quietly, positioning my arm forward and angled upward. "Take it back to here," she said, taking my arm back only a little ways. "Then bring it forward to here," she finished. "Ten o'clock, one o'clock, eleven o'clock."

"Ten o'clock, one o'clock, eleven o'clock," I repeated. I tried it, but cast too hard and watched the fly peak almost directly overhead and float down in front of me only a foot or two out on the pond.

"Too much wrist," Sarah said. I tried again, but again the fly fluttered helplessly overhead. I fought frustration and tried a third time, with nearly identical results.

"You're trying to overpower it," she said quietly, and moved behind me. She came up close, her right hand on my wrist and her left hand on my hip. "Keep your wrist stiff," she said, speaking softly from behind my ear. I could feel her breath on my neck, feel her body parallel to mine. I fought to keep my attention on fishing. "The motion is all in your elbow," she continued. "Let the rod do the work."

Slowly I raised the rod and took a deep breath. Sarah settled against me more closely, our bodies becoming one. "Ten o'clock," she breathed, her lips almost brushing my ear.

"Ten o'clock," I echoed.

"One o'clock," our voices low, our arms going back together in a single fluid motion.

"Eleven o'clock," our bodies leaning back and then rocking forward as the line snapped out over the water. I watched in exultation as the fly floated down into the center of the pond.

"Hold still!" Sarah uttered in my ear, and pressed herself around me to contain my excitement. I felt my heart beating, Sarah's breath on my cheek, our bodies clasped tight on the bank. The fly sank slowly beneath the surface. I held the rod out in front of me, waiting with trembling excitement for the moment when it would jerk and jump.

# TWO

AN HOUR LATER I had not caught any fish, but I was hooked. When Sarah said she had to get back home, I didn't hesitate to pack up and go with her. On the way back up the ridge, I asked her where she learned to fish. She told me about her childhood in Maine, where she had helped her father raise her younger sister. Her mother had died in the second childbirth, and from then on their father had taken both girls on his annual summer fishing trips.

"My dad was a wonderful man," she concluded, "but he was never the same after my mother died. I think he finally died of a broken heart himself."

"Your father's dead, too?" I asked. It did not seem possible that a double dose of death could visit such a beautiful morning. Sarah only nodded. When she asked me a moment later about my writing career, I understood that she was changing the subject.

"I used to be with the *San Francisco Call*," I told her. "The morning paper."

"We get it up here," she informed me.

"Oh. Well, I broke some stories that held the front page for almost a year, I got a raise, I got a Pulitzer nomination." It had been a great time, full of passionate feelings, intrepid reporting, and tens of thousands of avid readers. But it all changed so fast.

"When the corruption scandals hit the state capital," I continued, "the paper sent me up there. Within two weeks I tapped into this incredible source who knew everyone and told me everything. The politicians, of course, were furious, and the reporters who had been there a while were so jealous they couldn't see straight. Before long everyone was out to get me. Finally they figured out who my source was, and things went to hell from there.''

"Who was he?'' Sarah asked.

"She,'' I said. "A senate aide who worked for one of the most corrupt politicians of all. She finally wanted to come clean. The problem was that she had been collecting his bribes and laundering the money for years. People said I should have exposed her, too. They said she was guilty like the others and I was protecting her in exchange for sex.''

"Were you?''

I glanced up at Sarah. "It wasn't *for* sex, it was because of sex,'' I said. "I kept her identity secret because she had already been through hell. Her boss had been forcing her to have sex with him for years, by threatening to expose her. I was trying to do my job as a reporter and also give this woman a break. But we both got turned out, as they say.''

"What happened to her?''

"She left the state, went back to Kansas or wherever. I don't know.''

"And what did you do?''

"The paper called me back to San Francisco and put me on a lifestyle beat,'' I said. I didn't bother to conceal my disgust. "I tried it for a few months, but it was a joke. They wanted me to write about hemlines. *Radicchio*. Rich people's parties!'' My final shout hung in the cool morning air.

"So what happened then?'' Sarah asked.

"When I asked for another assignment, they started

talking about my 'journalistic judgement' and how I was hard to deal with. I got mad and made a scene. Next day they used an obscure clause in the union contract and fired me. I said fine, I'll go to work for a real paper. I went over to the city editor for the afternoon paper, but of course a phone call travels faster than you can cross the street. No one there would even talk to me. I sent out a couple dozen résumés, all over the state, and didn't get a call. The word had gone out, and that was that."

"I think it was very brave of you to protect that woman," Sarah said, "even if you got fired."

"Yeah, well, unemployment is no fun either," I informed her. "After I missed a rent payment I called my friend Doug, the guy who loaned me his rod, and asked if he could help. He pulled some strings with some people from England who were starting a new magazine. You'll never guess what Doug told them."

"What?"

"He said I was a lifestyle writer from the *San Francisco Call.* They were very impressed, said it would probably take me just a few hours to bang out a piece on the hot new hobby for the in crowd."

"Fly fishing?" Sarah was incredulous.

"Yup," I assured her. "It's the new thing. But writing is the *only* thing I know how to do, and this story is the only writing job I could get. If I don't make it work I'm in serious trouble."

When we got back to the house, Sarah went out to her car to get me some maps of the local area. I went into the bathroom to wash my hands, then came out again when I heard the phone ring. I couldn't see Sarah out the window, but I knew she would be right in, so I picked up the phone and said hello.

There was no answer, but I could tell that whoever had

called was still on the other end of the line. I spoke up quickly. "Do you want Sarah?" I asked. Again there was no answer. "She's right outside," I said. "I'll get her." But before I could put the phone down there was a click and then a dial tone.

When Sarah came in I told her about the call. She reacted without surprise, gliding past me to hang up her coat. "People don't expect a man to answer the phone here," she said.

"That's hard to believe," I said, half to myself.

Sarah turned to face me. "I've gotten used to being single," she said evenly. "It's surprising to me that I took to you as quickly as I did. I thought I had forgotten how."

"I thought I had forgotten, too."

We stood there silently for a moment, then Sarah held up the maps. "You can get these at the drugstore," she said. "And while you're there, get a pair of polarized sunglasses. They'll make it a lot easier to see the fish beneath the surface."

"Does that mean it's time for me to go?"

She nodded. "Even innkeepers have their own lives, I'm afraid."

"Well, if this is goodbye…"

"It's been fun," she said.

"It's been more than fun," I said. "You've been a life-saver. And there is something else."

She cocked her head. "And what might that be?"

"I really like you."

She looked at me with a smile that seemed to hold back as much as it let out. "I like you, too," she said. "But I'm afraid I'm not relationship material at the moment."

"Everybody is relationship material," I said. It was a

stupid generalization, but I couldn't help myself. Sarah laughed lightly.

"Go write," she said, and held the door open.

I FOUND THE MAPS I wanted, and some polarized sunglasses, in the little drugstore I had seen the night before. Across the street, the hotel looked even shabbier in the daylight than it did at night. Down a little farther, I found a small bookstore with a coffee counter and a rack of current magazines. I got some coffee and sat down at a small table near the window and leafed through the fishing magazine I had brought with me. The articles made more sense to me now, but there wasn't much I could steal for my own story.

I put the magazine aside, looked out the window, and waited for ideas to come. When I remembered Sarah's fish breaking the surface of the water, I paused to marvel once again. It seemed scarcely possible now to catch a wild animal you could barely see, with a line as fine as a human hair. Fine as a straw-gold hair, glinting with sunlight. Sunlit flecks of color in cool gray eyes, eyes that could see under water...

A while later I realized I hadn't been thinking about fishing for some time. My coffee was cold, the page of my notebook was still blank, and I was hungry. I left the bookstore, ate a sandwich at the deli next door, and went back to the drugstore for one of the bouquets of flowers I had seen there earlier. When the counter girl asked if I wanted a ribbon tied around the bouquet, I nodded. She smiled and I blushed.

Driving north in daylight, with the ocean stretching away to the left, I noticed the roof of the inn much sooner. As I measured the distance, I spotted a car turning into the inn's driveway just before I got there. To my surprise, I recognized the car: it was Sarah's. I turned in after her. But when I got up to the parking lot where I had met her the night before, her car was not there.

I looked around, then drove down to the far end of the lot. There I found another, narrower driveway that headed up into the trees behind the inn. I hesitated a moment, then went up. On either side of the drive, I saw small cottages built in the same Italian style as the main building. Each had a small terrace on the ocean side, but Sarah's car was not parked in front of any of them. It was not until I reached the end of the drive, well above the inn and past a grove of redwood trees, that I spotted Sarah's car. It was parked next to a sleek black sports car outside the most remote of the cottages. Suddenly, and with a rush of embarrassment, I remembered the phone call I had intercepted that morning.

Before I could look around for a way back down the hill, I noticed someone moving across the porch of the cottage. It was Sarah, greeting a young woman and going inside. I hesitated, not sure if I should take off or stay. I picked up the bouquet of flowers in my hand and looked at it. Romance had never been my strong suit, even when I held good cards. I just wanted to thank her, let her know that she had helped a guy out of a tough spot.

When I looked up again, the young woman was stumbling out onto the terrace and covering her mouth with both hands. She leaned over a railing, her dark hair falling around her face. I could not be sure, but it looked like she was about to be sick. A moment later Sarah reappeared and moved quickly to the other woman. She put her arms around her, stroked her head, and seemed to be trying to calm her down. Without thinking, I jumped from the car and ran up the path. Both Sarah and the young woman looked up at me in surprise, and Sarah spoke.

"Rigel, what are you doing here?"

"What happened?" I asked. Suddenly the younger woman leaned over the railing. This time there was no doubt about her being sick. Sarah quickly attended to her. I went to the doorway of the cottage and looked in to see what had caused so much upset on a serene forest hillside. On the queen-sized bed in the middle of the room was a man lying face down, apparently naked under the bedclothes that partially covered him. A strong odor issued from the room, and I stepped back outside to get a breath of air. I glanced at the two women, then went back into the room.

The air was close and warm with artificial heat. I pulled open some curtains and opened a window. The winter sunlight that came into the room gave everything a flat quality. When I turned back to the bed, I saw that the sheets were stained with what appeared to be regurgitated food. I laid Sarah's bouquet of flowers on a chair and picked up the man's wrist. The skin was cold, the arm was stiff, and there was no pulse.

I got a glass of water from the bathroom, went back outside onto the terrace, and gave the water to Sarah. The young woman was now sobbing and coughing, and Sarah made her drink the water before letting her talk. Evidently the young woman was the day innkeeper. She had been called up to the cottage by a housekeeper, who wanted to clean the room but could not rouse the occupant of the cottage. She had called Sarah, brought a passkey up to the cottage, and waited there.

At this point in the story the young woman glanced through the door of the cottage and began crying again. Sarah gently guided her down off the terrace onto the path where she could not see into the house. "Liz, I need you to get it together," she said quietly. In the still air on the hillside, her voice was clear and firm. "I want you to go down to the inn and call the diner. The sheriff almost always has lunch there on Fridays. His name is Fred Stone—Sheriff Stone. The diner's number is by the phone behind the bar. Can you do that for me?"

The young woman nodded through her tears and asked Sarah what she should tell the sheriff. "Tell him we had a medical emergency at the inn and we need him to come up to Hillhouse right away," Sarah said. "He'll call the ambulance. And don't tell anyone else what happened. At least not yet."

Liz collected herself and headed down the path. I came down to Sarah. "You okay?" I asked. She nodded. Neither of us spoke for a moment, then we both offered to stay and meet the sheriff.

Sarah shook her head firmly. "It's my responsibility," she said. "You can go."

"I'm staying," I said.

She looked confused now, and I realized she might not feel as calm as she looked. "I'm sorry," she said, "did I ask you why you were here? I mean, did you need something?"

My heart melted. "Hang on," I said, and went up into the room to get the flowers. Inside the door, I stopped. I had seen my share of dead men while working for the paper, but usually they were in a hospital bed surrounded by friends, or lying alone in a back alley on a frigid night. I had never seen someone dead quite like this.

Sarah appeared in the doorway. Neither of us moved or spoke for a moment. On a table by the door, I found a wallet and extracted a driver's license. "Richard G. Shammey," I said aloud, "from San Francisco." The face that looked back at me from the license was dark, handsome, confident. I went around to the far side of the bed. The face I saw was the same, but with the eyes closed, the mouth contorted. The half of the face that was turned up was bloodless white; the side turned down was blotchy red.

"I checked him in last night," Sarah said quietly. "He came in alone, got his key, and went up. He had a reservation for the weekend."

I turned back to the bed and gently pulled the bedclothes back. On the man's wrist, I saw a medical-alert bracelet stamped with bold letters:

SUBJECT TO ANAPHYLACTIC SHOCK.
NOT DRUNK. MAY BECOME INCOHERENT OR
LOSE CONSCIOUSNESS. TAKE TO HOSPITAL.

"Look at this," I said. Sarah came up next to me and looked down at the bracelet. "Anaphylactic shock is like an allergic reaction, except more serious. A friend of mine has the same thing. Did this guy eat anything last night?"

"If he did he brought it with him," she said. "Or maybe he ate some breakfast. There's a basket we bring to each room in the morning."

I crossed the room to a table. There was the basket, a paper wrapper and some crumbs, the remains of a muffin. Inside the basket was another muffin still in its wrapper, some granola, a small carton of milk, and some fruit. "How many muffins to a basket?" I asked. Sarah held up two fingers. "You know what's in them?" I asked her.

"We can ask in the kitchen," Sarah said. "We make them here."

I examined the remaining muffin and the discarded wrapper. "You know my friend Doug, who I told you about before?" I said. "If he eats certain kinds of nuts, or anything made with them, he could die. He wears one of those bracelets, too."

There was no response, and I looked over at Sarah. She was staring dumbly at something on a chair, as if unable to take her eyes off it. I had seen people go into shock around death, and I moved quickly to her side. She was staring at a bouquet of flowers tied with a ribbon.

"Um, I brought these for you," I said, plucking the bouquet from the chair and presenting it to her. Her face changed once, twice, and then settled into a lopsided smile as she took the flowers.

"I'm sorry," she said, "I should be more—"

"You don't have to say anything," I interrupted. "I just wanted to thank you for last night."

"I'm sorry you had to see this."

"Don't worry about me," I assured her. "I'll be fine."

Sarah just nodded, looked at her flowers, and stumbled out the door into the cool quiet of the afternoon.

THE SOUND OF TIRES on gravel heralded the arrival of a green and tan county car with SHERIFF in bold letters on the side. Sarah and I were waiting together outside the cottage. County Sheriff Fred Stone was a barrel-chested man slightly under medium height. He wore his sheriff's jacket over jeans and a starched plaid shirt. He looked at me and then addressed Sarah worriedly. "What's the situation?"

She stood aside and gestured into the room. Sheriff Stone went past her into the cottage. Sarah and I looked in through the open doorway. He stood still, gazing down at the body, and then blinked a few times in succession.

I glanced at Sarah, who was also looking at the dead man with strange absorption. It was as if they could not believe he was dead. When the sheriff finally looked up, it was not at Sarah, but me. He blinked again, and I suddenly had the feeling that he was confused and didn't know what to do. I opened my mouth to speak, but he turned and addressed Sarah.

"This how you found him?"

"Yes," Sarah said. "Actually, it was the day innkeeper, Liz Rizzo."

"The new girl," the sheriff said.

"She's from Mendocino," Sarah said. "She started last month."

"Tough thing for a kid like her," Stone said, half to himself.

"His wallet is there on the table," I said. "Sarah checked him in last night and apparently he hasn't been out of the room since."

Sheriff Stone made no move to examine the wallet or the license. "You know the guy?" he asked me instead.

"No. I'm a friend of Sarah's."

He gave a short laugh. "I don't believe I know you," he said. "I thought I knew everybody up here."

"I'm visiting. For the weekend."

"Oh, I see. Just get in?"

"Last night, actually."

"You staying in one of the other cabins here?"

I hesitated. Sarah spoke. "He stayed with me," she said.

Stone turned and locked eyes with Sarah. For the second time that day, I wondered if Sarah had more men in her life than she was admitting.

"You know," I said, "it may be that the guy died from something he ate."

Sarah pointed to the medical alert bracelet. "It says he has some kind of allergy," she said.

The sheriff walked around the bed and had a look for himself. "I never saw one of these before," he admitted.

"I got a prescription for a bracelet like that myself once," I told him, "but I never actually went and got it."

"What was it for? This?" Stone was pointing to the dead man's arm.

I shook my head. "It was for, um, poison oak," I said. Sarah and Stone looked at me. "I used to get it real bad when I was a kid," I mumbled. "The doctor said it would remind me not to go into the woods, but I didn't want the other kids to know."

"Ahh," Stone said, nodding.

"Plus it was a *bracelet*," I pointed out.

"They would have teased you pretty hard."

"Exactly. So I just stayed out of the woods."

There was an awkward moment of silence, in which Sarah looked understanding and Stone looked down at his shoes. Then he straightened up and looked around the room. "So the idea is, he ate something and died before he could throw it up?"

"Well, it looks like he…"

"Oh, yeah," Stone said, peering over at the sheets. "Maybe he tossed it up after." He glanced at Sarah. "Did he eat here last night?" She shook her head. Stone pointed to the breakfast table. "Is that the usual basket?"

Sarah looked into the basket. "It looks like it. I'd have to check."

"Right," Stone said, but he didn't move or give any instructions. Instead he blinked a few more times, and I had the feeling again that he was unsure what to do.

"You know," I said, "I think we need to get a doctor

up here, check the contents of the muffins, determine cause of death, that kind of thing.'' I said it as offhand as I could, but immediately I felt the air chill. I looked toward the window, but no breeze was coming in.

"Was this open like this?" Stone asked.

"I opened it," I said. "The smell was pretty strong at first."

The sheriff turned to face me. "I'd appreciate it if you wouldn't alter the scene anymore until I've had a chance to look around a little bit."

"I wasn't altering the scene, I was—"

"Was anything else moved or changed?" Stone interrupted. He was asking Sarah, though, not me.

"No," she said meekly. "We were just trying to help."

"If you want to help," the sheriff said, "why don't you step down to the kitchen and find out what was in that basket." I had a few other observations to share with the sheriff, but Sarah gave me a look that did not allow for argument. I shrugged, and we went out and down the path toward the inn. When we were out of earshot, I slowed down and turned to Sarah.

"What was that all about?"

"You offended him!" she exclaimed.

"But he didn't know what was going on. He didn't know what to do!" I protested. "We *were* helping."

"Fred is not stupid," Sarah said advisedly. "He just goes a little slower than I imagine you all do in the city. I thought it was nice what he said about the poison oak, about being teased by the other kids."

I frowned and folded my arms across my chest, but I kept quiet. The more I thought about it, the more I realized she was right and I was wrong. Fortunately, I didn't have to endure that painful realization for long.

When we reached the inn, my eyes widened. Floors, walls, and ceilings of polished wood glowed with light from a massive stone fireplace. Exposed beams provided a rustic quality, as did comfortable furniture positioned to give the best views through ocean-facing windows. The small, elegant bar that doubled as a reception desk gave onto a small room with small tables and comfortable chairs. The whole effect was sleek and stylish yet somehow still masculine. I wanted to move in and stay for about five years.

Liz appeared, nervously pulling on the ends of her long brown hair. She was younger than Sarah by about ten years, I guessed, with dark eyes and a friendly figure. In Liz's wake came the young housekeeper who had wanted to clean the Hillhouse cottage. She spoke little English but her story matched what Liz had described. Sarah dismissed her and they headed for the kitchen. It was small and compact, with ingredients and utensils crammed in every possible space. Sarah soon found the breakfast cook, a young man named Firenzio who spoke no English at all.

"I can't fish, but I can speak a little Spanish," I said to Sarah.

"That's okay," she said, and turned to Firenzio. In fluent Spanish she asked him what he used to make the muffins in the morning.

He immediately launched into an explanation, accompanied by a pantomime of pulling out various ingredients. One item he reached for was an unlabeled bottle above the griddle. It appeared to hold cooking oil, as did several bottles on the same shelf.

"We buy bulk oil in barrels, but there's no room for them in the kitchen so we refill these smaller bottles," Sarah told me. "I know that one of these contains olive oil, but I don't know about the others." She called over a chef and asked about the menu for the previous evening. The salad, he said, had been dressed with raspberry vinegar and walnut oil. "This is it right here," he said, and held up one of the bottles of oil. Sarah turned to Firenzio and asked him if it was the oil he had used in the muffins.

The young man colored with fear and confusion. He mimed making muffins in a great hurry while he explained that time is greatly short in the morning, especially when the inn is full with patrons and it is necessary to make many muffins in a time very short. He was not certain which bottle he took down from the shelf, but all were full of ingredients most excellent and tasteful. If the muffins were bad, it was no one's fault but his own.

When he finished, the young man asked Sarah if he was going to be fired for making bad muffins. She assured him that he was in no trouble, but he did not relax until she put a hand on his shoulder and thanked him for his hard work.

Back in the bar, Sarah sighed. "What do you think?"

"I think he probably used the walnut oil. But I don't think we should acquaint him with the consequences of his error."

Sarah sighed and shook her head sadly. "I should go tell Fred," she said. "I'll be right back."

"You want me to come up?" I asked. She gave me a look that said "better not," and left. I watched her go. A moment later Liz reappeared.

"How are you feeling?" I asked.

"Better," she said. "I never saw anything like that before."

"It's always hard the first time."

The young woman's eyes widened. "You've seen dead people before?"

"A few times," I said. "When you're a reporter for a big city newspaper, it comes with the territory."

"Wow!" Liz said. "I never met a reporter, either."

"We're just like everybody else," I informed her, "except more curious."

"Well, welcome to St. Horace."

I thanked her and told her my name. Her surname was Italian like the inn, and I remarked on it. We fell to chatting about the inn's operation, and I found myself asking what time Liz left the basket at the cottage, what time the housekeeper first went to the cottage to make up the room, and what time she asked Liz to wake the man on the bed.

"See what I mean about being curious?" I asked. "When you've been a reporter as long as I have, you just start asking questions about everything, even when it's none of your business."

"Well, it's okay," Liz assured me. "This is our one slow time of the day."

The phone behind the bar rang, and Liz answered. It was someone making a reservation for dinner. When Liz was done with the call, I informed her that according to Sarah, the man they had found that afternoon had a reservation for the entire weekend.

"Oh, God," Liz moaned. "He probably has a dinner reservation, too." She reached down below the bar and pulled out a small wooden box filled with reservation cards. Liz showed me how the person who took the reservation recorded the guest's name, address, phone number, and license plate number, plus related information about previous stays, dinner reservations, and so on. Only the license plate number caught my attention. It was a specialized plate, what in California is called an "environmental plate" because part of the extra money you pay is supposed to go to environmental clean-up or protection projects. I believe the generic term is "vanity plate," which captures the reason most people really get them. Anyway, Shammey's plate seemed to indicate his line of work: RT DEALR. When I asked Liz Rizzo who took the original reservation, she didn't hesitate.

"It's Sarah's handwriting," she said. "See how beautiful it is?" Liz continued to praise Sarah's organization, her teaching ability, her ability to pacify irritated guests—the list went on and on.

I remembered that Liz had started at the inn only recently. "Was it Sarah who hired you?"

"Oh, yes," Liz said, "and she's been teaching me the job ever since I started. That's why I called her today before I went in that room. She always tells me, it's better to bug her on her time off than make a big mistake."

"You didn't call her late this morning, did you?"

She shook her head without looking up from her cards. The phone rang again and I let my mind wander back up the hill to Sarah and Sheriff Stone. I wanted to know what was happening there, but something rooted me to my spot at the little bar. Finally my eye lit on a framed certificate hanging behind it. The certificate named the inn's official mushroom gatherer. When Liz got off the phone, I pointed to the certificate. "Now that," I said, "is a new one on me. Who certifies mushroom gatherers?"

Liz didn't know the answer to that question, but she knew the mushroom gatherer himself, a local man named Carl Larkin. Evidently one of the things the inn was known for was its use of exotic local mushrooms in its cuisine, and Carl Larkin was the man who provided them.

While Liz bragged about the inn's restaurant, I made a mental note about the mushroom business. As much as I detested the whole idea of "lifestyle" journalism, I had to pay the rent. I would have to find out more about the use of wild mushrooms in contemporary cuisine.

"...and we got the best one there is," Liz was saying enthusiastically. "I mean, Carl knows *everything* about mushrooms, and he knows where they all grow up on the ridge. I mean, he knows his way around in the woods better than just about anyone."

"Did you ever go out with him?"

"You mean on a date?" Liz asked, her eyes wide.

"No," I said, "I meant gathering mushrooms."

"Oh," she said, deflated. "No. But I bet he would take me."

"I just wondered where he goes, if there are special places or something."

"Oh, gosh, I don't know. He was up the hill just this morning, so I bet there's mushrooms all over up there."

"The mushroom guy was here this morning?" I asked. "By that cottage...?"

Liz's face darkened. "No," she said, "above there."

"How far above?"

Liz thought about it. "Not that far. After that it's just forest."

"You ever see him there before?"

"He's here all the time bringing mushrooms in before dinner," she said, "but he always comes in his truck, in the afternoon."

"Did you talk with him?"

"Oh, no," she said. "He was climbing the hill, so he didn't even know I saw him. I was picking up the breakfast baskets."

"How did you know it was him?"

"He's got this bright red hair," Liz giggled. "If you see that red hair sticking out of his cap, you can always tell it's Carl."

# THREE

BEFORE I COULD ASK LIZ any more questions about the red-haired mushroom gatherer, her duties called her upstairs and my curiosity called me back to the cottage up the hill. It appeared from his car, his license plate, and driver's license that Shammey was a successful San Francisco art dealer. If so, then I was the only newspaperman from the city who knew of his recent demise, alone and far from home. Even if it were no more than a few paragraphs in the morning editions, it would be an exclusive, a scoop. Newspaper reporters were trained to spot things like this and call them in from wherever they were—but of course I didn't have a paper to call in to. I stopped on the path and tried to think: how could I use this break, small as it was, to my advantage?

As I pondered this question, I noticed the filtered amber light that descended between tall evergreen trees and pointed up the hill. I sometimes walked in Golden Gate Park on winter afternoons when the light was like this, and I soon resumed my walk up the hill. As I approached the cottage, I heard Sarah and the sheriff talking. When I stepped inside, though, they were silent. Sarah stood with her arms folded and her lips pressed tight. The sheriff had the body exposed on the bed, and evidently had been going through the room with some care. The dead guy's suitcase was open on the floor, the furniture looked like it had been moved around, and all the lights were on.

"Ambulance will be here in a minute," the sheriff said without looking up. "Mind waiting outside?"

I looked at Sarah, and she gave me a quick nod advising me to go along. I stepped outside again, wondering about the tension I was suddenly feeling. Then my professional curiosity took over. I went back down the steps to the black sports car with RT DEALR license plates. It was locked and the windows were tinted on the inside, so I could not explore the vehicle in any detail. I did notice something on the floor behind the passenger seat: a white styrofoam cup with a plastic lid, the kind that roadside coffee shops gave to people on the go.

As I was about to leave the car and walk up around to the back of the cottage, the sun dipped below a heavy branch and a slender shaft of musty light illuminated the back seat of the car. On the rim of the white cup was a dull red smudge, roughly the shape of a woman's lower lip. I peered at the cup until the shaft of light slid away. I looked up to see the ambulance coming slowly up the driveway.

When the ambulance guys went into the cottage to remove the body, Sarah and Sheriff Stone came out. He was carrying the suitcase. I cocked my head toward the car. "The guy may have had someone with him last night," I said.

Sarah looked down at the car, then at me. The sheriff knit his brows and turned to her. "You see anyone with him last night?" Sarah shook her head. "You sure?"

"Yes, I'm sure. I told you he came in alone."

"You see any sign of someone else inside?" he asked, jerking his thumb over his shoulder. Again Sarah shook her head.

"Me neither," the sheriff said, "but we better check it out." He reached into his car and pulled out a radio handset. When it crackled to life, he barked orders to have the black car towed to a nearby county yard.

"I didn't see any signs inside, either," I said. "but I see one here."

"If there's something in there, we'll find it," the sheriff said. "Thanks for your help." With that he turned and went back into the cottage. I looked at Sarah, who stood up on the porch. She looked cold and tired. I remembered her flowers and went up to the cottage. As I got to the door, Sheriff Stone was stepping out. In one hand he carried the bouquet, in the other a black plastic bag that appeared to hold the dead man's personal effects. He pulled the door firmly shut behind him.

"We could just unlock the car and look inside," I suggested.

The sheriff handed me the flowers with a smile and a quick shake of his head. "Afraid not," he said. "But we'll get to it soon enough." I tried to think of another reason, but the sheriff didn't give me any time, or room, to come up with one. "Sarah tells me you're up here fishing," he said.

"That's right."

"Well, I sure do hope you stick to fishing. I'm going to put kind of a lid on this thing, and I'd be obliged if you would cooperate. Otherwise there could be unfortunate consequences."

This did not entirely surprise me. You elect an ordinary citizen as mayor, they think they can tell the newspapers what to write. You put an ordinary citizen in a uniform, they think they can push everyone else around. "What consequences?" I demanded.

Stone looked confused again, and I was beginning to wonder how he ever got himself elected sheriff. "For the good people who run this hotel," he said. "What did you think I meant?"

When I had no reply, Stone went past me, tipped his hat to Sarah, and drove off behind the ambulance. I watched until both vehicles were out of sight, then walked over to Sarah. I handed her the flowers, which looked a little worse for wear.

"How are you doing?" I asked her.

"I'm okay. And this is really sweet." She held up the flowers. I blushed for the second time that day.

"Liz seems to be holding up," I said quickly.

"Good," Sarah said. "She can hold the fort until I get back."

"Where are you going?"

"I'm not on duty for another hour, and I've got some things to take care of before that." She pulled her car keys out of her purse.

"Let me drive you."

"No, it'll be faster if I go by myself."

"Can I wait for you here?"

"I suggest you find yourself a place to sleep tonight," Sarah said.

"Whoops," I said. "I completely forgot."

She nodded. "Last night at my place was okay, but now I think it would be better if—"

"I understand," I said quickly. "I'll get a room somewhere. Now, what about dinner?"

"I'll be working," she reminded me.

"That's right. Damn."

I WENT DOWN to the inn, found the pay phone, and began calling the places listed in the small local phone book. Each one I called was full, and I began to think that perhaps fishing was more popular than I realized. After the fourth or fifth rejection I gave up. I came back out into the lobby and continued through it into the bar. Beyond it was a cozy enclosed patio with little round bar tables. I wandered into it, and heard the clatter of pots and pans coming from a passageway that led from the kitchen into the bar area. A moment later Liz Rizzo emerged from the passageway carrying a stack of dinner plates.

"Find a place?" she asked.

"Nope. And this place is hard to leave."

"It is," she said. "Too bad we're full."

"What are the plates for?"

"We serve food out here too," she said, pointing to the small tables in the enclosed patio area. "If you can't stay here, at least you could have dinner in the bar. That way you don't have to pay the fixed price for the whole dinner in the dining room."

This was interesting news, considering that Sarah would be working the bar this evening. But another idea had also occurred to me, one that required more immediate action.

"You know," I said, "You do have one room empty."

"No, look," Liz said, pulling out the reservation book. "All full."

"I hate to remind you of something unpleasant," I said slowly, "but someone checked out a little while ago, and he won't be coming back." Liz looked up at me, uncomprehending. Then she blanched, and for a moment I thought she was going to be sick again. I pressed my advantage. "The room's empty," I continued, "the sheriff has already searched it, and I'm the only other person that knows what happened. If I stay up there the next two nights, the inn still makes its money and no one else has to know."

"I don't think so," Liz said, fingering a strand of hair.

"Hotel rooms are the most perishable commodity there is," I reasoned. "Once a night in that room is gone, you can't ever sell it again."

"But that man is dead!"

"He's also gone. They took him away. It's over."

"But I can't just—"

"It's the best thing for everybody, Liz. Think about it."

"I have to call Sarah first."

"She's out doing errands before work. She won't be back until she starts work."

"Then you'll have to wait."

"I have a better idea," I said, smiling my most persuasive smile. "I'll go up and put the room back together so it's all ready when she gets back. Then I'll tell her myself. I'll take full responsibility. The worst that can happen is I have to go when she gets here."

"But by then you won't be able to find anything else."

"I already tried," I exclaimed. "If you don't take pity on me, I'm out on the highway."

Liz moaned in confusion, and I took her hand. "Come on," I said. "Just give me the passkey and some bed linens and I'll get to work."

"Are you sure the sheriff is done with the room?"

"Of course," I said. "I was right there with him when we finished up. He thanked me for my help. Sarah and I saw him off together, and we all agreed not to talk about what happened."

"Well, if you're sure," Liz said, and pulled out a passkey from under the bar. "The housekeepers are all gone, so if you don't do it I'll have to go back up there myself."

With a key and complete instructions on where to find

everything I needed, I headed back to the cottage on the hillside. The black sports car was already gone. I let myself into the cottage, turned on the light, and looked around. The bed was stripped of its sheets, although I could not remember when they had been taken from the room. The basket and muffin wrapper were also gone, leaving the table clear of everything but the glass decanter and two wine glasses. Most everything else was a mess.

I quickly began putting things to rights. When I had the bedroom put back together, I moved into the bathroom. This room had apparently been searched less thoroughly, because most things seemed to be where they belonged. Only the towels were missing, presumably taken out with the sheets from the bed. I tried to remember again when that must have happened, but could not picture it. When I examined the long clawfoot bathtub, however, I could picture Sarah's tub quite clearly, and her leaning over it to draw me a bath the night before.

I leaned over the tub a little closer. In the drain, nearly obscured by a white plastic plug, was a small mat of wet hair. Upon closer inspection, I saw that the hair was much lighter than the dark hair of the man who had died on the bed. In fact, this hair was red. As I pulled it apart, I discovered that the individual hairs were nearly a foot long. They belonged either to an auburn-haired woman, perhaps one who wore matching lipstick, or to a man who kept his hair tucked under a cap when he was out in the woods...

I stood for a while in the bathroom of the cottage, thinking. Was it possible that the well-to-do San Francisco art dealer had died while on a tryst in the countryside? Perhaps with a rich society wife, one with a name that sold an extra thirty or forty thousand morning papers? Was it possible also that the inn's mushroom gatherer heard or saw something and could provide the colorful details that would make the story jump off the page?

Carefully I preserved the hairs in a piece of tissue paper and put them in my shirt pocket. Then I went back out to the bedroom and looked around with a new appreciation. My eye finally fell on the decanter and wine glasses: fingerprints! I studied each item in its turn, and was disappointed to find that there were no fingerprints on any of them. I straightened up and tried to remember what Liz had told me.

Clean glasses and decanters were kept in a small maintenance room half way down the hill, where they were washed and refilled each day before being replaced in the surrounding cottages. Surely if these had been carried here from there, they would bear the prints of the housekeeper; if Sheriff Stone had examined them, they should have borne his prints as well. I picked up one of the glasses using a small hand towel, held it up to the light, and studied it closely. The glass was clear and unsmudged. Maybe Stone had completely missed them during his investigation. It was not hard to believe, considering everything else.

I went out to my car, brought in my stuff, and tossed it on the bed. Then I got into the car, drove down through the trees to the highway, and turned south to town. As I drove, I ran through the events of the afternoon in my mind. When I got to my own inspection of the cottage, I considered things more slowly. It was possible that a housekeeper had wiped the decanter and glasses clean herself, and that the sheriff had not bothered to examine them. The decanter was, after all, still full. If nothing had been drunk from it, there was no reason to suspect its contents. Still, I was not satisfied. My years as a reporter had taught me to think with special care about anything that had a perfectly good reason for you not to think about it.

I pulled into the parking lot on the side of the Pomo Bluff Hotel as the sun was sliding down toward the Pacific horizon. A chill wind blew streaks of high clouds out in long arcs that glowed pink and orange over the ocean. There was a telephone booth across the lot. I stepped into it and dialed my own number at home. It took me only a moment to confirm that no one had called me since I left. Ordinarily this news would have depressed me, but now I was glad I had no calls to return. I had plenty of people to call as it was.

My first call was to a woman in Berkeley, an artist I had dated at the height of my run at the paper. When my luck ran out, she found someone else to be seen with at San Francisco parties. I still remembered her number, though. When she answered the phone, the rush of her voice momentarily sucked me back a year into my past.

"Rigel, it's you! I can't believe it!"

I fought my way back to the present. "How are you, Corinna?"

"Oh, I'm grand. I was just at a dinner last night and somebody asked me about you. Isn't that a coincidence?"

"It's a small world."

"I told him I hadn't seen you for almost a year, and now here you are. He didn't call you, did he?"

"Who?"

"Never mind. I didn't like him that much anyway. But he remembered your work on the paper. You did leave the paper, didn't you?"

"I'm on another assignment now. That's why I'm calling, actually."

"You're calling me about a story? Is it about art?"

"Yeah, in a way. Did you know Richard Shammey?"

"Dick? Of course I know him, but I don't want you to put it in some article somewhere. He's so horrible, you know."

With a chill, I realized that to virtually everyone else in the world, "Dick" Shammey was still alive and well. I would have to keep things in the present tense if I didn't want to give my scoop away.

"Horrible in what way?" I asked blandly.

"The way he uses people! He treats art like it's just some commodity he can use to get ahead of other people. I can't believe the people who get involved with him. The poor things mustn't have a brain in their heads."

"Poor things?"

"Women, Rigel, young women. He's forever luring them in and then shucking them like old socks. And if they can paint or sculpt or anything it's even worse. He just sucks them dry and then all of a sudden they have no art left and he doesn't have any money they can get out of him, but somehow he moves to a new gallery and starts over. It's really horrible." She sounded like she was recounting the story of her favorite soap opera.

"How's he been doing recently, do you know?"

"Well, I heard he was in trouble again, that he was going to have to shut up his latest place unless he scored a major deal of some kind. But at this point, who would deal with him?"

"Certainly not you."

"Heavens, no! And none of my friends, either. I mean, we *have* to deal with gallery owners. It's unavoidable, but you can still avoid the ones that are the most horrible."

"Does he have any enemies? Anyone who ever threatened him?"

She giggled. "You sound just like a TV show!"

"I don't have a TV, Corinna, remember?"

"You should get one; I always told you that. They're better company than a cat and much easier to keep. So anyway, how was Christmas?"

"Lonely. Listen, I'm in a phone booth, so I've got to run."

"You still have a phone, don't you?"

"Yeah, but no one ever calls me on it."

"You could call me sometime." Her voice was softer now, almost believably vulnerable. Was it possible that the beauteous Corinna Geller had been alone for the holidays herself?

"I suppose I could do that," I said.

"I would like it."

"Thanks for your help, Cori."

"I mean it, Rigel."

"Me too. I'll call."

"Okay. 'Bye."

It was cold in the phone booth, but I felt more discomfort from the strange pressure that had started up in my chest. I blew out a long breath and dialed another number. This one, too, I still knew by heart. I breathed a sigh of relief when the phone picked up after the first ring. "Hello?"

"Bruce, it's Rigel Lynx."

"Hey, Rigel, I heard you got fired."

"I quit."

"That's not what I heard."

"Don't believe what you hear."

"Not even from you?"

"I need some information."

"Who you working for now?"

I thought it best to ignore the question. "I need some basic stuff from the Department of Motor Vehicles, that's all. You probably won't even want anything for it."

"We'll see," Bruce told me.

I gave him Richard Shammey's license plate number and waited while he tapped the keys on his computer. As usual, there was some jazz playing in the background. While I waited, I watched people walk in and out of the drugstore across the highway.

I had never met Bruce face to face, but he knew my work and I knew his. He had helped me on many stories in the past, because Bruce and his computer could do more snooping in an hour than most reporters could do in a week of interviews. I had never asked him how he got passwords to the computer systems of most of California's state and local governments, or if he had any kind of regular job. All I knew was that Bruce had unparalleled access to information and a full-blooded passion for baseball cards. I, on the other hand, have a vital need for information and a closet full of cards that I started collecting in kindergarten. It was a match made in heaven.

"Here you go," Bruce announced, and read out a stream of information about Richard Shammey. I wrote it all down.

"See how easy that was?" I asked. "This one will be even easier."

Bruce snorted, but he did not object when I asked for information about Carl Larkin. A moment later he gave me the address and phone number. I wrote them down.

"You got a driver's license on your screen?" I asked.

"Yeah. Average-looking guy."

"Red hair?"

"Black and white image," Bruce said. "He has freckles, though, which is common in people with red hair. Anything else?"

"I don't know," I said, and scratched my head. "Anyone else living at that address?"

The jazz played and the keys tapped as Bruce searched through the mountains of information the government sees fit to capture and keep.

"Uh-oh," he said.

I pricked up my ears. "What is it?"

"DMV lists a Melissa Sharon Larkin at that address."

"Wife or sister?" I asked.

"Can't tell."

"Why the 'uh-oh'?"

"Few years back she had a moving violation dismissed on a forty-five four hundred."

"Hey, I've got a couple of tickets I'd like to get rid of myself."

"Not that way," Bruce said. "It's a California Vehicle Code section that means you can't pay off the citation because you're in prison."

I pictured the wet red hair I had found in the bathtub, hair that may have been there during Richard Shammey's final hours.

"This Melissa, is she older or younger than Larkin?"

"Younger by about five years."

"No maiden name?"

"Melissa Sharon Larkin," he said, repeating the full name. "Sharon could be a maiden name or a middle name."

"That would make her a wife or a sister. What did she do?"

"How do I know?"

"You still have your password at DOJ?"

"For your information," Bruce said drily, "the State Department of Justice considers it a serious felony violation of privacy laws to access restricted information without prior written permission."

"That never stopped you before."

"No, but it raises the price."

"Come on, Bruce, I'm onto something here."

"It's my neck on the line, and they're getting better at tracking hackers."

"They'll never catch you."

"All the more reason to raise the price."

I thought hard for a moment about what would persuade Bruce to break into one of the state's most secure computer systems.

"Okay," I said at last. "Dave Winfield." One of baseball's best players throughout the 1980s, an All-Star at least a dozen times, thousands of hits, hundreds of home runs, and a class guy all the way. It would be hard to part with one of my Dave Winfield cards, but I knew it would go to a good home. To my surprise, Bruce yawned.

"I got a dozen Winfields."

"This is a rookie year."

"Got two."

"This one is signed."

"By who?"

I had to laugh. "He autographed the card in spring training just before his second year."

"How was the signature authenticated?"

"Well, I've got a photograph in my scrapbook, but I'm not giving you that!"

"You got the signature yourself? At spring training?"

"It was cool," I said, remembering it clearly.

"I'm not sure you should give that up, Rigel."

"I had to think about it, Bruce, but there's no one I'd rather trade it to."

There was a pause. Then Bruce spoke. "Department of Justice, here we come."

Again I waited on the line. This time it took longer, but it was worth the wait. Melissa Larkin was serving a sentence of 25 years to life on a first-degree murder rap, plus three years for using a gun. She was convicted of killing a marijuana grower from the north coast area while he was in San Francisco. The trial had been held in The City five years before. She would not be eligible for parole for another twelve and half years.

"Got a visual on her?" I asked.

"Yeah. Must be a sister, now I see her. Got the same freckles."

"Any chance she could be out early?"

"What, on parole? No way."

"Any other way?"

"She's in the Central California Women's Facility, in Chowchilla, okay? She breaks out of there, it's front page news."

"So it's not her," I murmured to myself, wondering if the red hair could possibly belong to her brother.

"What are you mixed up in, anyway?" Bruce asked.

"Can't say yet. Can I get one last search?"

"Secure?"

"No, just a library pull."

"Shoot."

"I need a recent, scientifically accurate, general interest article on anaphylaxis. It's an allergy." I spelled it and Bruce typed away.

"*Scientific American,* September nineteen ninety-three," he said at last. "Should be at any library."

"There's no library here. Can you download it to your computer from someplace and then fax it to me?"

"You're someplace they got fax machines but no libraries?"

"Exactly," I said. In the window of the drugstore across the highway was a banner proclaiming the number of the town's first facsimile machine. "Here's the number. And make sure you put a cover sheet in there with my name on the front. The people with the machine don't know yet that I'm going to use it."

"Will do."

"I really appreciate your help, Bruce. The card will come in the usual way, okay?"

"Take it easy, Rye."

"You, too. And thanks."

I stood in the phone booth and watched the sky go gray. I had the feeling of acceleration I get when an investigation begins to gel, when the individual facts start to add up to something greater, and I know for sure there are more to come. I didn't have a real story, of course, but I had the feeling. Dick Shammey of San Francisco dead in Pomo Bluff, Melissa Larkin of Pomo Bluff in prison for a San Francisco murder, red hairs in the bathtub, red hair on Carl Larkin...I dialed a third number. A voice rendered raspy by decades of cigarettes answered after four rings.

"Morgue, Hollis."

"Hi, Holly. It's Rigel Lynx."

"Hey, Rye, how are you?"

"I'm okay. No matter what they tell you, there is life after the paper."

"I feel the same way."

"Come on, you still work there."

"In the morgue? They should've just canned me."

"Seriously, Holly, how are you?"

"Seriously, Rye, I got a heart condition and one bad kidney. I can't drink anymore and I can only eat food that don't taste like food."

"I can't *afford* food that tastes like food."

"So we're in the same boat."

"Well, you're in the nice warm morgue and I'm out here in the middle of nowhere in a freezing-cold phone booth."

"You need something?"

"Yeah, I'm trying to dig up some stories on a murder trial, took place in the city about five years ago. Defendant was a woman, Melissa Larkin."

"I remember that case. I was on city desk then."

"Who covered the story?"

"No one. It was one of those cases, we buried a few summaries on the inside pages. Most of that we picked up from the other papers. It was just one of the many things that drove me to drink."

"You were already drinking by then," I reminded him.

"Drinking more, I meant."

I laughed. "What made you remember the case, Holly?"

"You mean aside from the fact that someone upstairs wanted us to keep a lid on it?"

"Yeah, beside that."

"They had just changed the sentencing rules, so if you used a gun you had to go to prison no matter what. It was the first case where it was a woman, not a man. She didn't seem like a killer at all, but the evidence went against her and the prosecutor was betting his career on a conviction."

"Can you fax me whatever you've got?"

"Sure, but it won't be much." I gave him the number

from the drugstore window, and scribbled a few notes in the waning light of the afternoon. Finally I was ready to ring off.

"Are you as much fun sober as you were drunk, Holly?"

"No, Rye, I'm not. Are you as much fun broke as you were when you had a job?"

"No, Holly, I'm not."

"Life is hard," he intoned, "then you die."

"Let's get together when I get back to town."

"It better be soon," he cracked. His laughter became an uncontrollable cough, and that was the end of our conversation.

I thought for a moment, then decided to make one more call.

"Hello?"

"Melodie? It's Rigel Lynx."

"Oh, hi, Rigel. We missed you at lunch today."

I laughed. Melodie was one of those ageless spirits who treated everyone she met as a friend she didn't see enough of. If you called her at six in the afternoon, she would say they missed you at tea. If you called her at nine in the morning, she would say they missed you at bridge the night before. It didn't matter if you drank tea or played bridge. It was her way of letting you know she liked you.

"Gee, Melodie, I'm sorry I missed it," I said sincerely. "I'm actually calling from out of town."

"Oh, are you going to put me in the paper again? My mother said it was the best story about me she ever read." I laughed. Melodie was Oklahoma by way of California, a master gardener who always looked like she had stepped out of a magazine. I met her during my brief stint as a lifestyle reporter, and she was one of the most enjoyable interviews I ever had.

"No, actually I need your opinion about something. Something having to do with mushrooms."

"The kind you eat or the kind you want to get rid of?" she asked. "I've got this one client, has this really wet side yard, she should turn it into a farm and at least get some money out of it. Otherwise it's just a sea of little toad-stools after every spring rain."

"That's kind of what I'm calling about," I said. "I ran into this guy, he's a certified mushroom gatherer for a local restaurant. I was wondering about writing him up."

"Is he cute?"

This threw me for a minute. "Why would that matter?"

"I mean, is he cute and single? Because if he's one of those gnarly old guys with a half-blind dog snuffling around in the woods, never mind."

"Are you saying that a mushroom gatherer would not make much of a story, even with all the food snobs in San Francisco?"

"Let's look at it logically," Melodie suggested, which made me smile. She had told me once that she was a completely intuitive gardner, and that logic had nothing to do with the color of a hydrangea. "Your guy's out of town, so we can't eat his fungus," she began. "That's what mushrooms are, you know, a kind of fungus. So we can't say, hey, I had some of Mr. Wood's marvelous mushrooms the other night drizzled with stone-pressed extra virgin olive oil, cilantro pesto and *pecorino romano*."

"No snob appeal," I concurred.

"Exactly. So if Stacy and Eleanor don't think he's cute and single, why would they want to read about him?"

"Stacy and Eleanor?"

"My friends, Stacy and Eleanor. They're both married for life, so they need a little something in the magazines to keep them juicy. Hunky guys who walk around in the woods would appeal to them."

"I don't think this guy is that type."

"Then it's a tough sell to Stacy and Eleanor, I'd say."

"So the idea is, nix on the mushroom man."

"Yeah, Rigel, sorry." She seemed sincerely unhappy that my idea was a dud, but then she perked right up. "Now if you want a really cool story, there's this guy I know who grows pears inside bottles and then puts brandy in the bottle and sells it to restaurants for, like, hundreds of dollars. Can you believe it?"

"You think that's the new food craze?" I asked, incredulous.

"Heck no, I think it's a sign we've all gone crazy." She laughed out loud, and I had to join her. We chatted a few more minutes, until I felt the cold of the day starting to seep into my bones. I said goodbye, zipped up my coat, and pulled open the door of the phone booth.

Before I could step out, a green and tan sheriff's car pulled up to the side of the hotel. Instinctively I stepped back into the phone booth. The driver of the car, just getting out, was Sheriff Stone. He went around to the passenger door on the other side and opened it. The man who emerged was thin and stoop-shouldered. He moved meekly, as if unsure whether to trust the sheriff who held him by one arm and spoke to him before letting him go.

The scene was suddenly reminiscent of many I had seen on the streets of San Francisco: a homeless person, a well-fed cop, and night falling. It always seemed to me that underfed people who had no homes or families deserved protection from the police, not harassment. But of course the same was true of ordinary citizens, people who were frightened by the sight of poverty and misery they could not comprehend. As I watched, the sheriff got in his car, backed out, and drove away. The other man shuffled out to the highway and began to walk away, past the front of the hotel.

I crossed to my car, got in, and drove out to the highway. The thin man was now well beyond the hotel, past the fringes of the town, and heading toward the bridge I had crossed on my way into town the night before. I felt an urge to help him, perhaps give him money for a meal, but I also felt pulled north to the inn and Sarah. Straight ahead, out to the west across the bluffs, the sun was going gloriously into the ocean, and I felt gripped by the irony that there should be homeless people even here, in one of the most beautiful places I had ever been.

When I looked back down the highway a moment later, the thin man had disappeared in the gathering gloom. I squinted in disbelief, but there was no one walking on either side of the road. When I looked out to the west again, the sun was down and the color was draining out of the sky.

# FOUR

WHEN I ARRIVED BACK at the inn, I sat in my car outside the cottage in the dark and studied its vague outlines. A man had died within its walls that morning, and I felt intuitively that there was a story attached to his demise. Many times I had stood in hallways and meeting rooms at the state capitol, visualizing the wordless meetings, discreet hand-offs, and back-door exits that I was eventually able to prove. I closed my eyes, took a deep breath, and tried to see…

First I tried to picture a red-headed woman going into the cottage with Shammey. What I saw in my imagination, though, was a woman coming out and going up into the trees. I opened my eyes and looked up the hill. I remembered what Liz had said about Carl Larkin, the mushroom gatherer, and realized that I was seeing him instead. But when I closed my eyes and tried to see again what Liz had seen, I saw someone coming down the hill and going into the cottage, not coming out. I opened my eyes again. For some reason I was getting it all backward. Perhaps I was just a little tired. Maybe I would try again in the morning.

Singing a few bars of ''Climb Every Mountain'' to encourage myself, I bounded up the steps into the cottage and turned on all the lights I could find. Everything was normal, ordinary, unremarkable—except for the implements of death that I had carelessly scattered on the bed before going to town.

A cold shot of fear coursed through me as I gazed on

my fishing gear. I remembered the missed rent payment, pleading with friends for work, agreeing to compose five thousand words on a subject I knew nothing about. I had forgotten all this, but now it flooded my brain. I had to start thinking about fishing, if I did not want to go home empty-handed. I swallowed hard and went into the bathroom to clean up.

Half an hour later, I paused outside the door of the inn. I still had to convince Sarah to let me stay in the cottage. Quickly I ran through my arguments, as I used to do outside the door of my editor's office. There was always something a reporter needed, and it was almost always an editor who could grant it: more time until deadline, approval on an expense sheet, permission to conduct just one more interview. When I was ready, I stepped inside and went around the corner to the small bar where Sarah would be stationed. She was not in sight, so I looked around the lobby and the seating area off the bar. It was still early. The few patrons that came in were escorted into the dining room by a smiling woman in a serving apron.

I was standing at the bar, gazing at the framed certificate on the wall, when I heard footsteps behind me. I turned to see Sarah coming toward me from the back passage to the kitchen. She wore a long knit dress that clung to her form, a shawl that draped subtle color over her shoulders, and a soft smile. She was such an eyeful that I almost missed the surprise in her eyes.

"Welcome back," she said, avoiding my eye as she glided behind the bar.

"Nice to be back," I said. "You look beautiful."

"Thank you. Did you find a place to stay?"

"Actually, I did."

"Good. Where did you wind up?"

"Not far from here, actually."

Now she fixed her eyes on mine, and I knew she was on to me. "You don't mean up the hill," she said.

"Yeah. I'm staying in Hillhouse."

Sarah's eyes became opaque, and then she turned away to ring up some dinner checks. I held my breath. Finally she turned back to me and spoke quietly. "Did Liz do that?"

"I talked her into it," I admitted. "She only went along with it because it was best for the inn."

Sarah looked at me coolly. "That's not your call, Rigel. It's mine."

"That's why I came to tell you," I replied. "The inn wants Hillhouse occupied by a paying guest, and the police want it off limits to people who don't know what happened. I'm the only person that qualifies on both counts. He didn't say you couldn't rent out the room, right? And it's better for you to have someone up there, so people don't wonder why you're turning people away when you have a prime place standing empty."

"I'm not sure Sheriff Stone would agree."

"I was going to ask you about Sheriff Stone."

"What about him?"

"I just wondered if you and he were…"

She looked at me, waiting for me to finish. I couldn't. Finally she shook her head slowly back and forth. "There are not that many single women in Pomo Bluff," she said quietly. "It makes the single men a little crazy sometimes."

"That's no excuse for acting like he owns you."

"I know."

"If you want to be alone, then he should back off."

Sarah looked at me, an eyebrow arched. "Does that apply to everyone, or just the locals?"

"Hey, I backed off already," I said, my hands raised in surrender. "I got a room of my own just like you said."

"Yes, but it's not a room I can let you have."

The phone on the bar rang and Sarah picked it up. The conversation was brief, but I understood immediately what it was about. When Sarah hung up, she was silent a moment. I waited.

"Well," she said, "it appears you were right about what happened. The doctor's report says our guest died of anaphylactic shock, and they're sending him down to San Francisco or wherever his people are."

"Was that Stone?" I asked. Sarah shook her head. "A deputy sheriff?" She nodded. "They did an autopsy already?"

"He said they took the body to a doctor who examined him and looked at the things they took from the room. The police are calling it—" She frowned, trying to remember.

"Accidental death?"

"That's it," Sarah said, nodding. "Accidental death."

"They're moving pretty fast," I said.

"I think it's not uncommon up here," Sarah said thoughtfully. "We're almost an hour and a half by car from the nearest hospital."

"No place to keep the body."

"Right, or even care for people who are in serious trouble. If someone falls on the bluffs and breaks a leg or something, they go inland to Santa Rosa in a helicopter."

"Wow."

"Well, we're out here by ourselves, pretty much."

I thought about it for a moment, then nodded. "Accidental death," I said. "I guess this means I can stay in the cottage, huh?"

Sarah looked at me. Her face was blank, but I could tell that she was thinking it through. Then she shrugged, opened up the reservation book, and slid a guest check-in card across the bar.

I SPENT THE NEXT few hours in a state of gustatory amazement, as Sarah served me a succession of dishes each more delicious than the one before. The woodwork in the walls, floors, and ceilings gleamed with candle light, and despite the proximity of other people in the small seating area off the bar, I felt I was in my own, intensely pleasurable world. One of the delights of that world was watching Sarah greet arriving guests, serve aperitifs to arriving diners, take reservations on the phone, and infuse all these activities with a genuine glow of warm hospitality. When she brought me a plate, or refilled my glass, I noted the length of her fingers and the fluidity of her gestures. I remembered being on the stream bank with her pressed against me...

With a start I remembered also that I had an article to write. The next time Sarah came by my table, I asked if I could have some paper to write on. She slipped a small notepad out of her pocket, pulled some blank pages free, and handed them to me. I watched her go, until I noticed that both men in a foursome nearby were watching her, too. Clearing my throat audibly, I busily addressed myself to making some notes for my article.

At last the bar was clear of arriving diners, and the inn's guests had all been checked in for the night. Sarah cleared empty glasses away from the few other tables around me, and then plopped into a chair.

"Innkeeper, barmaid, headwaiter—how much do they pay you?" I asked.

"Not enough," she assured me. "Would you like some more coffee?"

"I'm fine. Where did you learn all this?"

"I had to take over my father's household at a relatively early age, you remember."

"Yeah, I remember now. Sorry."

"It's okay."

"Whatever happened to your sister?"

"She lives in San Francisco now."

"Do you see her much?"

"Not as often as I'd like. She's married."

A number of my friends had recently married, and I now had to work hard to get them to spend an evening away from their wives and families. "Marriage is not jail, you know," I said irritably. "Your sister could get out if she wanted."

"I know," Sarah said. "But her husband is— He's in city politics. She has a lot of social obligations."

I knew San Francisco society only too well. I had soared into its higher elevations when I had Corinna on my arm, but it was a short flight and it ended with a sharp descent. "The society thing is pretty intense down there," I said finally.

"Actually, I think that's what's holding the marriage together. I don't think the relationship itself is very intimate anymore."

I became conscious of Sarah's downcast face, and quickly turned the conversation in another direction. "Speaking of San Francisco, there was something else I wanted to ask you. I saw this guy on the highway today, just walking off out of town, toward the river. I know this is weird, but he looked like he was right off the streets of the city.''

Sarah looked up. "Thin? Gray clothes?"

"Exactly."

She nodded soberly. "His name is Ben. Liz tells me he lives near the river somewhere."

"He has no family? No home?"

"I think he gets government assistance of some kind, for food and health care. I'm surprised that you saw him, because he usually stays out of sight."

"I didn't see him long. One minute he was there, the next minute he was gone."

"That's Ben."

"I wouldn't figure a homeless person could stand much of a chance out here in the country, especially in the middle of winter."

"He's been here for years," Sarah said. Someone called her name from the kitchen passage, and she quickly got up. "Be right back," she said.

I watched her go, then reflected on our conversation. There was something cool running through the middle of the warmth, and I wanted to melt it. When Sarah reappeared and sat down again, I turned the talk to the restaurant and the food she had served me for dinner.

"I never saw a certificate for mushroom gathering," I said enthusiastically, "but now I understand it. That soup was incredible."

"Yes, I had a taste in the kitchen."

"Does he get the mushrooms right around here?"

"I'm not sure where all he goes," Sarah responded. "The people who gather for a living don't like to reveal their spots."

"Yeah, I guess that makes sense," I acknowledged. "Since the mushrooms are just out there for the taking.

Like mining for gold." Sarah smiled at my analogy, and I smiled back. "What time do you get off tonight?" I asked.

"Shouldn't you be thinking about fishing?" she said gently.

I held up my sheets of paper, covered with words and phrases. "What do you think I've been doing?"

"You should get out earlier tomorrow because there will be lots of other people on the river."

"There was no one where we were today," I said, looking as innocent as I could.

"Don't you think people would like to read about places they can get to without trespassing?" Sarah riposted. "Like the Pomo River? Or C Ranch Creek? Just get those maps I showed you."

"I got them, but—"

She was already getting up. "I've got to drop in at a friend's house after work tonight," she said. "It's something I have to do."

She went behind the bar and out of sight. A moment later I heard her on the phone. I gathered up my papers and went to the bar. Sarah hung up the phone.

"How much?" I asked.

"For dinner? We'll put it on your room," Sarah offered.

"I've got to figure the tip," I reminded her.

"Buy me a drink sometime," she said.

"But you work every night."

"You could come in for dinner tomorrow."

"Again?"

"Sure. I like having you where I can keep an eye on you," she said, with a smile that made me blush.

EARLY THE NEXT MORNING I followed one of the maps to a muddy dirt road that ran along the north bank of the

Pomo River. I could see dawn-gray sky high above me through the tree tops, but down in the river ravine it was still nearly dark. I pulled off the road where I could hear the water running, gathered up my gear, and waded through deep ferns toward the river. Wet to the waist, I looked ten feet down a steep, slick slope at the water swirling past me. There would be no fishing from this spot, and I looked up and down the river for a better position.

Half an hour later, I found a gravel bank along the river that was dry enough to crouch on and set up my equipment. But before I could even assemble my rod, I heard footsteps crunching the gravel a hundred feet upriver, beyond some willows. I looked through the willows and watched as another fisherman approached the bank. The guy had gear hanging from his belt, his vest, his pants—he apparently owned everything the fishing companies made, and had brought it all to the edge of the river. Even his clothes matched.

I returned to my own preparations, but looked up every few moments to watch the other guy. Once he let the line slip out of his rod and was trying not to step on it as he gathered it back up. I chuckled to myself, remembering exactly the same trouble the day before. Another time, the guy was on his hands and knees, probably hunting for a fly he had dropped on the gravel. I shook my head in sympathy and tied on my own fly.

When I was ready, I stood up and scanned the river. I quickly realized that the willows around me didn't give me room to cast properly, so I clipped my fly onto the rod near the handle to keep the line taut, and prepared to work my way upriver. Before moving off, though, I turned to watch the other fisherman cast. I still did not have the trick of making the line fly out over the water consistently, and hoped I could learn by watching someone else. After watching the guy hook his own hat a couple of times, I decided I would have to learn by doing instead. As I emerged from my spot and circled well up the bank, the guy spun a quick glance at me. I raised my hand to tip my hat in greeting, but he had already turned his back. I let my hand fall and went on my way.

Half a mile upriver in growing daylight, I saw a bend in the river where the gravel bank provided room to fish. I made for it eagerly, then slowed down as I saw not one, but two long lines flicker through the air and land on the water. I circled back up the muddy slope and approached the scene quietly. The two men fishing this spot were out in the stream some distance apart, but their lines were long enough to overlap each other's territory. I watched as they systematically cast each part of the bending river and let their flies sink deep into the current. A couple of times I thought I saw fish break the surface of the water, but neither man had a strike.

I longed to join them, to be working the water the way they were, but I knew there was not room for one more. So I got out a small notebook, looked around at the water, trees, and sky, and began to describe the scene in quick phrases. Soon, though, I became cold and stiff. When the two men pulled in their lines and waded to shore, I picked up my rod and worked my way carefully down to the bank. One of the men was lighting a cigarette while the other one changed flies. When I strolled up, both nodded their heads briefly in acknowledgement.

"Having any luck?" I asked.

One of the men snorted. The other man glanced at me, or rather at my rod. "Luck has damn little to do with it," he said, and returned to his work. Neither of them said another word to me, and I felt my cheeks burn. When they turned and went back to fishing, I headed off up the river with my jaw set in determination. The going became increasingly rough, however, and twenty minutes later I had managed to get only as far as the upper edge of the river bend. Breathing heavily, I came out of a thicket onto a small rock and looked down the river. My fury at the two fishermen had ebbed, and soon my curiosity got the better of me. I guess it's the reporter in me. Things in life make me angry sometimes, but eventually I become more interested than upset.

The man nearest me was casting across the water, where the river undercut the bank and a dead log lay half in, half out of the water. It appeared he was trying to get his fly to go under the log. This seemed to me a good way to get the line snagged or broken, but he kept at it. More interesting to me was the way the man had a pile of loose line at his feet, which he played out with one hand while he cast the rod back and forth with the other hand. I looked down at my rod and reel to figure out exactly how this technique would work, then watched again to see the result. After a series of mid-air casts, the fisherman finally landed his fly near the far bank of the river. The current carried it to the log, where the water swirled up and over.

Suddenly a silver flash exploded on the underside of the log. The fishing line that had been lying on the surface of the water flew up into a taut diagonal from the surface of the water to the man with the fishing rod. He had hooked a fish! As I watched, the diagonal swung in my direction: the fish was heading up the river, *away from the log!* The surface of the water exploded again, and my heart leaped as the fish twisted and lunged in the air. Now the diagonal swung back downriver, and I saw that the fisherman was quickly drawing in the line to keep the fish on the near side of the log. The other fisherman had reeled in his line to give his partner plenty of room to work.

Twice more the fish leapt from the water, and both times I caught my breath at the beauty and power of its struggle to break free. Finally the fish was swimming back and forth in just a few feet of water near the bank of the river. The fisherman kept the line taut while his partner came over to help. I thought the other man would bring a net, but instead he brought a camera. When the fisherman waded farther out into the water, the fish began to thrash wildly. Carefully the man worked his way closer, until he was able to lift the fish out of the water. It was over a foot long, and he held it just a moment while his friend snapped a couple of quick pictures. Then he held the fish under the water while he worked the hook from its jaw. Finally he released the fish and waded back up the bank. His friend clapped him on the back and the two of them gestured and talked animatedly.

I realized I was gripping my own rod tightly, as though I were fighting the surging steelhead myself. Inspired, I turned and looked up the river. Not too far off, the gravel bank fingered out into a broad stretch of river. I would have to work to get to it, but I could fish from the spot without obstacle. When I arrived at the place I was hot with exertion and anticipation. I loosened my fly, shook it out onto the water at my feet, and pulled several measures of line out from the reel. "Ten o'clock, one o'clock, eleven o'clock," I repeated to myself, as I looked behind me and then in front of me. It was time.

With my feet firmly planted, I made my first cast of the day. To my surprise, the line flew out from the rod in a lovely arc. To my dismay, the fly with its twelve feet of transparent leader dropped in a heap on the water, well short of the end of the neon green line. I had seen the other fishermen drop their flies first, followed by the leader and the line, and I wanted to do the same. But try as I might, I could not. I thought the secret was in the mid-air casting the others did, which had the additional benefit of lengthening the line and allowing a much longer cast. As near as I could tell from the fishing magazine, this technique was called "false casting," because it had all the qualities of a real cast except letting the fly land on the water.

But when I tried swinging my rod back and forth to keep my line in the air above me, I caught the fly on the gravel bank, or worse, I had to duck as the fly and its metal hook came straight back at my head. Then I jerked my rod back so fast one time that the leader snapped and the fly flew off out of sight, leaving the light-weight leader flapping impotently in the breeze.

For another hour I tied on heavier flies, replaced broken leaders, and tried different stances. The idea of actually catching a fish had all but disappeared from my mind. I just wanted to make one good cast. Sometimes I would come close, but more often I would shake my head, pull in the line, and start all over again. Even when I was successful with one part of the cast, I usually was not able to repeat it a moment later. Trial and error, I finally concluded, is mostly a trial.

THE SKY WAS fully blue when I saw a group of three or four other fishermen headed my way. I considered going farther up the river to regain my privacy, then decided to get off the river and have breakfast. An hour later I was seated in a small diner across the highway from the hotel, on the southern edge of town. From inside I could see the ocean, the mouth of the river, and the highway bridge that crossed the river. Checking my maps, I determined that the land south of the bridge was the historic C Ranch, deeded to an early California grandee by the Mexican government. It was all private land now, but there was public access along C Ranch Creek for fishermen during steelhead season.

While I ate, I thought about my magazine story. I needed a way to start the story, what writers called a "lead." Sometimes a lead was obvious, sometimes not. Sometimes an editor with her own ideas would rewrite a lead entirely. But that didn't matter now. I knew from experience that once I had a lead in my mind, the rest of the outline would fall into place. I let my mind drift through the morning's events, testing each one as a potential starting point. None of them clicked, and I chuckled to myself. Catching a lead, I realized, was like catching a fish: luck had damn little to do with it.

After breakfast, I paused in the parking lot before walking down the highway a bit and picking up the faxes I expected from Bruce and Hollis. I just wanted to take a moment and look at things while the sun was bright. Not far behind the hotel, the land sloped up steeply to the east under a thick blanket of evergreen forest. The tree-covered ridge went north and south as far as the eye could see. I was turning around to have a look to the west when I caught some movement up on the bridge that crossed the river. At first I thought it was a crow, but crows didn't get that big. Then the dark shape disappeared.

Without stopping to think I unlocked my car, jumped in, and raced out of the parking lot. It took only a few seconds to get to the bridge, and not much longer to traverse its length. There was no one in sight, except in the cars that passed me going the other way. On the far side of the bridge I slowed down and looked carefully at where the bridge ended and the guard rail of the road began. It appeared that there was a break between them, and that a person could slip between them and go down the slope.

I quickly accelerated, found a turnout, and parked. When I walked back to the end of the bridge, I saw that there was indeed a narrow, almost hidden trail leading down the slope. Holding onto bushes and roots, I clambered down until I came to a flat ledge alongside the massive concrete anchorage of the bridge. Above me I heard cars whiz by on the roadway. The ocean breeze swirled around my legs and the river glided by below.

I let my eyes adjust to the dim light under the bridge, then looked across the underside of the bridge to the other side. The far anchorage was not a square block, as the one on my side appeared to be. In fact, it was shaped like a fat, stubby horseshoe with the opening facing out toward the river. If there was a similar opening on my side, I realized, it would make a relatively cozy little hideaway. Carefully I began working my way around the anchorage and under the bridge.

A few moments later I stared in wonder at the strangest "workshop" I had ever seen. On tables made of rocks and driftwood planks lay the skeletons of a dozen different birds, each at a different stage of reconstruction. Individual bones were sorted into abandoned boxes, cans, and bags. A curious assortment of tools lay here and there, as if I had interrupted an eccentric ornithologist in the middle of his work. The complete skeleton of a large gull stood apart on a flat rock, its wings outstretched as if it were just taking off from the beach. I marveled at it, reached out to touch one of the wings, and was startled when the wing folded in and collapsed against the body of the bird.

"It ain't broken," said a voice behind me. I whirled around. Ten feet away but almost invisible in the shadows stood a thin man dressed in shabby gray. "Here, I'll show you." He shuffled past me and went around behind the gull to demonstrate. "See?" he said, as he made both wings flap up and down. "He still works. Light and strong, that's how they're made." The man reached under the "table" and pulled out a mantle of gull feathers. Carefully he draped the feathers onto the skeleton and attached them under the wings. "You see, it's the feathers that make 'em the size they are. These skinny little bones make big wings when they're all dressed up." Again he made the wings move, but this time the currents of air created by the feathered mantle swept the dust at our feet. The man looked up at me. "Now all he needs are his insides back, and he could fly on home."

"That's fantastic," I said softly.

"There's birds all over out there," he said. "Birds and bones." He looked up at me, and for a moment I thought he was going to cry.

"I'm sorry to disturb you," I mumbled. "My name is Rye. You must be Ben."

"Who told you my name?"

"Sarah, at St. Horace."

"I know someone that works there."

"It's a nice place. But this is really something." I gestured around me.

"This is just the work area," Ben said.

"The noise doesn't bother you?"

"Ain't many cars after dark."

"It must get really dark down here."

Ben smiled, his teeth surprisingly white against dark

weathered skin and a wiry brown beard. "I got light," he said. "Fresh water, too. Only thing I don't have is a place for company." When he shrugged, his own long arms resembled wings.

"That's okay," I said.

"Something you want?"

"I just wondered why the sheriff had you in his car yesterday," I began. "It didn't seem like you were doing anything wrong."

Abruptly, Ben stalked past me to the far edge of the ledge, near where it emerged into daylight. Then he spun and walked back to where he had been. I held my ground and kept my attention on him.

"The sheriff," Ben said. "The sheriff."

"He had you in his car, by the hotel."

"I know, I know," Ben said impatiently. "I spent the night there."

"You spent the night?"

"Inside there, they have a little bed and such."

"Where, Ben? Did the sheriff— Did you spend the night in jail?"

Ben looked at me defiantly. "*Office,*" he said. "Sheriff's *office.*"

I shook my head, my anger rising. "Why did he run you in? What does he say you did?"

Again Ben jerked into motion, walking past me and then back behind the rock. Carefully he returned both feet to where they had been before. "I went to town. New moon, I always go."

"All you did was go into town?"

Ben rolled his lower lip between his front teeth. "Talked to some people. By the store."

"They don't have any right to hassle you, Ben. If you're not breaking any laws or disturbing the peace, they don't have any right to arrest you or put you in…the sheriff's office. Would you like me to talk to them about it for you?''

"Don't matter now," Ben said darkly, and spun on his heel. I thought he would go a few paces and then come back to the rock, but this time he kept going, around the corner of the anchorage. I hustled after him and saw him up the hillside, filling a pan of water from a pipe that came out of the hillside. He appeared to be talking to himself, or conversing with someone I could not see. When the pan was full, he brought it back under the bridge and put it down on one of the rough plank tables. When he went around the other corner of the anchorage, I waited. He soon reappeared with a kerosene stove and two mugs, and set about making tea.

I was silent, then began talking to Ben about his work with the birds. When the tea was ready, Ben went back to his position behind the rock where the large gull stood with its feathered wings outstretched. I picked up my mug and sipped the strong, dark tea. For a while neither of us spoke. I raised the subject of the river down below, but Ben seemed uninterested.

"Guess what I saw," he asked instead, his mouth smiling like a child's. For the first time, I began to wonder what had driven him out of society to live under a bridge.

"Where, Ben?"

"In the office."

"You saw something in the sheriff's office?" Ben nodded. "Was it yesterday?"

Again he nodded. He had not moved his feet since returning to his position behind the rock. "It was him all right."

"Who was it, Ben?"

"Ambulance brought him in."

Suddenly I knew who Ben was talking about. But I still didn't understand why a dead man was so interesting to him.

"Did you know him?" I asked.

Ben's face changed, suddenly defensive. "I said I seen him."

"I mean, did you ever see him before yesterday?"

There was a long pause, while Ben bit his lower lip and I waited. Finally Ben spoke. "Up the ridge. Harvest time."

"Harvest time," I said. Up here that meant September, maybe late October. But it didn't mean anything legal. "Was it a good crop?"

"My friend had it."

"You were helping a friend bring in his crop."

Ben looked at me, surprised. "You know Carl?"

"Carl Larkin?"

"He was my friend," Ben said, and looked down at the gull. He made one wing flap up and then down.

"But the man you saw yesterday, at the sheriff's office," I said. "That's wasn't Carl. That man's name is Richard."

"No," Ben said somberly.

"I'm pretty sure about it," I said gently. "I was there when they found him."

"Dick," Ben stated. "Ambulance brought him in."

I understood now that I was the one that was confused about things, not Ben. "I'm sorry," I said. "I didn't understand. I thought his name was Richard, but it's Dick."

Ben nodded. "I saw him yesterday."

"I'm curious, Ben. Was Dick visiting Carl when you saw him the last time?"

Ben shook his head sadly. "No," he said, "it was…"

"Who, Ben? Who was he visiting?"

I held my breath. Again Ben made one wing of the gull flap once, up and down. I kept waiting. The name he finally uttered, which sounded like "Gibbie," was almost inaudible. It was also meaningless, until I remembered that Melissa Larkin was convicted of murdering a man from Pomo Bluff named Gibson McPhail.

"Dick was visiting Gibbie," I said, keeping my voice calm. "They knew each other." Ben nodded, and made the gull wing flap again.

So Dick Shammey's last trip to Pomo Bluff was not his first, and he knew both Carl Larkin and the man Larkin's sister was supposed to have murdered. I couldn't believe how rapidly the plot was thickening. Of course, it could all be the product of a mind that was no longer whole, but there was also something incestuous about it that fit my notion of small towns. Even San Francisco seemed like a small town sometimes.

"Tell me, Ben, do you remember which year you saw Carl and Gibbie up the ridge with Dick Shammey?" Ben flinched. I waited a moment, then continued, more slowly. "You said it was harvest time. That's in the fall, right?" Ben did not look up, but his head dipped a moment.

"Try to remember, Ben. Was it the fall before…what happened? To Gibbie?"

Ben looked down at the ground and began shaking his head back and forth strenuously. Finally he began talking to himself, but too quietly for me to hear.

"I'm sorry, Ben, what did you say?"

Ben looked up and glared at me.

"I said what I said. But nobody listens. You can't bring him back, can you? You can't do that. You do what you can do, and they done it. The only question is, now

what? Can things go back like they were? You can't
bring him back!"

I held up a hand gently, hoping to slow Ben down.
But he continued with a flood of words that would not
be stopped and that I could not follow. When he finally
paused and seemed to remember that I was there, I
quickly thanked him for the tea. He stared at me, like I
had just arrived on his doorstep. He began speaking to
me in a voice that was surprisingly clear and direct.

"You know what?" he began. "The county says I'm
schizophrenic. That's what they say: Too bad, Ben,
here's some money. Every month: Here's some money."
He stuck one arm straight out from his side, with his palm
up as if he were receiving payment. "You know what?
The county pushes me out of the store. Out of the town:
We don't want you, Ben! Don't spend any money here!"

He stuck his other arm out, making his body a gaunt
cross under the humming overpass. He flapped both arms
up and down, staring at me. "So who's schizophrenic?"
he demanded. "Me or them?"

# FIVE

I RETURNED TO my car and drove back into town, my mind burning with possibilities. It appeared that I had stumbled onto something more interesting than the accidental death of a San Francisco art dealer. The story of Shammey's demise now looked like it could hold the front page on speculation alone. Of course, I didn't have a paper to write the story for, but that was secondary. If I had a hot enough scoop in my hands, the paper would have to take me back. Or even better, I could refuse an offer to come back to work, but charge them through the nose for exclusive rights. As I say, my mind was burning.

The fire got a bucket of cold water, though, when I cruised up to the drugstore and saw the "back after lunch" sign hanging in the door. I got out of the car and checked, but the door was securely locked. I couldn't see the fax machine advertised in the window, but I was sure my faxes about Melissa Larkin's murder trial were in there somewhere. I stood outside and looked around, considered my options. I could wait until the proprietor returned, but there was not much to do in town and I was still full from my late breakfast. Also, I didn't want to hang around quite so conspicuously.

Then a light came on. If I couldn't get more information about Melissa Larkin from long distance, I could try to get it up close. It would be tricky, but one could prepare. One could take precautions. After a brief stop in the grocery store I got into my car and consulted my notebook. The address I needed was in the notes from my conversation with Bruce, and one of the maps told me where to find it. I pulled out of the parking lot and headed north on the highway.

I made a few false turns on the way, but I eventually found the place I was looking for. I sat in the car and looked up from the road, through the iron gates that stood ajar halfway up the long driveway. Then I pulled farther up the road, around a curve, and parked out of sight. Quietly I walked back down to the bottom of the driveway and waited. It didn't take long for the dogs to appear. They stopped inside the gate and watched me, silent but quivering with energy. I had heard from some of my buddies on the paper that the most dangerous dogs were the ones that didn't bark. That was why I had taken the precautions.

I began talking quietly to the dogs about their sleek coats, their bright eyes, their obvious intelligence. I could have praised their impressive musculature, sharp teeth, and heavy leather collars, too, but I was trying to keep my courage up. When one of the dogs finally sat down on his haunches, I carefully unwrapped the chunks of meat I had brought and tossed two halfway to the gates. The standing dog hesitated, but his companion quickly trotted out and lapped up both treats. Now the standing animal came forward expectantly. I knelt down slowly and held out a few more chunks of meat.

By the time the red-haired man appeared at the top of the driveway and looked down, I was petting both dogs and apologizing to them, quietly, that I had not brought them more good things to eat. When I noticed their owner, I stuffed the meat wrapping deeper into my jacket pocket and straightened up with a smile. The man whistled shortly and both dogs leaped up the driveway toward him. I waved and called out "Good-looking dogs!"

"They're not usually so friendly," their owner called back. "You got dogs of your own?"

I took a couple of steps up the driveway toward the gates. "Not just now," I said, drawing out my vowels a bit and looking like I was mighty sorry about my dog-less state. "Livin' in the city is no place for dogs like these."

"I hear you," the man said. He paused outside his gates, not inviting but not unfriendly either. His hair was pulled back and tied in a pony-tail. "You visiting somebody up here?"

"Fishing," I said. "I never saw a crowd on the river like I saw this morning, so I'm looking around for someplace a little quieter."

"Not much water up here."

"Well, I figured maybe I could get over the ridge, hike down to the north fork."

He nodded, possibly impressed. "It's a ways from here," he said, "but you could do it."

"Any fish in the fork?"

"Some. I don't fish myself, but I got friends who've been there. They usually take an easier route."

"Is there a trail anywhere?"

The man nodded and petted the dog that leaned against his leg. "There's trails all over this ridge," he said. "You can get pretty much anywhere you want if you're willing to walk a while."

"It's beautiful country," I said. "And it looks like you got yourself a mighty nice slice of it right here."

The man pushed open his gate a little. "Come on up, take a look," he said. I strolled up the driveway, then turned back to the west and took a deep breath. At the end of a rich green carpet of forest the ocean stretched away silvery blue. One of the dogs licked my hand and snuffled against my jacket, and Larkin laughed. "You got some kind of way with dogs," he said.

"They're good dogs, is all."

"Well, I appreciate your sayin' it."

"Name's Rye."

"Carl. Nice to meet you."

"Same. This is mighty pretty. How much of it is yours?"

"About ten acres," he said. "I don't have any neighbors nearby, so it feels like more."

I turned and looked at the house, which was modest but snug and secure. The roof was lined with solar panels, and beyond the house there was a windmill turning at medium speed in the breeze. There was a small barn, a pumphouse, a satellite dish, and a cottage that looked quiet, as if its occupant was gone for a while. A good-sized late-model pick-up truck was the only vehicle in sight. The perimeter, or at least as much of it as I could see, appeared to be well fenced all the way around. There was no evidence of a woman's touch anywhere on the property.

"You get much power out of the windmill?" I asked.

"As much as I can use," Larkin said.

"How come everyone doesn't do it?"

"Number of reasons. Chiefly they don't know how. I got the equipment from a guy in Denmark, he designed the gearing and the generator himself."

"And you heat your water on the roof," I observed.

Larkin nodded soberly. "The sun and the wind give us so much energy we don't use," he said. "It's hard going down in the big cities and seeing how people have forgotten the basic machinery of the planet."

While he talked I got a good look at him. He had a square jaw, a lightly freckled complexion, and clear eyes.

He was a little taller than me, and more solidly built. In his jeans and pullover, he reminded me of the models for casual wear that filled the mail order catalogs. He was, after all, the handsome single guy Melodie said he needed to be.

"From the way you talk," I ventured, "you might be an engineer or something. Am I right?"

"No," he said, "but I work with guys like that sometimes."

"Architecture?"

"No," he said again. "I do a little construction, a little this and a little that. People up here are more self-reliant, I guess. We learn how to do things, take care of themselves, take care of each other, you know." He stroked the side of his face with the opposite hand, then pinched his chin between the thumb and forefinger.

"It's a good way," I affirmed. One of the dogs was angling to get at the pocket of my jacket, the one that had the meat wrapper in it. I turned away, ostensibly to look out at the view, and gave the dog a couple of good thumping pats. He lifted his head, and I scratched the top of it like I had seen Larkin do. Then the other dog wanted the same treatment. Larkin smiled down at the two of them like a fond parent. I scratched and patted his animals until I felt awkward, and then pointed behind Larkin at the cottage. "Mighty cute," I said. "You build it?"

"As a matter of fact, it came with the place," Larkin said. "Of course, it was just a shed then."

I studied the cottage as if sizing up some real estate. It was obviously closed up, with the curtains pulled and the walkway overgrown. "What did you have to do to it?" I wondered aloud.

"Plumbed the toilet, ran in some electrical, the usual. Except I put the shower out back, an open-air deal."

"No kidding?"

"Have a look." He walked me around the back of the cottage, which was completely private from the rest of the compound and shaded by tall pines that marched up the hillside into a thick wood. The dogs snuffled around the base of the cottage while I examined the shower. It was actually a cozy redwood nook built out of the wall of the cottage, with a smooth deck beneath it, a broad bench tucked into the side, and pegs for hanging clothes. It was better than most of the indoor showers I had seen.

"This is a feature," I said.

"We get the water from right up the hillside there, so it just seemed natural to put the shower out here, too."

"Wait a minute," I said. "You've got wind power, solar heat, spring water—do you pay any utilities at all?"

"Not hardly," Larkin said matter-of-factly. "I compost most of the garbage and recycle the rest."

By this point I had forgotten that Larkin was a potential witness to a suspicious death, or the potential subject of a story about wild mushrooms. Instead I was making mental notes for an article about Carl Larkin, paragon of environmentalism. But the paragon's next comment brought me back to reality.

"It was my sister got me onto all this conservation," he said, "when she was living here." Again he rubbed the side of his face with the opposite hand. I couldn't believe that he had mentioned his sister, a convicted murderer, so casually. Then I remembered that as far as he was concerned, I was a total stranger who didn't know anything about Melissa and Gibbie and Dick Shammey.

"I can't believe anyone would move away from here," I said half-aloud, turning to look up into the woods.

"She'll be back," he said flatly, and stared off into the trees. I kept my face a blank, but the silence that followed was hard. I couldn't really console Larkin for something I was not supposed to know about. I cast around for a new subject.

"You know," I said, "this kind of reminds me of the place I'm staying down the highway."

He looked up. "Mar Vista?"

"No," I said, "it's the Italian place."

"Saint Horace," Larkin smiled. "Livin' rich."

"It was the only place I could get," I said earnestly. "Believe me, I tried to get a place in the hotel."

"The inn's okay."

"You ever eat there?"

"Not often. But I sell 'em some mushrooms."

I raised my eyebrows. "Pick 'em wild?"

Larkin nodded and I gave a low whistle of admiration. "They're all over up here, if you know where to look," he said modestly.

"Yeah, but half of 'em can kill you."

"Well, there are other things beside mushrooms up here that can kill you," he said. "You just have to learn what's what."

"I guess you have to learn your way around, too," I said, "or you take a walk in the woods and you don't come back."

Larkin laughed. "It's not that dangerous. Like I say, there's trails all over."

"Well, if that's the way it is, are there any trails down there by the inn? Any way I could get over the ridge from there?"

Larkin looked thoughtful. "From there," he said, "it's a little tricky. You can pick up a trail after a while, but it's rough woods at first. You would have to know your way, or have someone show you. It'd be easier just to go up the highway, or down across the river."

"C Ranch Creek?"

"Yeah. Though it may not be too solitary down there, either."

We laughed, and one of the dogs licked my hand. I held both hands out. "Listen, have you got any place I could wash up?"

Larkin smiled and we strolled back out toward the main house. I felt sorry for him, knowing his wait for Melissa would continue for twelve more years, at least. I wanted to know if he had seen anything around Dick Shammey's cottage the day before, but now the ruse I had used to get into his home was working against me. In fact, I felt guilty about my duplicity. Carl Larkin, with his basic values and direct manner, was the kind of man that made other guys proud to be men.

When we got to the house Larkin showed me into the bathroom. As I washed my hands, I spotted several matching zippered pouches on the back of the toilet. After hesitating a moment, my reportorial instincts kicked in. I left the water running and went over to look closer. The quilted pouches reminded me of the ones Corinna would bring to house parties in Carmel for the weekend. One pouch was open and gave off a strong scent of perfume. Inside were a number of cosmetics, including several lipsticks. I returned to the basin, rinsed my hands, and dried them on a nearby towel. I found Larkin in the kitchen, putting a kettle of water on the stove.

"Well, this was mighty kind of you," I said. "I think I'll take your advice and go check out that creek."

"Good idea," Larkin said, and walked me outside. The dogs accompanied us to the gates, and I gave both animals a hearty rub and several sincere pats of appreciation. Larkin waved goodbye from the top of the driveway, and I waved back.

"Nice guy," I said to myself. "I wonder who's visiting?"

I got in my car, turned around, and headed back down the hill. At the first intersection I came to, I could not remember which way I had come up, and went left. It soon became apparent that I was not heading downhill, and I turned around to go back to the intersection where I had gone wrong. As I slowed for the turn, a car came up the hill and sped through the intersection in the direction of Larkin's house. The woman in the passenger seat glanced out her window at my car, and I slammed on the brakes. It was not the cover-girl beauty of her face that caused my reaction. It was not even her long red hair. It was the car she was riding in, and the person driving it.

"WE'VE NEVER HAD anyone get this many pages before," the woman behind the cash register told me. "And we've never had anyone use it from out of town. This is really exciting!" She carefully counted the fax pages, and then counted them again, while I waited impatiently. "Let's see, twenty one pages, four dollars for the first page, and two dollars for the following pages...that comes to forty-four dollars!" She beamed at me proudly and held out her hand. I paid her the money and stuffed the sheaf of paper in my bag. "Do you want anything else?" she asked.

"Not at these prices," I said, and walked out. I walked across the highway to the pay phone, looked up a San Francisco number from my notebook, and dialed it. When a man with a clipped British accent answered, I apologized for calling him at home. After that I did not beat around the bush.

"I need you to wire me some expense money," I said.

"The story's going great, but things are much more expensive than I thought."

"We're happy to pay your expenses upon receipt of the story," my editor assured me.

"Then advance me ten percent of the fee. Lord knows it's not that much."

"Against policy, I'm afraid. Can't you use a credit card or something?"

I fought a combination of embarrassment and anger. "I would if I could," I said slowly. "But I need all the credit I have to cover the hotel. A couple hundred dollars in cash is all I need to get through the weekend. You'll have the story a week from today."

"I know this sounds heartless, Rigel, but I'm simply not authorized to extend funds in advance of receipt."

Not heartless, I thought. Spineless. "Sorry to bother you," I said, and hung up.

I stared out the window a moment at the sky, turning leaden under a high overcast. The ocean was already slate gray and dotted with white caps. I zipped my jacket and made another call.

"Hi, Marcy, it's Rigel. Is Doug there?"

"Sure, Rye, hang on."

A moment later Doug came on the line.

"Hey, Rye, how's the fishing?"

"Great."

"That means you caught something."

"Well…"

"I told you, there's good fishing and great fishing—"

"I know."

"—and great fishing is when you catch something."

"Right."

"So you've been having *good* fishing."

I sighed. "Actually, it's been a little rough. The women are catching more fish than I am."

"You brought women?"

"I met someone up here."

"Listen, are you fishing or fooling around?"

"I'm fishing, Doug, believe me."

"The rod working okay?"

"Fine. Listen, I wanted to ask you about your allergy to nuts."

"You mean, nuts like you or the kind you eat?"

"Thanks, pal."

"You mean anaphylaxis."

"Right. Did you ever eat a nut by accident?"

"Yeah, and I don't want to do it again."

"Can you tell me what happened?"

"Is this what you called to ask me?"

"I met this guy, I think he has the same problem."

"If he does, he either knows about it or he's dead," Doug declared.

"Those appear to be the choices," I agreed.

He went on to tell me about a time before he was married, when he had eaten some birthday cake with shaved almonds under the icing. He had enjoyed a brisk walk home to his apartment when his throat began to constrict. "I knew right away what was happening," he continued, "so I pushed myself off the chair before I passed out."

"How did you know?"

"It's not like any other feeling in the world. Your whole body is trying to reject this poison any way it can. It's like your insides want to leave your body through every orifice."

"Why did you want to get out of the chair?"

"So I could get some blood to my head. Otherwise I

would pass out and stay passed out and that would be the end of that. When I came to, I saw the front door of my apartment and started crawling toward it.''

"Did you make it?"

"Yeah, but later we figured out it took me about half an hour to go ten feet. I kept going unconscious when I would lift my head to crawl some more."

"So you knew what was happening, and you kept fighting to get to the door."

"Yeah, and I was lucky. I fell against the door when I reached up to open it, and the landlady heard me. She came up with a key and opened the door."

"Did you throw up?"

"In the ambulance, I believe, or on the stairs. I was not taking careful notes at the time."

"So the main thing is, you didn't just die."

"Right. I had a chance to get help."

"I'm glad you made it," I said sincerely. I pictured Doug sitting in his spacious living room with an unob-structed view of the Golden Gate Bridge. "Can I ask you something else?"

"Shoot."

I swallowed hard and asked Doug to loan me some money until I was paid for the magazine story. To my relief, he did not hesitate.

"There's one condition," he told me. "You've got to catch a fish, and show me proof, or pay me back double." It was a tough bargain, but the only one I could scare up on short notice. I told him the name of the local bank, thanked him for his help, and ended the call with a prom-ise to somehow catch a fish and get a photo.

Half an hour later, my wallet full again, I walked out of the bank, crossed the highway, and went into the small bookstore I had visited the day before. The owner was putting up signs for a poetry reading that night, and when he brought me my coffee he left a flyer on the table alongside the cup. I nodded but did not look up. I was reading my forty-four-dollar faxes, and I wasn't going to be cheated of a single penny.

As Hollis had told me, the trial of Melissa Larkin made headlines principally because she was the first woman subjected to the harsh new sentencing laws for people convicted of murder involving firearms. But I didn't care about that. I was more interested in the picture that emerged of her alleged victim, Gibson R. ("Gibbie") McPhail. Evidently McPhail was a known cultivator of marijuana. This was not unusual for a man living on the economically depressed north coast of California, because marijuana was often the top cash crop after lumber. But McPhail was also a promising painter whose artistic career was cut prematurely short. He had exhibited some paintings in the city the summer before his death.

According to the prosecution, McPhail was ambushed in San Francisco and shot dead by Melissa Larkin in late autumn, after he had sold a large marijuana crop. McPhail was shot a few blocks from her apartment, with a small-caliber, scaled down pistol of the type Smith & Wesson had recently introduced for women. He was shot several times from up close, indicating that he knew his assailant. His watch and wallet were found in Larkin's car. The money was never recovered. McPhail and Larkin were both unmarried. Both were born and raised in the area around Pomo Bluff.

It looked like an open-and-shut case, and I remembered Ben's diatribe about schizophrenia. It occurred to me that, yes, the county may be a little split in how it treated him, but that didn't mean he wasn't nuts himself. I remembered one homeless man in San Francisco who believed he was the mayor's chief aide. He showed up every morning at city hall and had to be forcibly turned away.

Maybe Ben had concocted the whole story about Shammey and Gibbie and Carl Larkin. Maybe Melissa knew about Gibbie's harvest, invited him to visit her after he did his deal, and plugged him when the money was in the bag. Maybe Shammey just ate something he shouldn't have while on a pleasant weekend in the country. Maybe I should be thinking about my fishing article instead of chasing notions I couldn't prove.

The last fax about the trial showed a courtroom artist's rendering of the trial in progress. It had the usual line-up of defendant, attorney, prosecutor, and judge. When I got to the face of the witness on the stand, the hair on the back of my neck stood up. The last time I had seen this dark, handsome face was on the drivers license belonging to Dick Shammey. I quickly scanned the story until I came to a passage that I reread a number of times:

The defense's final witness, Union Square gallery owner Richard G. Shammey, stunned defense attorney Rosalie Cordova by apparently contradicting Larkin's testimony on a number of key points, including her whereabouts during the time McPhail is believed to have been killed.

When Cordova asked Shammey to confirm Larkin's testimony, that they had spent the evening together except for a short period when she went to a nearby store for groceries, he testified that "it was more like an hour." Cordova then pressed Shammey to say that he and Larkin had spent the night together. He replied that he went to sleep before she did, and that he "did not know what time she came to bed.''

Under cross-examination, Shammey also failed to support Larkin's testimony that she hated guns and had never owned one. In response to close questioning from prosecutor Aaron Sugarman, Shammey testified that the defendant had stated an intention to acquire a handgun for self-defense because of the high crime rate in her neighborhood. Cordova's hearsay objection was overruled by Superior Judge Grady Banshaw.

Shammey concluded his testimony by emphasizing that he had ''enjoyed his time'' with Larkin and expressed a hope that she ''has not done something she will be sorry for later.'' Both attorneys are scheduled to make closing arguments on Monday.

I looked again at the rendering of the courtroom scene. Melissa Larkin sat at the defense table with her head in her hands. The defense attorney was shown standing by the witness stand, with her arms spread in theatrical disbelief. The prosecutor was writing something down. The judge was looking at Shammey. Once again, the hair on the back of my neck stood up. I remembered now what Hollis had told me on the phone, that some people thought Melissa Larkin was framed. He also said that city hall had leaned on the paper to kill coverage. That was not something city hall did for young women fresh from the countryside. It was not unheard of, however, in cases involving well-heeled men and women who owned chic shops and galleries in the area around Union Square. People like Dick Shammey, for example.

I read the report of Shammey's testimony one more time. If I was reading it right, Melissa Larkin had somehow become one of Shammey's ''young women,'' as

Corinna put it. At the very least, Melissa and Shammey were sleeping together. But that was not all. She had counted on him as a witness in her defense—a confidence that was evidently misplaced. She was in prison for murder, and Shammey was dead in her old home town. "Ben," I said half aloud, "I take it back. It's not you, it's them."

A man and woman at a nearby table looked up at me like I was schizophrenic or something. I smiled at them and returned to my reading. The *Scientific American* article about anaphylaxis ran on more than a dozen pages, but I didn't get far into it before returning to contemplation of Melissa Larkin. It was not hard to imagine her living in the little cottage on her brother's property, and then moving to the city with high hopes. It dawned on me that if what Ben said was true—that Shammey had visited Carl Larkin earlier that fall—then it might have been Melissa that introduced Shammey to her family and friends back home. She and Shammey were lovers, after all. She must have been proud to show off someone so glamorous and sophisticated. Someone who may have used her mercilessly, then framed her for murder.

It was sad, really. False hopes, dashed expectations, murder, prison, and death. I had spent plenty of time sitting around in bars with reporters who worked the crime beats. To these men and women, everyone was guilty until proven innocent, everyone was lying and covering up, and nothing was shocking any more. To tell you the truth, it was one of the things that got me into political reporting. There was still room for ideals, for preserving the public trust. Politics might be full of bad people and bad deeds, but it rarely left people dead.

I put down my coffee, raised my eyes, and looked out the window toward the highway. The afternoon was coming to a close, and it was time to head back to the inn and rig up for tomorrow's fishing. But a weight had settled in me, and it took an effort to lift myself from the chair and walk outside to my car. The death of Gibbie McPhail, and the subsequent incarceration of Melissa Larkin, both seemed tragically unnecessary. The fact that Shammey, too, was dead, seemed to cast an even deeper shadow over the whole business. I wished now that I had never looked into this dark corner of country life, and that I would have things more clear in my mind before I saw Sarah again that evening.

WHEN I RETURNED to my cottage at St. Horace I took a long shower, put on my last clean shirt, and spread out my fishing gear on the bed. The last leader I had used that morning was gnarled and knotted, and it had to be replaced. While I worked, I thought about my visit to Carl Larkin. I had guessed from Ben's remarks about Carl Larkin's autumn "harvests" that Larkin might be selling more than mushrooms. That was why I had gone to Larkin's house expecting to find dogs. I had been surprised that the gates were open, but now I understood why: Larking was expecting visitors. Or more precisely, he was expecting his house guest to return. Evidently Larkin had no reason to hide the fact that he had a woman staying with him, because he had let me use his bathroom without hesitation. But if the red-headed woman was a guest from out of town, where was her car?

I finished tying on a new leader and opened my small plastic box of fishing lures. I studied several different flies, noticing how they were basically metal hooks wrapped with different colors of thread, twine, and feathers. At last I selected a relatively long, slender fly and hooked it on the front of my shirt. I went to the closet and removed the piece of folded tissue paper I had tucked into the pocket of my shirt the day before. I came back to the bed, unfolded the tissue, and extracted the long red hairs I had found in the cottage bathtub. I studied them a while, then pulled the fly off my shirt and carefully wrapped the hair around it. When I had tied off the hair and clipped the ends, I held the fly up to the light. "You are one chubby dude," I said.

This reminded me of Sarah's explanation about adopting the perspective of the fish you were trying to catch. I realized that I had used the same technique with my source in the state capitol. I made sure to appear as someone she could tell things to, someone who would understand her point of view. This was not just a pose, by the way. I did understand. In fact, I understood too well. But that was ancient history. I began to speculate on how to present myself to the red-headed woman in a way that would induce her to tell me what she knew. I could find out if she had come up to Pomo Bluff with Shammey, when she had taken her bath, and if she was there when...

Suddenly I had an intense feeling that someone was in the room with me. The hairs on the back of my neck stood up and I felt goose bumps raising on my arms. I stood up and looked around, trying to shake off the feeling. Finally I flung one of the pillows from the bed onto a chair, just to hear a sound. The crisp white linens were barely wrinkled, and I remembered I was staying at an inn. "It was the housekeepers," I said, half aloud. "They came in to make up the room." I looked around a little more, and realized that the housekeepers had not only come in but had done a very thorough job. This must have been Sarah's instruction to them, and I got a little glow inside. Dealing with the fishing gear could come later. Now it was time for dinner in the bar at St. Horace.

# SIX

W<small>HEN</small> I <small>CAME INTO</small> the inn, Sarah was just coming down from the second floor. I met her at the bottom of the stairs, and to my surprise she took my hands in hers and leaned forward to plant a quick kiss on my cheek. Before I could react, she was slipping away again. At the last moment, I managed to hang onto one of her hands and press my lips to it. Sarah smiled, gently extracted her hand, and sauntered away into the bar. I watched her go, feeling quite debonair, until I realized that a young couple had come in the door behind me and watched the whole thing. Quickly I followed Sarah into the bar and sat down at the table where I had spent the previous evening.

To my chagrin, the young couple also came in and took a table nearby. They were talking in low tones and laughing, and I forced myself to look away at a cat perched on a railing outside the window. Soon enough Sarah was standing above me, looking down with a cat smile of her own. "Would you like anything to drink, sir?"

"Oh, yes," I said brightly. "Have you anything in a nice, dry martini?"

"I'm so sorry, sir," Sarah said, playing along. "Wine and beer only, I'm afraid."

"Ah. Well then, a nice cold beer."

"Very good, sir," she said, and left with a wink.

As I sat in the cozy room and looked around at the calm, well-ordered, and thoroughly hospitable surroundings of the inn, I began to feel a little silly about hiding the hairs from the bathtub in my fishing gear. If I really suspected foul play, why didn't I turn the evidence over to the police, tell them what I knew, and let them do their job? I would still be the only professional press on the scene. I could still break the story in some paper, somewhere, somehow.

There was also the little matter of my nearly empty checkbook. The deal I had made with Doug seemed like a foolish bargain, because there was no guarantee I was going to actually catch a fish. The story about fishing, on the other hand, was on the hook. I just had to land it. So if I had my priorities straight, what I really needed to work on was the paying assignment I had come up here to do. Especially if I was going to hang around the swankiest place in town so I could watch Sarah bring me dinner.

I resolved to make some notes on the article while I ate. There was just the one question to clear up with Sarah, and I could do that later. I had brought my briefcase with me, and as I sipped my beer I made notes about the two fishermen I had watched that morning. I wrote down the remark about luck having nothing to do with catching fish. I looked up at Sarah as she served some wine to the young couple next to me. Perhaps luck still had something to do with catching women.

Suddenly I realized that I could easily burn up a few hundred words describing places for fishermen—and fisherwomen—to stay while they were visiting the north coast. Lifestyle readers ate up that kind of thing, didn't they? I turned a page in my notebook and began describing St. Horace. I figured I could write up the inn, the Pomo Bluff hotel, and the place that Carl Larkin had mentioned, to cover the range of accommodations in the area. Of course I would have to find that third place, but I was sure Sarah could tell me where it was.

She, however, was kept busy greeting diners and pouring wine for the restaurant. Every few moments a waiter or waitress would appear from the back passage and take away a tray in the other direction, across the lobby toward the restaurant. Finally the restaurant's hostess appeared to collect the young couple. The lobby was empty too, and I was momentarily alone with Sarah.

"Would you like me to run through the entire menu," she asked, "or just start with the list of appetizers?"

"I don't think I can repeat last night's performance," I smiled. "How about going directly to the entrees?"

After taking my order, Sarah looked down at my notebook. "How's the article coming?"

"Plenty of notes," I assured her. "Listen, do you know a place called Mar Vista?"

"Sure," she said, and told me where it was. "Are we no longer to have the pleasure of your company?"

"Don't worry," I said, as I noted down the address. "I'm just describing different places people can stay."

"How did you hear about Mar Vista?"

"I met someone up on the ridge today who told me about it."

"I was up on the ridge today myself," she said.

"Really?"

"My sister is in town visiting an old friend of hers, and after we had lunch I drove her back up there."

The memory of Sarah's car going through the intersection up on the ridge went through my mind in slow motion. The red-haired woman in the passenger seat, the woman Sarah was driving up to Carl Larkin's house, the woman I believed was in the cottage with Dick Shammey, that woman was... "Your sister," I said, dumbly.

"Rachel," Sarah said, looking at me with a hand on her hip. "Remember, I told you about her?"

"Sure," I said quickly. "I was just— I mean, I didn't realize she was here. She came up today?"

"Last night, I think."

"She's not staying with you?"

"The old friend is really an old flame," Sarah said with a wry smile.

"Ah."

"I'm going to put your order in."

Sarah disappeared and I stared down at the table top. My mind had begun to spin, and I struggled to get it to stop. I looked first at one hand, then the other. My left hand was the mysterious woman with the long red hair, the woman I believed was in the cottage with Dick Shammey. The right hand was Sarah's sister, visiting her "old flame," Carl Larkin. I held my hands apart, then brought them together. Could the mysterious red-head and Sarah's sister be the same person?

When Sarah came back, I looked up at her hopefully. "Can I ask you a weird question?"

"You want to change your order?"

"No, I wonder if there's any chance that your sister knows that guy. Dick Shammey."

To my surprise, Sarah looked around to see that we were alone. "I wondered about that too," she told me quietly. "Her husband's father has a big house full of art, and she meets people he knows all the time, at parties and gallery openings. When I saw the license plate on the guy's car I wondered if she might have met him before, at a party or something."

"What's her husband's name?"

Sarah told me, and I nodded. I knew both the husband and his father by reputation. The older man had been

President of the county Board of Supervisors before I became a reporter. He had also married the last descendent of one of San Francisco's oldest society families. The woman's family had lost virtually all its former wealth except for a Pacific Heights mansion full of old paintings and furniture. I had heard that the father's last supervisorial campaign was financed by the sale of a famous old master painting, although it was never revealed who bought it—or who arranged the sale. A number of city museums that had been counting on a bequest were surprised to find the painting gone without a trace.

Sarah returned to her duties, and I returned to my riddle. If Rachel had arrived on Thursday night, not Friday night, it was possible that she came up to Pomo Bluff with Shammey. It seemed unlikely, though, that she would get a ride up with Shammey, take a bath in his tub, and then go to stay with her old boyfriend instead. Even if she did, how did she get from St. Horace to Larkin's house? It was possible that Larkin had picked her up at the inn Friday morning, but that presupposed that she spent the night with Shammey in the cottage's only bed. It also left unexplained Larkin's presence at the inn the following morning, alone and on foot, heading up the ridge through the woods. The whole situation was off somehow, as if the pages of a book had been bound in the wrong order.

A young waiter appeared from the kitchen with my dinner, and I fell to it with a delighted palate and a distracted mind. Some more people came in and sat down while waiting for the tables in the restaurant, and I ate in silence. When Sarah returned a short while later, my plate was empty.

"That was fast," she said.

"Listen," I said quietly, "is it possible that your sister

came up here with Shammey on Thursday night?" Sarah's eyes widened, and I added quickly, "I mean, could she have gotten a ride with him?"

"I spoke with her on the phone Thursday night," Sarah said. "She had a fight with her husband and she was really upset."

"Was she in the city?"

Sarah lowered her voice, but the sharp edge of familial protectiveness was unmistakable. "She didn't say where she was. And what makes you think she has anything to do with what happened here?"

I glanced at the other tables, whose occupants did not seem to notice the sudden tension between their hostess and me. "Let's talk about it later," I said. The phone rang in the bar, and Sarah left.

The next time she came to my table, she asked if I wanted coffee or dessert. I asked for coffee and weighed my options. When the people at the other two tables went into the restaurant, I made up my mind. I could not see Sarah's eyes as she poured my coffee, but she seemed to be relaxed.

"Can you sit down a moment?" I asked gently. She sat down and put her silver coffee pitcher on the table. I put a hand on her arm, and she did not move or push it off. "When I went into the cottage yesterday afternoon, after everyone was gone, I found some hair in the drain. It was long, it was wet, and it was red." Sarah raised her eyes and looked at me in wordless surprise.

"I saw you and your sister driving up on the ridge today," I continued quickly. "so I know what kind of hair she has. That's why I wondered if she was in the room at some point."

Sarah picked up her arms and folded them across her

chest. I could see her jaw set. "Are you saying my sister had something to do with that man dying?" she asked.

"Just wait a minute—"

"You said yourself it was from the muffin!"

"I'm not saying she did anything," I said, keeping my voice low. "I'm saying she might have been there. If she didn't do anything then the best thing she can do is come forward and tell what she knows."

Sarah looked at me accusingly. "Rachel has enough problems," she declared, "without you coming up with a story like that."

"I've been thinking about the muffin," I continued. I was past the point of no return as far as upsetting her, so I figured I should at least learn what I could. "If the guy did eat something that he was deathly allergic to, it's more likely that he would have been trying like hell to get someone's attention, not lying around on the bed. That guy didn't look like he was fighting for his life, he looked like he had fallen asleep after getting laid."

As the last two words fell from my lips, I began regretting them. Sarah's jaw dropped and her eyes blazed. "Is that what you think? That my sister screwed that guy and then *killed* him?"

"I didn't say that, I just—"

Abruptly she stood up. "Are you up here fishing, or driving around spying on me behind my back?" With that she grabbed the coffee pot, spun away from the table, and disappeared into the kitchen. The silence was deafening, and I could feel my cheeks burning again.

"Damn," I said aloud. A moment later I heard movement and looked around. One of the waitresses was peering out from the back passage to the kitchen, as if investigating a loud noise or bad smell. Seeing only me, her eyebrows went up and she ducked back out of sight.

I groaned inwardly. A moment later Sarah swept back out from the kitchen and went into the bar without acknowledging me. I got up and walked to the bar. She was busily pulling corks on bottles. "Hey," I said softly. "I'm sorry."

She thrust a check across the bar at me. "Twenty-three dollars," she said, and yanked another cork. I couldn't think of anything to say, so I pulled out some money and put it on the bar.

"Thank you," she said, and put the money in a drawer below the bar. When she looked up at me, I wanted to kick myself. Her composure, the gliding calm that gave her such aplomb, was shattered. I wanted desperately to restore it, but I couldn't think of what to say. "I think you better go," she said, her voice small. "We're really busy."

A group of four people swept into the bar and Sarah greeted them briefly with a smile she surely had to fake. I lowered my voice.

"Sarah, I'm sorry."

She looked up at me. "If you knew what Rachel has been through in her life—" Her voice broke and she turned away. She set four glasses on a tray and picked it up. "I have to go," she said in a low voice, and went out to the table where the four people had just sat down. I cursed myself quietly, then strode to my table, stuffed my notebook in my briefcase, and put on my jacket. I wrote "I'm sorry" on a scrap of paper and left it on the bar as I stalked out of the inn into the night.

I WAS TRUDGING UP the path to my cottage when I saw the county patrol car and the two uniformed men standing on the porch. I was glad for something else to be interested in besides my own stupidity.

"What's going on?" I called as I approached the cottage.

"You the occupant of this room?" one of the deputies called back.

"Yup," I responded, and bounded up the steps. The deputy that had addressed me was in his fifties at least, with silver-black hair and a kind face. His partner was about my age, but taller and heavier. Both men looked uncomfortable. "What can I do for you?" I asked them. The older deputy responded.

"We've got instructions from the County Sheriff to search this room, its occupant, and his motor vehicle," he said, speaking slowly. He probably figured I was unused to police talk, men in uniforms, and so on.

"You're a day late," I said. "They took the guy away already, and towed his car. You should've called before you came."

The younger deputy pointed at me with a long, heavy flashlight of his own. "You said you're the occupant of this room."

My sympathy drained away. "The guy you want—the dead guy—is already gone," I said, looking from one deputy to the other. Neither reacted. "I checked in afterwards. Sheriff Stone already searched the room and questioned everybody. If you want to search something, ask Stone if you can search the guy's car. That's where you should be looking."

The older deputy scrutinized a piece of paper. "These instructions came from Sheriff Stone. I'm sure he knows what ought to be searched and what—"

"I'm telling you, he searched this room himself," I interrupted. "I'm Rigel Lynx, not Dick Shammey."

"He said the occupant of the room," the younger deputy said, once again pointing his flashlight at me. I pushed the flashlight aside with my arm.

"Go ahead and look in there if you want," I said. "But you've got no reason to search me or my car."

I moved toward the door of the cottage, but the younger deputy blocked my way. For a large man, he moved with surprising quickness. The older man put a hand on the younger man's arm and spoke to me.

"We have all the reason we need," he said. "You cooperate, we get it done a lot quicker. And it seems to me you ought to worry about finding another place to stay instead of arguing with us."

"What do mean, find a place to stay?"

The older man read from the paper. "Said accommodation to remain unoccupied until such time as a police report pursuant to affidavit is filed with the Superior Court." He looked up at me. "That means you can't stay here."

"You can't kick me out at nine o'clock on Saturday night!" I protested. "Where am I going to find a place now?"

"Seems to me they shouldn't ought to have put you in here," the older deputy said. "You want to argue with someone, go see the innkeeper." I rolled my eyes at this suggestion. The older deputy continued. "Deputy Anderson here will drive you downtown to the hotel so you can check in there, or maybe call around and find someplace else. We'll bring your car down to town when we're through."

"You can't run me off like this," I said. "Maybe it works with your local kids, but I'm not that stupid."

The younger deputy patted his open palm with the flashlight. "You think we're stupid?" he asked.

"I think this whole thing is stupid."

"Maybe a night in jail," he suggested, "would change your mind for you."

"You arrest me, I'll make you wish you hadn't," I told him. I had been pushed around by far larger, far angrier cops than this muscle-head. It was a point of pride with reporters, at least in the big city, never to back down to a cop unless you had to stay out of jail to get a story. I had been arrested several times when the police had been sweeping up homeless people in their paddy wagons, simply because I would not stop recording what was happening. The cops involved always got an official reprimand, although they probably got a pat on the back in their own station house.

"I don't like to mention this, but you're giving us grounds," the older deputy said. "Obstructing justice, preventing a peace officer from doing his duty, threatening an officer—"

I pulled my notebook out of my satchel. "False arrest," I said, "police harassment, altering a crime scene. You boys want to play hardball, step up to the plate." I began to write down their badge numbers. This was one of my favorite maneuvers, because it played on all cops' fear of personal accountability.

The younger deputy evidently had a favorite maneuver of his own. He unclipped a pair of handcuffs from his belt and held them up. The two of us locked eyes. The older deputy ended the contest by stepping between us. His belt buckle was no more than an inch from my own.

"I don't know who you are or how you got mixed up in this, son, but you're gettin' in the way," he said gruffly. "We came down here fifty-six miles on county business, and we're not going up home without doing what we came to do. You want more trouble than you got already, we'll arrest you. Or you can just move on and go fishing somewhere else. It's up to you.''

I looked from the older deputy to his partner, who obviously favored an immediate arrest. ''Just take a ride down in the patrol car,'' the older deputy continued, ''and we'll bring your car down there in a while. You mess with me, you're going face down in the back seat with handcuffs on.''

I was outnumbered, I was upset, and I needed time to sort things out. I put my notebook away. ''You take me down,'' I said to the older deputy. ''So he doesn't make me puke all over your nice clean patrol car.''

I STOOD ON the plank sidewalk outside the hotel and watched the patrol car roll back up the highway. I had not been able to get him to talk about the instructions from Stone or when they had been issued. Instead he had advised me to head home and let the whole thing just blow over. That had ended our conversation. Now I looked up the highway toward the bookstore. Even from a distance, it was easy to see that the place was packed, and I remembered the flyer for the poetry reading. I looked over at the pay phone in the parking lot, standing forlornly under its yellow streetlight, and felt the wind cut through my jacket. I turned and went into the bar.

To my surprise, it was not nearly as boisterous as it had been at the beginning of the weekend. The crowd was still overwhelmingly male, and the smoke was still thick, but there was a seat at the near end of the bar where it wrapped around to the wall. I swung up onto the stool and waited for the bartender to work his way down.

While I waited, I looked around. In my jeans and jacket, I didn't stick out as much as I had before. I saw also that the inside of the bar resembled the outside of the hotel: old, worn, and well used. The wood floor was uneven but worn smooth, the dusty mirrors on the walls all advertised different brands of whiskey, and the ceiling fans seemed designed to distribute the smoke more evenly, not remove it from the room. A snake skin stretched for nearly twenty feet above the mirror behind the bar. What kind of snake, I wondered, could get that big and then find its way to Pomo Bluff? I also noticed a series of cracks in the mirror, way up high. It occurred to me that you would have to throw something heavy, like a beer mug, to make cracks up there. I smiled. I liked this place more every minute.

The bartender came at last. His mustache made him look like a friendly walrus. The woman bartender I had talked to the first night was not around.

"Any rooms?" I asked.

"Juice?" he said, cocking an ear.

I raised my voice. "Any rooms in the hotel?"

"All full up," he said. "You just get in?"

"No, I was just tossed out."

The bartender laughed sympathetically. "What'll it be?"

I hesitated a moment, then ordered my second beer of the evening. While I waited I looked around. A bulky old guy in a fishing vest and brimmed hat was holding court at a table near the wall. He had a bulging wallet chained into one back pocket and a big buck knife chained into the other. He was drinking rosé. The men surrounding him, all younger and drinking the same brand of beer, one by one displayed with parted hands the size of their recent catches.

I sighed and remembered my promise to Doug to catch a fish and get a photo of it. At the moment, catching a $400 fish seemed easier than figuring out what had happened to Dick Shammey—and if anyone else was involved in his death. More than anything, I wished I had waited before suggesting to Sarah that her sister was mixed up in it. If I had waited, I could have cleared Rachel entirely or explained her involvement. As it was, I had upset Sarah with nothing to show for it.

When the beer came, I thought about my options. I could go outside in the cold and wind and call a bunch of places that were all full. Or I could sit right here in this warm, friendly bar and try to sort things out. At the very worst, I could let an hour go by before calling Sarah back and apologizing again. Perhaps she would even agree to take me in for another night. From where I sat I could see the whole room and most of its patrons. There was also pretty good light from a large illuminated plastic dog that perched precariously on the end of the big wood-framed mirror that stood behind the bar. I pulled out my notebook and my pen, opened them both up, and took a long drink of crisp, cold beer.

After a while I turned to a blank page, and wrote down a list of names. First was Gibbie McPhail. Next to his name I wrote, "Pomo grower dead in SF. $ gone. Who did it?" Next was Melissa Larkin. Next to her name I wrote, "Took the fall. Did Shammey tip her over?" By Shammey's name I noted, "SF dealer dead in Pomo. Companion gone. Who did it?" I considered the symmetry of the notes on McPhail and Shammey, with Melissa in the middle. I took another drink of beer and looked around the room. Things were beginning to make sense.

I skipped a line and made another list of names: Carl Larkin, Rachel, and Fred Stone. By Carl's name I wrote in, "Motive (Melissa). Opportunity (Liz). Means?" I looked at Rachel's name and then wrote in her last name,

Gordon. This made me remember Sarah's face behind the bar. I shook my head, not so angry now but still full of regret. Finally I opened my eyes and concentrated on Sheriff Stone's name. I looked at it for a long time before writing in, "Whose fingerprints wiped off? Carl's? Shammey's?" Suddenly I had a flash of insight.

I sat back and let it unroll in my mind. Corinna told me that Shammey needed some quick cash to bail himself out of financial trouble. Ben said Shammey had come to Pomo Bluff before (after the marijuana harvest), no doubt to do a deal—perhaps even to set up the deal that resulted in Gibbie McPhail's death. It was not hard to imagine that Shammey had killed Gibbie McPhail himself, and framed Melissa. The money, after all, never turned up. Now I imagined Carl Larkin sending his former lover Rachel Gordon to Shammey to offer a new deal. Like Corinna said, Shammey would find it hard to resist an attractive young woman with money attached. Shammey's ride up to Pomo Bluff with Rachel in the passenger seat must have seemed to him like another double score, but in fact Rachel was delivering him into the hands of Melissa Larkin's big brother. A man with revenge on his mind. I drained the last of my beer and wrote one word next to Rachel's name: "Bait."

I looked up as the bartender put down another beer and picked up the empty bottle. "I figured you were too busy workin' to ask me, so I just brought it," the bartender said with a friendly smile. I pulled a bill out of my wallet and dropped it on the bar, then raised the bottle in salute. The bartender nodded, picked up the money, and left. I took a drink and looked around.

There were a few couples dancing to jukebox music now, and I studied the women. Most seemed girlish from behind, with long dresses and thick braids down the middle of their backs. But when they turned around I could see they were sturdy, mature women with rouged cheeks and tight smiles.

A teenaged boy with a shaved head and green side-burns moved through the dancers in search of someone in the bar. Either he was visiting from the city or his parents had a satellite dish with MTV. I decided it was the latter, because he came over to a middle-aged man and woman sitting at a table not far from me and leaned over to speak to them. After a few exchanges, which I could not hear over the noise of the bar, I saw the man's hand come out of his pocket holding a shiny foil package about the size of a matchbook. The boy quickly slid it into his pocket, kissed his mother on the cheek, and went out the front door of the bar with purpose in his stride. A gust of cold wind blew into the room as the kid left. I smiled to myself and turned back to my beer.

I looked down at the second list of names in my note-book and thought back to where I had left off. Rachel would make ideal bait for a Shammey trap, which Larkin had set up so he could administer frontier justice. Once Shammey was dead Sheriff Stone was there to smooth everything over. It would have all gone off without a hitch, except that a reporter from the big city brought flowers to a woman who had given him a place to stay, and that woman happened to be the innkeeper where Larkin took his revenge. That was why Stone had told me not to say anything, and why he had called in his rein-forcements: to chase me out of the inn and out of town. Larkin and Stone wanted to sew up Shammey's ''acci-dental death'' before anyone could react, much less stop them.

''So now what?'' I said aloud, and the grizzled old

guy next to me turned on his stool. He had been sitting quietly alone for almost an hour.

"We have another beer," he said, and set his empty down on top of the bar, loudly.

"I'm still working on this one," I said affably, as I closed my notebook and put my pen down on top of it.

"By the time he gets here," the man said, indicating the bartender, "you'll need another one."

"Tell you what," I said. "Watch my stuff while I hit the head." I poked around until I found the bathrooms, near the rear exit from the bar. When I found the swinging door into the men's room, I noticed that it had been kicked open by the toes of many boots. I kicked it open myself, relieved myself, and washed my hands. When I got back to my stool, the old guy held up the two fresh beers triumphantly. I laughed, and we touched our bottles together. I noticed from the change on the bar that I had paid for both beers. It didn't matter.

"What you writin' about?" the guy wanted to know.

"Fishing," I said. Even sitting next to someone, it was necessary to raise my voice to be heard.

"You writin' a book? Or just keeping notes?"

"Magazine article," I said. The guy nodded.

"Guy I know, he writes down everything he did every time he comes back from the river. Every cast, just about. Says it helps him prepare for next time."

"I bet it helps him," I said.

"Oh, sure."

"Plus he gets to go fishing twice."

"How's that?"

"Once on the river," I explained, "and once when he's writin' it down."

This idea pleased my new friend immensely, because he laughed until he began coughing, then kept coughing more and deeply. When the bartender materialized with a glass of plain water and another man got up from his stool and came around to pound the guy on the back, I understood that they were handling a situation they had handled before. No one needed to say anything, they just took care of their own. I sat quietly by and waited until everything was calm again, then apologized to the old guy for having set him off.

"That's okay," he told me. "Gets the phlegm out."

"Maybe you shouldn't sit in here with all this smoke," I suggested.

"Hell, I came through the depression," the man told me. "You got to go with what you got, because you don't know what's coming along."

This reminded me, in my beery haze, that I had been kicked out of my room and relieved of the keys to my car. I still had to find a place to stay for the night. Without thinking I kicked the bar, then felt sheepish and looked down to see if I had left a mark. Even in the bar light, I could tell that there were way too many marks to find the one I had made, if I had made one. I straightened up. I wanted to keep studying the situation with Shammey and the others involved in his death, but it was getting late. It was time to drink up and hit the phone. I stuffed my notebook in my satchel, dropped my pen in after it, and reached for my beer.

Behind me the door opened and a rush of cold wind blew my napkin off the bar. I watched it fly away, then noticed the bartender looking at whoever had come in behind me. Two or three more heads turned along the bar. Quickly I looked over my shoulder, expecting to see the two deputies with the keys to my car. Instead I was looking into the agitated face of a strikingly beautiful woman with her hair tucked up under a black knit watch cap. She parted her lips to speak, but not to me.

"Hi, Luke," she said to the man next to me. "Can you loan me your stool for a minute?"

The old fellow got up as if levitated by an unseen force. "Sure, Rachel," he said. "Sit on down."

# SEVEN

RACHEL SLID UP ONTO the stool next to me. She resembled Sarah in the shape of her face and her complexion. After that, she was someone else entirely. Her eyes were greener, her cheekbones were higher, her lips were fuller, and the auburn hair that tumbled around her shoulders when she pulled off the cap was like a mane on a strange and wonderful animal.

A crusty old columnist for the paper wrote once about how a woman's beauty changes the behavior of everyone around her, until she has no chance of being "natural" anymore. I tried to see the ordinary woman inside the extraordinary beauty before me, but it was hard. Whoever that woman was, it looked like she was wrapped pretty tight inside.

The bartender appeared and asked Rachel if she wanted anything. With a reflexive smile she shook her head and turned to me. For a long moment she fixed her eyes on my face, as if she could read my mind by studying my features.

"You're Rigel, aren't you?" Her voice was lower than Sarah's, almost theatrical.

"Call me Rye."

"Sarah says you're very sweet."

"Well, so is she. When I—"

"You have to understand that what I'm telling you is very important," Rachel interrupted. She was shaking her head and looking upwards with a worried expression. "You have to understand that it's…"

"What?" I asked.

Rachel looked over one shoulder along the length of the bar, over the other toward the door, then back at me. "You know what this is about, don't you?" I nodded. "Then you have to know that he is not like other people. It doesn't excuse what happened, I don't mean that, but you have to understand how a person could... How you could... How you could feel different around him."

I nodded again, more deliberately.

Rachel leaned in closer. "You understand?"

"Dick Shammey," I said.

Rachel nodded up and down, causing her hair to fall down around her face. When she swept the offending locks out of the way with a backhanded motion, I had to lean back to avoid getting whipped by the flying tresses. I wondered for a moment if she were under the influence of something besides her own personality.

"He's magnetic," she announced. "That's what he is. He's magnetic, and people find that very attractive. To feel yourself being pulled toward someone, you feel alive, you feel like your life is going faster than it was before. And you are! You are going faster because of that pull, because of the magnetism, you do things you would never have done with another man. It's so *exciting*."

She looked at me for some kind of agreement, I suppose, because when I didn't react her face fell into a mask of earnest concern. She leaned in toward me, her hair brushing my shoulder, her eyes on mine. "I don't just mean intimate things," she said dramatically, "although they feel very intimate, he makes you feel intimate. I just mean, with someone like that, you find yourself— Things sweep you along. You get swept along in the current."

I was close enough to smell her perfume, to feel her breath, to touch her just by shifting my weight. But for all her beauty and allure, she was not more attractive to me than her sister. I eased back away from Rachel and reached for my beer. "Are you sure you don't want anything?" I asked her.

"I want you to *understand*," she said, "about a young woman."

"About a young woman," I repeated, understanding that Rachel was about to talk about herself.

"Yes," she said. "You leave here and go to the city and meet that man and your whole life changes so fast you don't have time to react. You go through things—" She stopped and pressed a hand to her mouth.

It felt strange listening to someone talk about her life as if it had happened to someone else, but in my line of work you get used to it. I had interviewed many people who were sent out on the streets when California closed its mental hospitals under then-governor Ronald Reagan. Those people frequently talked about themselves as if they were someone else. The important thing was not to challenge the mental construct. If you did, you sometimes lost the person entirely. Otherwise they could be surprisingly lucid. With Rachel, I just had to keep her talking long enough to learn what she knew about Dick Shammey's death.

"I want to understand," I said. "About the young woman. I want to know what happened."

"He's also very bad," she blurted out, looking up at me. "He's so very, very bad. You think you can help yourself, but you find out he is totally unable to discriminate the way other people do. It's not something you could change even if you wanted to so, so much." She closed her eyes, as if pressing down a pain, then shook her head and opened her eyes.

"That's the way he is," she continued sternly, "and

that's why you don't understand. You think he is the one who knows so many people and has so many friends and has been everywhere and seen everything. That's the one you want.''

I noticed a couple of guys along the bar were watching us. I stared at them pointedly until they turned back to their beers. I turned back to Rachel, who had continued talking.

"...she could not believe she had found someone like him so quickly, I mean, that he picked her out of all the other girls in the city. There are so many people everywhere there. She loved the country but meeting him was the reason she went there, to see things and meet people that aren't here. Do you know what I mean?" I nodded. Suddenly her attitude changed and she looked down into her lap.

"You live there, you know all about it," she muttered, and wrung her hands. For the first time she was using the word "you" to mean me rather than herself. I felt how vulnerable she was and put a hand on her arm. To my surprise, she snatched it away as if I had poured boiling water on it.

"I'm sorry," I said quickly, "just tell me, don't worry about it.''

She looked into my face again and pressed her palms together at her lips, but she didn't say anything. I knew I had to be patient, but it was hard. I forced myself to breathe deeply, to observe, and to report to myself what I observed. Her hands were smooth, and her long fingernails were bare. She wore a wedding ring. She had slender wrists that disappeared into her leather jacket, and she did not wear a watch or bracelets. I looked again at her wrists. There were dark marks, like bruises, where you would grip someone in order to subdue them or hold them down.

Abruptly Rachel pulled her hands down and buried them in her lap. When she sneaked a glance at me, I caught her eyes and eased her back into conversation. "You were talking about the city."

"Everything seemed so perfect there, you know?" she said, like the memory pained her. I nodded sympathetically and Rachel went on. "She had a home, she had this wonderful man. People wanted to know her, they wanted her to be a part of their lives. She wanted to help them, because so many of them were so tense and nervous all the time."

I laughed softly in agreement.

"She wanted to give them the peace you get here in the country but you can't hardly find in the city," Rachel declared. "That's how she met him, that's how it started."

"How what started?"

Rachel's eyes blazed, and in that instant she looked so much like Sarah that I blinked in disbelief. "You said you understood what this was about," she said accusingly.

"I do, I do," I soothed her. "I just want you to feel free to tell the whole story." Now there were even more people at the bar watching us, and I quickly scanned the room. In the far corner an elderly couple were standing up and putting on their coats.

"Come on," I said. "Let's get a table." I grabbed my briefcase and left my beer and the wrinkled bills on the bar. We cut through the few couples dancing to the juke-box and approached the table. As soon as we sat down I realized that there was a speaker almost directly over our heads. It would be harder to hear each other than at the bar, but harder still for anyone to overhear us. I put my briefcase on the floor, pushed the table out from the wall, and slid my chair closer to Rachel's. We had to nearly put our heads together to talk, but the arms of the chairs would enforce a discreet distance between us. All things considered, it was an improvement.

"Sorry," I said briefly. She nodded absently, like a person used to being led around by men. I felt genuinely sorry for her then, but she was not paying much attention to me. She seemed to be talking more to herself.

"He... He encouraged her... He *convinced* her...to violate a trust she had with someone else. That was how it started. It didn't seem so bad, being in the city. Instead of at home where everyone knew what you did. He said it was natural to love people and to express your love. But it was wrong. She shouldn't have done what she did."

She was folding and unfolding her hands on the table, staring at them like they might reveal something. I saw the diamond ring on her finger and it dawned on me that Rachel was more than bait for Shammey. She had also been his lover. She might, in fact, still love him.

I remembered what Sarah said about Carl Larkin being Rachel's "old flame," and a shiver went through me. Was Rachel's adulterous affair with Shammey all part of the plan, a cover to get him back up to Pomo Bluff without suspicion? Or was Larkin getting revenge on both Shammey *and* Rachel, by using the woman who had left him to kill the man she now loved? If that was the case, then this whole business was even more cold-blooded than I thought.

"Oh, God," Rachel moaned, and dropped her head down on her hands. Her hair spilled off her shoulders, out across the table, onto my arm. I remembered the hairs

I had hidden among my fishing gear, and remembered the deputies who had come to Hillhouse to search it— was that what they were looking for? Traces of Rachel's presence that the sheriff might have missed? I plucked a single hair from the table and held it up to the light. I was still staring at it when Rachel straightened up. She forced a small smile, gently pulled her hair together, and corralled it on the far side of her neck. The exposed skin had a thin red scratch that ran from behind the ear around to the base of her neck.

"You've been through a hard time," I said. "But that part is over now."

"In some ways," Rachel said. Her voice was not so theatrical now. It sounded almost calm, rational. "But not in others. She's still paying for it every day. Every single day that goes by. I think about it all the time and wish for her that she had never left. If she had stayed here none of this would ever have happened."

"I'm sure you had plenty of good reasons to leave," I said. "It's not your fault that other things happened."

Rachel turned slowly, her eyes narrowed in suspicion. "This is not about *me*," she said.

"I realize it's really about Dick Shammey," I replied quickly. "I'm just saying that you—"

"Melissa!" Rachel hissed, her eyes furious. "I've been talking about *Melissa!*"

Another chill passed through my body, this time like a cold wind through an open window. I pulled my jacket closer around me. Rachel was staring at me, accusingly.

"He led her into *total destruction*," she said, emphasizing the last two words. "Before the trial I went to the jail to see her, and she was like a train had run her over a hundred times. She actually *wanted* to go to prison. She didn't want anyone ever to see her again and she would never have to face people who knew what happened.''

I scrambled to put things in order, to shuffle the pages of the book so the story made sense. "What did happen?" I asked.

Rachel looked at me as she had when she first came in, like she was searching my face for signs that she could trust me. I tried to look as trustworthy as I could considering my mind was spinning even faster now, trying to reconstruct our entire conversation with Melissa, rather than Rachel, at the center of it. I suddenly felt an urge to get another beer. I wanted clarity, even the false kind you get out of a bottle.

"People here loved Gibbie," Rachel said. "Some of them still do, even though he's been in the ground five years." Her eyes were locked on mine, and I felt there was meaning beyond her words. I had to stop the spinning. I had to get the meaning clear.

"Did Melissa kill him?"

Rachel looked surprised at first, then relieved, like this was the question she had been waiting for all night. "At first I thought maybe she did, because of— There was the betrayal— That must have hurt her, made her confused.''

"You talked to her? Afterward?"

Rachel nodded. "In the jail. I could see how confused she was. And the way she talked about him... She just wanted him back, she was crazy for him.''

"Who, Gibbie?"

Rachel glanced at me. "No," she said darkly, and I knew then who she meant. "When I got to know him," she continued, "when I found out how he works, I changed my mind. Melissa wasn't hard enough, she wasn't— I don't know. But him— He would do anything, to anyone. I don't think she ever knew what happened. But he knew all along."

"Rachel," I said. "I have to ask you something."

"What?"

"Were you with Shammey the other night? Before he died?"

Rachel tossed her head and looked down at the table top. Then she swung her head up to look at me. A small sarcastic smile flickered across her face. It was a smile I had seen before on the faces of attractive women, the kind of women men couldn't leave alone. It was a smile that said, *I know what you want.*

"Is that what you came up here for?" she asked. The theatrical tone was back. I didn't care.

"I came up here to go fishing," I said. "Were you with Shammey?"

"Sarah said you were writing about something."

"I'm writing about fishing. But I'm in this mess up to my eyeballs and I want to know what happened. Were you with him?"

Rachel stared out into the room. When she spoke, I had to lean forward to hear. "That was the loneliest night I have ever spent in my whole life," she said. I waited, but that was all she said.

"You had a fight with your husband," I prompted.

"Does Sarah tell you everything I say to her?"

"You got in the car with Shammey—"

"I thought you were a friend."

"I am. I like Sarah. Very much."

"Then why are you hurting her?"

"How am I hurting her?" I demanded. The conversation had suddenly turned against me and I had to beat it back. That was when the man in the dark coat materialized next to the table. The light was behind him, making it impossible to see his face. When he spoke, though, I felt the shock of recognition.

"Let's go," he said. It was Carl Larkin, and he wasn't talking to me.

"Wait a minute," I said, "we're talking here."

*"Now,"* he growled, and took hold of Rachel's arm. She seemed to go limp, allowing Larkin to yank her up out of her chair and spin her toward the door.

"Hey," I yelled, but I was wedged in behind the table. Heads were turning all over the bar, and Larkin already had Rachel halfway across the room. I reached down behind me for my briefcase, pushed the table away from me, and scrambled for the door. I reached it just as it swung shut on Larkin's heel. I yanked it open again and plunged out the door.

Waiting just outside in the bright yellow light of the hotel porch, obviously expecting me, were Sheriff Stone and the big deputy I had seen earlier at Hillhouse. Stone was in full uniform with his arms folded over his chest. The younger deputy was dangling my car keys from the little finger of one hand, like a treat he might give an obedient dog. My car was parked among the other cars in the narrow strip between the hotel and the highway.

Larkin and Rachel had paused at the end of the porch that led to the parking lot on the side of the hotel. He had her firmly by the arm. She gave me an imploring look that pierced my heart. Instinctively I moved toward her, but the young deputy stepped into my path. Stone barked out something to Larkin, and he yanked Rachel down the stairs and out of sight. I turned to Stone.

"What the hell is this?" I demanded.

"We're here to see you off," Stone replied calmly.

"Who said I'm leaving?"

Stone shook his head and frowned. "I was hoping you

would see this as doing you a favor," he said. "Getting you out of the little trouble you seem to want to get yourself into."

"He has no right to jerk her around like that," I said, pointing toward the end of the porch.

"That's part of what I'm talking about," Stone said. "That poor girl is very unhappy, almost to the point of being disturbed. She came up here to be with her family and her friends, not to get all riled up."

"*She's* from the city!" I protested.

"But she's still one of ours," Stone said. "You see, this little town, it might be one of the prettiest places on God's green earth, but it's kind of delicate, you know what I mean? It's an ecosystem, that's what it is. You put something in a ecosystem that doesn't belong there, you mess it up."

"It's mighty pretty," I snapped. "But it looks to me like your economy runs on hospitality. You're running a tourist attraction, Sheriff, not an environmental preserve."

Stone smiled back, but it wasn't friendly. "We manage to keep body and soul together by making things nice and clean for you all to visit," he allowed. "That's why we can't have it messed up. When one of you comes up here and makes a mess, we do our best to clean it up and send it back where it came from. Otherwise we got unfortunate consequences."

To my right, Carl Larkin's truck spun out of the parking lot and headed north up the highway. "I don't care about your consequences," I told Stone. "I care about the truth. I just want to know what happened."

His face hardened. "I believe we already know exactly what happened," he said, as if my question were a new one. "I also believe I know what's going to happen now."

I looked at the younger deputy, who had one hand on the nightstick hanging from his belt. Then I pulled myself up to my full height, which enabled me to look down at the Sheriff. "Why did you have your boy here search my room?"

"No one was supposed to be in that room and you knew it," Stone said. "Aside from the obvious need to go over the room again, I wanted to make sure you knew we would not be tolerating your breaking the rules."

I snorted in derision. "So are you all through with your little investigation, Sheriff?"

Stone folded his arms across his chest again. "Deputy Anderson?"

The younger deputy pulled a small notebook from his jacket pocket, flipped it open, and recited from it. "Richard G. Shammey of San Francisco, being found dead, apparently of natural causes, in an unincorporated area of Mendocino County, his body has been examined by a resident physician in good standing with the county Medical Association, in consultation with the County Medical Examiner. The deceased having no companions accompanying him, and there being no next of kin or marital estate, the attorney of the deceased has instructed the county to return the body to the City of San Francisco for cremation according to the decedent's last will and testament. The body was received at Curtis Brown mortuary in San Francisco at approximately eleven-thirty a.m. today."

I looked at Stone. "You left out cause of death," I observed.

"Appears to have been a very serious allergic reaction," Stone said smoothly. "I believe the doctor's report refers to 'facts consistent with sudden respiratory failure from anaphylactic shock.'"

"He could have been poisoned."

"Where do you get that kind of notion? From movies?"

"What about the cup in the car?"

Stone inclined his head toward the deputy, but kept his eyes trained on me. "Did you find any drinking vessels in the decedent's vehicle, Deputy Anderson?"

"Yes sir."

"Did that object reveal the presence of any other passengers in the motor vehicle?"

"No sir."

"Where is the vehicle now?"

"Returned to the attorney of the deceased. There's an automotive delivery service out of Santa Rosa, they arrived yesterday at—"

"That's fine, Deputy, thank you," Stone said.

"There was someone with him," I said, "and you know it."

"If you can't prove it, you might as well not say it."

"What if I have evidence?"

"Then you would be guilty of withholding that evidence from a police investigation," Stone said.

"We would have to prosecute you to the full extent of the law," said the ever helpful Deputy Anderson. He was dangling my keys from his little finger again.

"We could let a judge decide that one," I told him.

Stone shook his head, like he was truly sorry about my inability to comprehend. "You see, this brings me back to my original point," he said. "We're trying to do you a big favor by just turning you around and sending you back down the highway. We're convinced that what you really want to do is go on home and write your fishing story. You don't want us to throw you in jail and muss up your hair and all that. You really don't.''

"I'm not sure I'm the one who'll be going to jail," I said, and folded my arms across my chest.

Stone snorted, then pulled out a small paper sleeve, the kind police use to hold small pieces of physical evidence. Carefully he extracted and held up a long red hair. It was coiled in a spiral, as if it had been wrapped around something small and compact, like a dry fly. Stone admired the coiled hair a minute, then reached out and plucked a long red hair off the sleeve of my jacket. I looked down in surprise, and saw strands of Rachel's hair on my sleeves and on my collar.

I looked up at Stone, who was grinning nastily. He held the two hairs up, twisted them together between his fingers, then dropped them onto the windy porch. In an instant they were gone. Our eyes locked. "Now, what was that again," he asked, "about evidence?"

It was bad enough that Stone had found the hairs I had hidden in my room at St. Horace. They were my only proof that someone had been with Shammey when he died. But now I could not even mention them, because Stone would claim I had collected samples of Rachel's hair in the bar at the hotel, not in the bathtub at Hillhouse.

I couldn't believe this pair of country cops had gotten the better of me. I set my face in defiance and tried to think. Up the highway to the right, a crowd began spilling out of the coffee house. In the light of the bookstore doorway, pulling on her coat, was Liz Rizzo. Instinct took over.

"Okay, Stone," I said. "You win. I gotta say goodbye to someone, then I'm out of here. Hey, Liz!" I called out, as loud as I could. Both Stone and the younger deputy turned to see who I was calling to.

The instant their heads were turned, I snatched my car keys from the deputy's finger and stalked down the steps off the porch. I didn't look back until I had squeezed through the row of parked cars and crossed the highway. The deputy was on the bottom step of the hotel stairs, but Stone was yelling at him. I strode up the highway and soon caught up to Liz in the parking lot.

She smiled brightly in recognition. I greeted her with truly breathless enthusiasm. "How was the reading?" I asked.

"It was great!" she said. She held up two books. "I bought the books!"

"I'm sorry I missed it," I said. "Would you tell me about it?"

"Okay," she agreed. "But I have to get up early tomorrow."

"Me, too. Want some coffee?"

As I steered her back into the bookstore, I glanced across the highway. Sheriff Stone and his deputy were disappearing through the door into the bar of the Pomo Bluff Hotel.

I ORDERED COFFEE for both of us while Liz sat down at a table. Then I went outside to the pay phone on the wall of the tourist boutique next door. I dialed the number at St. Horace and waited until a woman's voice answered. It was not Sarah, so I asked for her.

"She's unavailable at the moment," the woman said. "May I ask who's calling?" the voice inquired. I told her my name and offered to hold. A long minute later, the same woman came back to the phone. "I'm sorry, Sarah has gone home early. I believe she was not feeling well."

"Do you have her number at home?"

"I'm sorry, no, I don't."

"Can you get it?"

"I believe it's not listed, and we don't give out the home numbers of our employees, sir. Would you like to talk to the restaurant manager?"

"No, never mind."

I hung up and leaned against the wall. A cold wind flowed along the side of the building and under my coat. I could feel the alcohol now after sprinting up the highway. I could feel my tiredness at the end of a day that had begun in the dark. I could feel my frustration that something bad was going down and I was powerless to expose it, much less prevent it. And I could feel a swollen place in my heart where my feelings for Sarah were lodged. I didn't want to go home now, for a whole lot of reasons. But I had no place to stay the night. I sighed and went back inside.

The room was still warm from the crowd, and I took off my jacket. Liz chattered about the evening and read me a few of her favorite poems. I tried to concentrate on what she was saying, but it was hard. As soon as it was possible to work it into the conversation, I told her that the police had decided to close Hillhouse for a while. Her eyes got wide.

"How come?"

"I'm not sure," I said. "Probably it's just routine."

"But where are you going to stay?"

"Well," I said, as if I were just working it out in my head, "on Thursday night I stayed at Sarah's house, but then her sister came up on Friday, so I can't stay with her tonight."

"I don't think her sister is staying there," Liz said. "I think she's staying with Carl Larkin. You know? The mushroom guy?"

I put a look of surprise on my face. "Really? Are they friends?"

"Helen at the drugstore told me they were together for, like, two years. Then Sarah's sister went and married this guy from San Francisco. Helen said that this guy, he was from this big important family or something, and he came up here for some vacation, and he saw her—Sarah's sister, I mean—and then—"

"Rachel."

"Right, Rachel. So anyway, he saw her and he found out who she was and then he started sending her letters and stuff, and presents, and then he got her to come and visit him in the city and then she moved down there and married him!"

"Wow," I said. "That sounds really romantic."

"Well, I guess," Liz said. "But I don't know why he takes her back, I really don't."

"Carl, you mean."

"Yes. I mean, like, wow, the poor guy!"

"Love is complicated."

"No kidding!" Liz agreed.

I steered the conversation back to my need for a place to stay, adding in the additional problem of needing to keep the cost as low as possible.

"It's really too bad," Liz informed me. "I got a bunch of calls from people today who were looking for a place. When I tried to refer them to the other inns and places we send people, they said they already called those places. They were being referred to *us!*"

"Boy, I sure don't want to sleep in my car."

"Yeah," Liz agreed. "That would be gross." While she tried to think of a place for me, I suddenly had an idea. Or at least I pretended it was sudden.

"If it wasn't too much trouble," I said lightly, "I

could just crash on your couch or something, how about that?"

I knew right away that it was no good. Liz was speechless, her eyes wide. I immediately withdrew the suggestion, and then waited while Liz apologized and told me about her parents letting her move down to Pomo Bluff by herself and how she had such a little place and she really wanted to help. Finally her face brightened. "Come on," she said, "I know what you can do." She stood up and headed out the door. I put on my jacket, went to the window of the café, and studied the front of the hotel up the highway. My car was still there, which surprised me at first. Then I remembered that they wanted me to leave. I had to have my car for that.

There were no patrol cars in sight, so I went out to the parking lot and joined Liz by her car. To my chagrin, she was opening up the trunk and pulling out a sleeping bag. "Stirrup Beach is the best place at this time of year," she said.

"Stirrup Beach," I repeated. "That's south, right?"

"South of C Ranch even," she said. "The trees there are so thick it's like sleeping indoors. Even if it rains you don't get wet."

I hefted the sleeping bag. "Is this rated for oceanic temperatures?"

"It's not that cold by the ocean," she laughed. "And this is a really good sleeping bag. I've used it in the mountains and everywhere."

"Well, this is really sweet of you."

"It's better than sleeping under a bridge someplace!"

I looked up. "Like Ben," I said.

Liz appeared surprised, then pleased. "Do you know Ben?"

"I met him the other day. He showed me his workshop."

"Isn't it cool? I think it's just the most amazing thing!"

"I was impressed."

"I'm so glad you got to meet him. Sometimes I think I'm the only one in this whole town who talks to him. Everyone else acts like he's invisible or something."

"Except the Sheriff, evidently."

Liz rolled her eyes. "That is the most peculiar thing of all," she said. "Ben goes into town hardly ever, like maybe once a month. And the Sheriff, it's like he's always waiting for him. He arrests him and puts him right in jail, and then he lets him go the next day. It's the weirdest thing."

"Yeah," I agreed, remembering it. "I saw him let Ben go yesterday afternoon."

"But that's not the weird part. What's *really* weird is that the Sheriff buys him all this food, and gives him clothes and everything."

This did not square with my picture of Sheriff Stone. "How do you know this?" I asked.

"Once Ben showed me. I saw where he got some socks and a sweater. Also a case of soup in cans, I forget the kind. And the doctor came to see him, too, Ben said." She pulled her coat closer around her as a gust of wind chased through the parking lot.

"That's interesting," I agreed. "Why does the sheriff help him, do you think?"

Liz looked at me like it was a major mystery. "I sure don't know the answer to that one," she said. "Most of the time he looks like he'd just as soon kill Ben as do anything nice for him."

WHEN I WALKED across the highway to my car, the coast was clear. I wondered if they had messed up the car, but I didn't want to stick around for a complete examination in front of the hotel. I figured I would get out of sight, find Stirrup Beach, and then make sure everything was still intact. I was worried about Doug's fishing gear, though, so I threw open the trunk of the car. The rod and pouch were there, and it looked like they were more or less intact. My clothes though, were a hopeless jumble. I threw Liz's sleeping bag in the back seat, got into the car, and headed down the highway across Ben's bridge into Sonoma County.

I had gone a mile or two when a pair of headlights appeared behind me. It was dark on the highway, which had no lights of its own and wide open country on both sides. I checked my speedometer and continued along, thinking about Rachel and the way she had looked at me before Larkin hustled her off the porch of the hotel and into his truck. I slowed for a sharp curve. When I came out of the curve onto a straightaway, the headlights I had seen behind me were surprisingly close.

I quickly got back up to speed on the straightaway, but the vehicle behind me closed the distance in no time. It must have been some kind of truck, because the head-lamps seemed to shine directly in through the rear window. When I flipped my rear view mirror down to cut the glare, it didn't make any difference at all. Soon the truck was so close that the lights filled my back window and I could hear its engine along with the sound of my own. I pressed down on the accelerator and shot ahead.

My lead evaporated in a few moments, and I sped up even more. Now I was careening around curves, barreling through straightaways, and plunging down hills. Still the headlamps behind me shone high and hard. I began to understand that the driver of the truck was not just an impatient person eager to get home in time for the news. Then I realized that I was nearly out of control on a wet two-lane road in the middle of nowhere: playing their game, on their turf. I immediately took my foot off the accelerator and let the car slow.

In an instant the glare of headlamps filled the rear window so brightly that I was sure I was going to be hit. Still, it was a shock to feel the impact. My throat was suddenly tight, and my heart was beating uncomfortably fast. Intimidation was one thing. Vehicular assault was another. I saw a gravel patch on the shoulder of the road up ahead, hit the brake to flash my tail lights, and began to steer off onto the shoulder of the highway. Again the headlamps blazed and again the truck rammed me from behind. Compared to this hit, the first impact was just a nudge. I lurched forward against my seat belt and felt the car skidding through the gravel toward a rail fender. With adrenaline pouring into my veins, I pulled at the wheel and fought the car back onto the paved surface.

By the time I got the car under control again, I was seething with anger. The headlights remained at most a dozen feet behind me, so I drove on, furious. I willed my breath steady and fought the fear that welled up in my chest. When I spotted a pair of headlights coming toward me, roughly a mile away at the far end of a long, level curve, I longed for some way to tell them what was happening. Of course, it wouldn't have mattered if I could. Calling the cops was pointless when it was the cops themselves who were trying to force me out of town. There was only one way to take advantage of the presence of another car, and before I could weigh the pros and cons of that option, I pressed down on the accelerator and shot forward.

The headlights behind me fell back, then charged forward to catch up. Just as they did, I swerved into the oncoming lane and mashed the accelerator to the floor. Now the other car was zooming straight toward me, nose to nose. I clutched the wheel and clenched my jaw. The headlights behind me were coming up fast, and they were still in the right lane. Just a few seconds more...

The driver of the car coming toward me was now frantically flicking his headlights on and off. There was no shoulder on his side of the road for him to run to, and stopping in his lane would only lessen the impact of my car when it crashed into his. He had only one choice to avoid a head-on collision. "Move over, damn you, move over!" I roared. At the last possible moment, he did.

At the instant we passed, each of us in the other's lane, my car went airborne off a slight incline in the road and then bumped back down onto the roadway. As soon as I had control of the car, I looked in my rear view mirror. Receding in the distance, a pair of stationary headlamps illuminated the rail fence by the side of the road. The tail lights of the other car were disappearing around a bend and out of sight. I turned my attention back to the highway in front of me, and sped away.

Soon the road turned into a forested area of tight switchbacks. I wrenched the car through them until I came to a left turn up the ridge. I accelerated up the grade until I reached the top and found a small secondary road. I pulled into it, went down half a mile, found a flat spot off the road, and turned off my engine and my lights. My breath was short and my heart was pounding. I wanted to kill the bastards; I was scared to death they would find me; I couldn't believe I was mixed up in this mess.

I cracked the window a little so I could hear an approaching car, but the woods were quiet except for the wind. I forced myself to think of what to do next. I didn't want to go back to the highway, much less back to town. The idea of sleeping outside, by the ocean, in this wind, did not appeal to me, either. For the first time since I had arrived, I thought seriously about just driving home. The idea didn't stick, though. There were too many things left unresolved. I had Liz's sleeping bag, for one thing. I hadn't caught my four-hundred-dollar fish yet, either. There was also the matter of Sarah. I told myself that my feelings regarding her were all out of proportion to the small amount of time we had spent together. Of course, there was a word for that state of mind. It wasn't a word I used much, but I was familiar with what it meant.

I shook my mind free and pulled out the maps I had bought. It took a while, but I finally figured out I was on a ridge road that ran almost all the way back up to Mendocino county. In fact, the road dead-ended at the county border: the Pomo River. I rolled my window down all the way and listened for a while. Finally, I started the engine and rolled quietly down the dark, winding road between tall trees that tugged at the wind. The last mile was a curving plunge down through bigger trees, which completely blocked the sky. When I got to a place where the sound of the river was louder than the sound of the wind, I pulled off the road under the canopy of branches. By emptying the back seat and reclining the front, it was just possible to lay back, pull the sleeping bag over me, and sleep.

# EIGHT

I AWOKE IN the dark, in my car, in the woods, in the middle of winter. I dismissed it as a bad dream, but the sensations of cold and discomfort were so real that I struggled toward consciousness instead of falling back into sleep. Immediately the recollections started pouring in: I had been forced out of the inn, lured out of the bar, and pushed down the highway at seventy miles an hour. With a groan I kicked off my shoes, wriggled into the sleeping bag, and zipped it up. I blew on my fingers and flexed my toes until I could feel them again. I glanced down at my briefcase to make sure I still had it. Then I closed my eyes and tried to go back to sleep.

Ten minutes later, I gave up and opened my eyes. I kept seeing the imploring look on Rachel's face before Larkin yanked her down the stairs in front of the hotel. At the time, I thought she wanted to be rescued. But that was because I had been thinking of myself as the fisherman and Rachel as the fish. Now I realized that Rachel was the lure. I was the fish. Once Larkin and Stone found the evidence I had hidden in my fishing gear, they sent her to the bar to keep me there and shed more hair all over me. Her imploring look was not a plea for help. She wanted me to understand that she had no choice, that they were forcing her to do it. She wanted to be forgiven.

I shook my head at myself for being taken in so easily, and wondered once again how much Rachel really knew about what was going on. I believed the story she told me about Melissa Larkin was accurate—and that it applied equally well to Rachel herself. I no longer doubted that she was in Hillhouse with Shammey. The question was the timing, and her knowledge of events.

It was possible that she knowingly drew Shammey to Pomo Bluff, but was in the dark about what Larkin and Stone had planned for him once he got there. She was, after all, the perfect lure. Shammey had taken advantage of women like her many times before, and he no doubt knew the power he had over her. He knew that if he wanted to set up a drug deal, for example, she would help him if he asked her to. She knew how to contact Larkin, someone Shammey had already met once before. She knew a secluded, neutral place in the woods where they could do the deal.

All this made it possible that Larkin and Stone were using her without her consent. Of course, it was also possible that she was in it up to her eyeballs—that she had set me up last night just as she had set up Shammey two nights before.

It was getting light now, and my stomach reminded me about breakfast. Reluctantly I struggled out of the sleeping bag, pulled on my boots, and got out of the car. The huge redwoods around me dripped heavy drops onto the soft, loamy ground. I could see my breath in front of my face, and high overhead, a gray sky. I stomped my feet a bit to get the blood flowing, then opened the trunk of the car. It took a while to sort things out, but everything was there. As I put the fly box back together, I examined each fly until I found the one I had wrapped with Rachel's hair. It was its old skinny self again, and I gave it a sour look. "Some help you were," I said, and dropped it back into a compartment with its mates.

When I got back up on the ridge I saw that it was a bleak January day. The sky was gun-metal gray, the distant ocean a swollen reflection of a sullen sky. Even the trees seemed a darker green, although that could have been my mood. I slowed the car as I came down the ridge and approached the highway, but there were no patrol cars. There was hardly any traffic at all, in fact, and it occurred to me that it was Sunday morning.

I sat at the intersection for a few moments, wondering whether I had anything to fear from Stone and his cohorts in broad daylight. They might, of course, believe that their show of force had chased me down the highway and out of their way. They could also be around the next bend, waiting. I finally pulled out onto the highway and headed north, toward Pomo Bluff, but well below the speed limit. When I came to a long, shallow curve I slowed down even more. I thought I saw skid marks on the shoulder of the road, right near a rail fence on the other side of the highway. I continued down the road, looking for the spot where I had been hit while pulling off the road.

It made me furious all over again. If I had gone out of control here, on an empty highway at night… The image of paramedics, doctors, and flashing lights played in my mind. I saw myself being put into an ambulance, unconscious, while Fred Stone told a doctor in a white coat that I had spent the evening in the hotel bar, drinking. The doctor was nodding and the paramedics were closing up the ambulance, and then suddenly I came to my senses—not in the daydream, but in real life.

What had Stone said in front of the hotel? Something about a doctor's examination, and "facts consistent with anaphylactic shock"? I pressed down on the accelerator and rocketed up the highway toward Pomo Bluff, my mind buzzing. I parked between two camper-sized vans behind the hotel, then walked around the side to the phone. I looked through the business directory in the skinny little phone book hanging on a chain. There were four phone numbers to choose from.

I dialed the first one and looked around me as the phone rang. An answering machine picked up after half a dozen rings, but I didn't leave a message. I dialed the second number, which rang without any response. The third number triggered an answering machine, but this time the message advised evening and weekend callers to try another number. I scrambled to write it down before the message was through.

I hung up the phone and took a deep breath. There were cars on the highway now, and a few people heading into the hotel. I remembered the hotel had a restaurant of its own. Probably served breakfast. It didn't matter. I rehearsed my plan in my mind, then dialed the number I had written down.

"Hello?" It was a woman's voice, one that was no longer young. I put my hand over the mouthpiece and lowered my voice.

"Good morning, Mrs. Clark?"

"Yes, who is it?"

"It's Deputy Anderson, Ma'am. Sorry to call so early."

"Deputy Anderson?"

"Yes ma'am."

"Oh, yes, I'm sorry. I just didn't recognize your voice." I coughed again and pinched one nostril shut.

"I'm a little under the weather, that's all."

"Oh, I'm sorry. Did you want to see Jim about your cold, is that it?"

"Actually, I'm calling on county business. Is Doctor Clark at home?"

"County business?"

"Yes, Ma'am. For Sheriff Stone."

"Is it about that poor man at the inn? I thought that was all through."

My heart skipped a beat. I had to concentrate to keep my voice low. "That's right, Ma'am. Just one thing I need to check on."

"Well, I'm very sorry, but Jim's just gone out. It's Sunday, you know."

"Yes, Ma'am, I know, I just wondered if—"

"He goes fishing every Sunday this time of year, I thought everyone in town knew that!"

"Yes, Ma'am," I said. My mind was racing. I couldn't keep this up much longer, but I was too close to give up. "I was kind of hoping to do a little fishing myself today. You have any idea where he might be going?"

"Heavens, no. But I think he would advise you to stay home on a day like this, and get some rest for that cold of yours."

"Yes, Ma'am, I'm sure he would." I said, as disappointed now as I had been excited the moment before. "Thank you for your trouble."

"No trouble. Shall I tell him you called?"

"No, that won't be necessary," I said quickly. "Sheriff Stone can call him on Monday."

"All right. I'm sorry I was unable to help you."

"That's okay. You have a good day."

"Thank you. And take care of that cold."

"I will."

"Goodbye."

I coughed and hung up.

WELL, PERHAPS BREAKFAST was in order after all. I was hungry, and that at least was a problem I could solve. I thought briefly about going in the hotel, but after what had happened the night before I thought better of it. The diner across the highway served a pretty good breakfast, and I got a good table overlooking the ocean. I cast an eye up toward the bridge into Sonoma County every now and then but most of the time I gazed glumly out the window and chewed or swallowed. There was a newspaper left on the next table, but I ignored it.

Maybe there was a murder to be investigated, and maybe it would make a sensational newspaper series. But I had no more leads to follow, no physical evidence, and plenty of local opposition. I did have enough dirt to pitch the story to the paper when I got back to town, and if an editor took the bait I could come back and work the story for as long as it took. In the meantime, I had a contract for an article that I had not even started writing yet. My rent was due in ten days. Even I, Rigel Lynx, ace investigative reporter, had to face facts.

One of those facts, curiously enough, was that I enjoyed fishing. It was a surprisingly pleasant thing to think about when you weren't doing it, and when you were, it was totally engaging even if the fish ignored you completely. When I turned my mind to the technique of casting, I discovered that a part of my brain had been puzzling out the proper motion all the time I had been doing other things. Before I knew it I had my right arm raised and was drawing it forward and back in a rhythmic gesture, trying to synchronize my ideas about casting with the body that had to execute them.

"Pause before you come forward," said a voice behind me. I flushed, then looked around behind me. "You've got to stop a moment and let the line get straightened out behind you," continued the white-haired gentleman sitting at a table behind me. The woman next to him, probably his wife, smiled sweetly and returned to the newspaper.

"Otherwise you're just stirring it up over your head," he said. "See what I mean?" He brought his own imaginary rod back, and made an exaggerated locking motion to show how he had stopped the rod to let the line come back. "Now the line goes out behind me," he said, looking over his shoulder. "When I come forward"—he brought his arm forward with authority—"the line goes straight out in front. You have to do the same exact motion in reverse as you want to do in front of you."

I nodded through this explanation. Inside my head, the part of my brain that had been working on casting technique was shouting one word over and over: "Yes! Yes! Yes!" Suddenly I could not wait to get back on the river and fish.

"I see what you mean," I said. "If you come forward too soon the line's still over your head. It can't come forward because it's still going backwards."

"Exactly," my new instructor said. He looked like the kind of guy you'd put in a movie about elderly outdoorsmen: wise, gentle, and completely nuts about fishing. "You hold onto your line as it goes back, then let it loose to fly out in front as you come forward. You can cast it out there pretty far if you wait long enough on the backswing."

"I'll give it a try," I said, meaning it.

His wife looked up and smiled again. She was perfect for the movie, too: white hair in a bun, apple cheeks, and twinkling eyes. "I made him stay home and have breakfast with me one Sunday morning," she told me, "and he still manages to go fishing right here in the restaurant!"

Her husband turned to her in consternation. "I was just trying to help," he said. She winked at me.

"I really appreciate it," I said.

"There, you see?" he said to her. He turned to me over his shoulder. "Get a couple for me, huh?"

I assured him I would do my best, and he turned back to his breakfast. I, however, could not turn around to mine. Across the highway a woman was getting out of her car in front of the Pomo Bluff Hotel and going inside to the dining room. I kept watching, and a little while later she came out onto the porch of the hotel. She pulled her coat tighter around her as she looked up and down the highway, then crossed it and came toward the diner. It was Sarah, and she was looking for someone. I turned back to the window and stared dumbly out to sea.

The embarrassment I felt from the night before was still fresh enough to burn my cheeks. I tried to remind myself that I had been right—Rachel *was* involved in Shammey's murder—even if the facts were a little sketchy and I had been a little premature in my presentation. I knew this was all true. It just didn't help.

I heard the door open and felt a rush of cold air. I took a deep breath and held still, as if I was looking out the window at the waves. I tried to push the swelling feeling in the middle of my chest back down to wherever it had come from. Then I felt her arrive next to me. I looked up into her face. She looked down into mine. Neither of us said anything for a moment. She put a hand on my shoulder. I put my hand on her hand. She pulled out the chair next to mine and slid into it. We were sitting side by side, like friends.

"I was afraid you had gone," she said at last. I shook my head.

"Not without seeing you," I said. She smiled a brief, wry smile.

"I'm so sorry about what happened last night," she said. "I didn't find out about it until you were already gone."

"I'm sorry, too," I said.

"I mean about Hillhouse. Never mind about the other thing."

"I meant the other thing."

"Really, it's not important," Sarah said, a little sternly. "But they should have told me about the search and all that. Maybe they're allowed to do it that way, but I couldn't believe they would. It's not how people do things up here."

"That's not all they did," I said, lowering my voice. "I was driving south from town to go sleep on the beach, and some bastard in a truck rammed me from behind."

"Was he drunk?"

"It was intentional, Sarah. They're trying to get me to leave."

Her face became grave. "I can't believe that."

"It happened twice. It wasn't an accident."

She looked down and shook her head. "I have to talk to Fred. This is nuts."

"It doesn't matter," I told her. "I'm leaving anyway."

She looked up at me. "When?"

"I've got a little more research to do, then I'm out of here."

"You're going home to write your article?"

"Yup."

She frowned and shook her head again. I pretended to look out the window so I could study her somber reflection in the glass. "I can't believe this is all happening," she said quietly. "It's usually so quiet up here, especially in the winter."

"I feel like I brought most of it with me," I said softly.

"No."

"Yeah. Especially about what happened between us, last night."

"Oh, Rigel—"

"I mean it. For some reason I thought we were on the same side, that I could think out loud. But it was stupid. It was your own sister I was talking about, for Christ's sake."

"We *are* on the same side," Sarah said.

"But that doesn't mean I can just—"

"You don't have to apologize. I overreacted."

"You had every right—"

"I know," she said firmly, and laid a hand on my arm. "That's why I was looking for you. I knew you would feel terrible, and I wanted…to see you."

I glanced down at her long, slender fingers. They belonged to a hand I had once kissed. I looked up at her. "I called last night, but they told me you went home or something."

"They were just protecting me," Sarah said. "I had to work."

"Ah."

"There is one thing I want to say about last night."

"What?"

She stole a glance over her shoulder. The diner was full now, and noisy. She leaned a bit closer and lowered her voice. "Whatever else may have happened, Rachel did not kill anyone." Our eyes met. "I know her better than anyone does, and she's simply not capable of something like that. But she is capable of *thinking* that she did something like that, and that's what I'm worried about."

I turned and looked out to sea. The gray was tinged with green now, and streaks of milky white stained the tide. The sinking feeling I'd felt in the bookstore the day before came back, as I realized again that this whole mess was darker and colder than I knew. I could easily imagine Larkin and Stone working on Rachel's fragile psyche, convincing her that she had killed Shammey. She had been so tense in the bar, so preoccupied with Melissa and Shammey and what happened in the past. I now recalled her imploring look on the porch of the hotel, and saw it in a new light. Yes, she wanted to be forgiven—but for something far worse than betrayal.

I wanted to say more, to tell Sarah everything I had seen, everything that had happened. But something held my tongue. Without evidence, proof, or witnesses, all I had was a strong suspicion that something bad was happening. The most I could do was offer a warning. "If I were you," I said at last, "I would get your sister out of Pomo Bluff and keep her out. This is not a good place for her, even with you here."

"She's leaving soon."

"Good."

"We just want things to go back the way they were."

I glanced at Sarah, who was staring out at the horizon. Even in this unflattering light, with a troubled expression on her unadorned face, she looked lovely to me. There was something pure about her, something clear. The swelling sensation came up again in my chest. I forced my eyes away. After a while she let one of her hands fall onto my upturned palm. I spread my fingers and she twined hers among mine.

"This has been pretty awkward," she said.

I laughed quietly. "Boy meets girl, girl teaches boy

how to fish, boy loses girl…" I looked out toward the water. There were dark clouds on the horizon.

Sarah turned to me. "So where did you sleep last night?"

"In my car, down by the river," I said. "Liz gave me her sleeping bag."

"You slept in your car? You must be exhausted."

"I've been better," I said. "You forget what a hot shower's all about until you don't get one."

"I think you should come home with me and take a hot bath," she said.

I glanced at her and caught a glint in her eye. I remembered the bathtub, the heat, being naked in her room, and wanting her, wanting her with a fierce tenderness I had not felt in years. I shook my head and withdrew my hand. "It's a mighty attractive proposal," I said. "But I've got to go fishing."

"You could fish the stream behind the house," she suggested. "Bath before, bath after."

"I think I better stick to places where I don't have that temptation hanging over my head," I said. "I still haven't been to C Ranch Creek, and I've got to head home soon."

"Will I get to see you before you go?"

"Well," I said, "I still have to pay my bill at the inn, and I've got to return Liz's sleeping bag."

"I start at three," she said.

"This afternoon, then."

"Good luck on the river."

"Thanks."

BY THE TIME I got down to C Ranch Creek, it was raining and the temperature had dropped precipitously. I pulled on an extra sweater, tied a bandanna around the top of my head, and jammed my hat down. At least the bad weather had discouraged everyone who didn't have a magazine deadline. There was just one car parked near mine, and as I clambered down a slope and approached the creek, there were no fishermen in sight. "All right," I thought. "Let's find some fish."

I remembered how the two fishermen from the previous morning had found a curve in the river and were casting to the deep water where the current cut the far bank. On average, C Ranch Creek was not as broad as the Pomo River, or as deep. There were, though, some spots marked on one of the maps. All of them were on bends of the river. For the first time in my life as a fly fisherman, I had a plan.

As I worked my way upriver on a muddy trail, it occurred to me that "fishing" was a strange name for what I was doing. Guys with shotguns in the woods or rushes did not call what they were doing "deering" or "ducking"; they called it "hunting." It seemed to me, moving quietly near a stream with my rod in my hand and scanning the water for a spot where large fish were likely to be hiding, that I too was hunting.

I realized now why the guy said luck had little to do with catching fish. Maybe "fishing" entailed some luck, but hunting was about using every advantage you had to find and capture a wild animal. You spent all morning sneaking up on fish, anticipating which way they would be going, using specialized equipment to lure them to the boundary between their world and ours. Once you had a fish at the boundary, the challenge was to bring it out of its watery world into our world of earth and air. I was in the first phase of this hunt, looking for a place where I could move on to the second phase.

The rain let up a bit as I came around a thicket of

willows that obscured the stream. Ahead was a broad stretch of creek where a huge dead tree had fallen into the middle of the stream. I pictured myself standing on the tree, almost in the middle of the creek, casting upstream. Suddenly it didn't matter if the trunk was slick, slanting, or dangerous. I had to try it.

The tree was bigger than it looked from a distance, and it had fallen over from far up the bank. I had to climb nearly to the soft, broken roots and moist bowl of earth at the base of the tree before I could find a way to get up onto it. From that point it took a while to work my way back down, but it was worth it. Where the tree angled down into the water, a smooth dead stump of a branch made a rough foothold. There was clear access for casting both up the stream and down.

I quickly assembled my rod and tied on a big fly with a shiny silver body, long orange tail, bright orange mantle, and two silver eyes popping out on top. I couldn't really believe a fish would mistake this thing for food—and then I understood that it was the way the fly was presented that made it seem like food to a fish. This bright orange and silver thing was not doing the hunting: I was. I gave the knot an extra tug to make sure it was strong, clipped off the extra bit of leader, and got ready to cast.

A light rain was falling again when I took my stance on the log a few feet from where it disappeared into the flowing stream. The water was light brown and mostly opaque. I had a strong sense that there were fish under the water, and I was ready to hunt them. First I shook the fly out on the water and let the current help me pay out some line, downstream toward a riffle. Then I pulled four or five yards of line off the reel and let it fall at my feet. I ran through the sequence in my head: take the rod back to the one o'clock position while holding onto the slack line in my left hand; pause to let the line get all the way behind me, then come forward to the ten o'clock position and let go of the slack line so it could shoot out the tip of the rod.

And it worked. The line did glide out, and the fly did land on the water farther out than I had ever cast before. I looked around to see if anyone was applauding, but for some reason the audience had forgotten to attend. I looked out at the fly, which had dipped beneath the surface. The line, too, was sinking after it. I pulled them back with a sweeping tug. I decided I would now cast twice as far, using the technique of casting back and forth in the air like Sarah had done, letting a little more line out each time.

It didn't work. Instead I got the fly and the leader tangled around the rod and had to spend ten minutes pulling it all apart again. My heart sank during most of those ten minutes, and I had to get my enthusiasm back up before I could cast again. I thought back to the old guy in the diner, and replayed his lesson. In my mind's eye I saw him turn over his shoulder and look back at the imaginary line. A light bulb lit up in my head. I set up, drew the rod and the line back, and this time I looked backward over my shoulder to actually watch what I was doing.

This astonishing technical advance enabled me to see the line as it went back, and to know exactly when to start the forward motion. It was so much fun I did it again, casting back and forth in the air. Each time I looked back and chose the precise instant to end the backcast and begin coming forward.

At last I remembered the slack line in my left hand. On the next forward cast, I let go of some line. It shot out so fast I heard it hiss up the rod. The sight and sound of this new effect mesmerized me, and I stopped moving. I'll never forget what happened next. The line continued to fly out in a vibrating strip of neon green, parallel to the surface of the stream. When there was no more slack line to come, the far end of the line—the fly, that is, the lure, the thing that I was chiefly trying to manipulate—dipped down toward the water. The line seemed to float up a bit in compensation, before it too settled down onto the water...after the fly. It was perfect. A broad grin broke out across my face and my eyes watered. Tears of joy, let it be said, are both hot and sweet.

Soon the current pulled the entire line out straight, and there was nothing to do but reel it in slowly. Carefully I set myself up again, and this time took a few deep breaths. Despite the deep satisfaction of the previous cast, I already wanted more. I wanted to cast all the way to the riffles I could see downstream. To accomplish this, I would have to be able to false-cast a number of times, letting out more line each time, before I let the fly fall onto the water. I ran through the steps in my head, and drew back the rod. I knew now that the pause at the back of the cast had to be matched by a pause at the front. The rod and the line would do all the rest of it for me.

Once again I looked over my shoulder so I could see when to begin the forward cast. When I came forward, I released some slack line. It shot out from the rod and straightened out. But before it could fall to the water, I snapped the rod tip back. The line reversed direction and began flying backward. Again I looked over my shoulder, waiting until the line was flat out behind me. Again I came forward and let more line fly free from the end of the rod. Again I waited for it to lengthen out before drawing it back. With each false-cast, I had to wait longer for the line to reach its full length. When I finally let the fly fall onto the water, it was only a yard or two above the riffles. I was in heaven. The rain, the cold, having to keep my balance on a slick slanting log—none of it mattered. Casting like this was a thrill all its own. What could be more exciting?

I found out a moment later. I had pulled eight or ten feet of line free from the reel and was letting it run out the rod. The fly went into the riffles and dipped below, out of sight. An instant afterward, the entire rod in my hand jerked to life with incredible force. The reel emitted a high-pitched "screeeee" sound as it spun out more line. My jaw dropped. I had caught a fish.

I don't really remember the next few moments, but instinct must have taken over. The power I felt in the rod was electric. It bowed and bucked and danced like a living thing. With my left hand I steadily, artlessly reeled in the line. I had heard the phrase "playing a fish," but this was serious. The stream was not wide and there were plenty of snags and willows and things to break a line on. I wanted to see the fish, I wanted to pull it out and believe my eyes. That was when the fish leaped out of the riffles into the deeper water above.

It was an indescribable sight—and that's coming from a person who lives by describing things. This wild, shining bullet shot out from under the water into the air, a place of certain death under ordinary circumstances. But now, in a fight for its life, the fish was attempting to fly toward freedom. My heart leaped into my throat as the fish disappeared again under the water. He was running laterally now, and I reeled faster. It was not that big a fish, but it was my first steelhead, my first fly fish, and it was worth an awful lot of money in story value (not to mention loan terms). I kept reeling. My heart was beating like a drum.

As I drew the fish nearer, it hit me that I had to get him onto dry land somehow. I had not handled a live fish since childhood, and then I had been sitting next to my dad in a big, flat boat. Now I was balanced on a wet log near the middle of a flowing stream, all alone. I swallowed hard and stole a quick glance at the bank. Even if I could somehow work my way up the log and then off it without losing the fish, the edge of the stream was a muddy slope. If I went too far up the log, to where the ground was firm, I risked snagging or breaking the line.

Finally I had the fish in sight, swimming slowly back and forth just a foot or so under the water about eight or ten feet away. It seemed tired from its ordeal, but I had no time to feel sorry for it. I looked again at the bank and had an inspiration. From where I stood, I could pull the fish out of the water and swing it up the bank onto firm ground. After that I could just walk down and get it. This little maneuver was not going to win me any style points, but there was no one watching and dead fish tell no tales. I looked back at the fish, making slow figure eights in the water. I let a little line back out so I would have enough to get the fish well up onto the bank. I looked down at the log to position my feet for the right balance and leverage, then looked to my left to pick a landing spot for my flying fish.

Suddenly I heard a swirling "ploosh" of water against the log, followed an instant later by a tug on the rod. By the time I could look down, the fish had plunged with surprising force under the log right where I was standing. I yanked the rod up hard. The line was caught tight, and the rod bowed deeply. Then it suddenly snapped straight and the line pulled free. Too free. There was no fish on the end of the line, or any fly either. Several feet of leader swung back and forth impotently in the breeze, and then the entire line slid back down the rod and made a pile at my feet.

THE WORST THING about this cold shaft of fate was its location in the heart of a sweet happiness only moments old. Part of me was still rising in exhilaration while the rest was collapsing in despair. And it was my own cowardice that caused it. If I had just pulled the fish out of the water and grabbed it in my own hands, I would still have it. Instead I was trying some scaredy-cat short-cut so I wouldn't have to get my feet wet. I cursed myself for a while, but it didn't make me feel any better.

The rain had stopped and there were holes in the clouds to the west. That meant the storm was breaking, which meant there would probably be a swarm of fishermen before long. I remembered the two guys from the day before, and it cut me deep to remember the guy wading out into the river to get the fish, and holding it in his hands. He had actually *caught* his fish. I had only hooked one. The difference may seem slight, but to me the gulf was enormous. I realized also that my fish had tricked me, had let me think I was a big, successful hunter before diving under the log and breaking the leader.

This sparked some competitive fire in me, probably from the same tinderbox that had fueled my success as a newspaperman. When other reporters would get a better slant on a story than I had, or break a story I should have known about first, it lit a small fire inside me that would not go out until I did something to quench it. It was not my colleagues on the paper I was competing with, it was my own standards. Probably the others felt the same way I did. We all wanted to be the best we could be, because that's what it took to tell the public the truth.

Once I felt that fire was lit, I poured on some lighter

fluid. "It's not bad enough that you'll owe Doug twice what he loaned you," I scoffed. "He'll remind you the rest of your life that this was the only trip his fishing gear ever went on without catching a fish." I threw on some kindling. "Dear Editor," I imagined, "Was it not possible, out of all the writers on the planet, to find one who knows how to fish?" I tossed on a log. "No, Sarah, I didn't catch anything. I hooked one, but he got away."

Now the bonfire was blazing. I notched the butt of the rod against a stump of a branch, laid the rod in the crook of my left arm, and pulled out the fly box. Inside I found the fly I had wrapped with Rachel's hair. It looked a little worse for wear, but I didn't care. "You get another chance," I announced. "Don't blow it."

The next hour was cold, wet, and long. As the sky cleared, a chill breeze came up. Casting into the wind was harder work, but I would not turn my back to the wind and cast upstream. I told myself it was because the current would just drag the fly back down into the line and spook the fish, but I didn't really know that. What I knew was that I had hooked a fish down at the riffle below. That was a certainty; everything else was conjecture. So I kept casting to the riffle, letting the current carry the fly down, and then reeling it slowly in. It was probably stupid, but I couldn't help myself.

Eventually I decided to change the fly. I reeled in but let the line hang in the current while I stood the rod up in the crook of my arm and rubbed my fingers together. They were mighty cold, and I needed them warm before I could dig into the fly box and tie knots. As I brought my hands down to the pouch on my belt, the rod slipped out of the crook of my arm and tilted away from me. I reached to take hold of it with my right hand, but it had already fallen beyond my reach and was tipping over into the stream! Instinctively I stabbed at the air with my left arm while fighting for balance with my right.

I won the fight to grab the rod, but lost the fight to regain my balance. I teetered on the log a moment, then fell hard onto my right hip and nearly slipped off the back side of the log into the water. Some benevolent god, though, had hooked my right arm around the stump of a branch, giving me enough purchase to kick and scrape with my legs so that I did not go backwards into the water. Finally I was lying still on the top of the log, with my heart pounding in my chest. My hip ached and one of my feet was soaked all the way up the calf, but I was all right. I had the rod clutched in my left hand, lying across my body and pointing downstream. It was all right, too. I breathed a sigh of relief and lay back on the log, thanking my stars I hadn't fallen in.

I was just about to sit up when the tip of the rod jerked and the line went stiff where it slanted under the water downstream. It appeared that the current had caught the line. Then the line went slack, and I turned my attention back to getting up off the log without dropping the rod or falling in the creek. Suddenly the rod was jerking again, but the line wasn't dragging downstream now. It was angled back from the rod tip in my direction, as if the line was being taken under the log by some strange force.

Then it got stranger. The line began to run off the reel with a high-pitched whine. I almost fell off the log again as I realized what was taking the line out. I scrambled to sit up and then turn onto my knees. When I got my balance I held the rod with my right hand and froze the reel with my left. The rod bowed down sharply toward the water, jerking with the same powerful vibrations I had felt before. My mind soared into elation: I had another fish on the line!

There was only one problem: the line went into the water on the downstream side of the log, but the fish had taken the line under it to the upstream side. There was no way to play the fish, except to try to pull him back under the log to the downstream side. I kept the reel from giving up more line, and carefully inserted the tip of the rod under the water, so that I could pull the line directly back under the log without snagging it. But when I had two feet of the slender, flexible rod under water, the fish began fighting harder and the rod was bowed against the log. I remembered Doug's final instruction: he didn't care about flies or leaders, but I was not to damage the rod. Cursing my luck, I let the reel run free so I could pull the rod back out of the water. Line ran out as the fish went further upstream. Somehow I had to get the line around to the upstream side of the log.

Necessity soon became the mother of invention. I sat down onto the log like it was a horse, letting both legs dangle into the water. It was cold, but I didn't care. I let the reel run free so I could bring the rod up onto the log. I passed the handle down between my legs and lay down on top of the log with the rod under me. Now the rod couldn't go anywhere I didn't go, and no more line could run out. More important, the line was now clear of the water on the uphill side of the log. I could see it, and by lying full length on the log and reaching out as far as I could, I was able to take hold of the line on the upstream side of the log.

Carefully I sat up again with my ankles locked together under the log. It was not the most elegant position, and my legs were mostly under icy cold water, but that didn't matter: now I could play the fish. I couldn't use the rod, but I didn't need it. I sat back up and held the line, feeling the wild pull of the fish at the other end. The instant there was any slack at all, I pulled the line in hand over hand. It was slick, and once when the fish leaped from the stream I let it slip a few feet, but I was not about to be distracted by the beauty of nature. I did not care about form, or style points, or impressing anyone. This was hunting, and the point was to bag the game. All I cared about was getting the fish close enough that I could pull him out of the water with my own two hands.

When I had pulled in all the green neon line and had only ten feet or so of leader left, I could see that this was a much larger fish than the first one. I held still and felt my breaths coming fast and my heart beating faster. This fish, too, did tired figure eights at the end of the leader, but I wasn't buying the act this time. I sat up straight, then got one leg out of the water and onto the log behind me. Carefully I drew the other leg up and crouched on the log. I kept my eye on the fish the whole time.

When I was ready, I began to pull the leader in, hand over hand. It was much finer than the line, and cut into my hands. I didn't care, because I could hardly feel them for the cold. Soon the fish was thrashing in the water near the log. With a grunt I pushed myself up to a standing position and drew the fish from the water. He swung in the air, flailing furiously, but I held my arm high to keep him from hitting the log or its stumps of branches. By twisting my line hand I was able to wrap the leader around my wrist and reel the fish another foot or so higher, so I could slowly reach out and grab him by the tail. Quickly I twisted up the slack in the leader so that I had the fish taut: one end by the hook in his jaw and the other end by his triangular tail. Now I could catch my breath and admire the fish up close. He was almost two shimmery feet long, and though he was suffocating in the morning air he was still very much alive.

I put the fish against the log and planted my foot on this tail to keep the fish taught. With my free hand I pulled out my pocket knife and clipped the leader free where it met the green fishing line. Then I took the end of the line, looped it over the log a few times to secure the rod, and then took the fish by the tail again. Carefully I straightened up and made my way up the log. Sometimes the fish shook angrily, other times he was still. When I hopped off the log I went along the bank until I found a small boulder. There I waited until the fish became still, then took it by the tail in both hands and smacked its head hard against the rock. Now it was no longer suffocating, and no longer able to get away from me. I had my fish at last, and he was a beauty.

I laid him on the boulder and worked the fly loose from his jaw. The hook was flattened a bit, and the hairs and wires that made the hook a lure were nearly all shredded away, but the fly had done its job. I tucked it in a pocket of my vest, then went back up on the log to retrieve and disassemble the rod. When I was ready to walk back down the creek, I used the piece of broken leader from the fish I had lost to make a carrying loop for the fish I had caught. With my trophy dangling by my side, I set off for my car.

I got as far as the willow thicket where I had first spotted the log when I met two fishermen coming up the river. I didn't recognize them at first, but when they greeted me I knew their voices.

"I guess we're headed in the right direction," said the one in the khaki hat, pointing to my fish.

His companion, wearing a blue vest, laughed. "Unless you already caught and released the rest of 'em," he said.

"I did hook one other, but he released himself," I admitted. They laughed. They were the two guys I had watched on the river the day before. It was only one day, but it seemed like a lot longer.

"This is a real beauty," said the hat.

"The other one was a lot smaller," I told him.

"*Most* of 'em are smaller than this," the vest said, and we all looked down at the fish a while. When they asked me what I used to catch it, I pulled the beat-up fly out of my pocket. The guy in the hat examined it closely, but he finally gave up and asked me what it had been before the fish chewed it up.

"Well," I said, "I don't know. This is the first fish I ever caught on a fly. I don't know what any of them are called yet."

"This is your first?" asked the vest, incredulous. I nodded. He put out his hand. I shook it. "Congratulations," he said. "There's nothing like the first one."

"Listen," the hat said, "you want a picture? I got a Polaroid, it only takes a minute."

A smile spread across my face.

While he pulled the camera out, his partner opened his fly box and held up a couple of flies. I pointed to one that matched the one I had used. He nodded and hooked it on the outside of his vest. "I'll try it," he said.

I told them about the downed tree, and then it was time to pose for a photo. While the first one was developing, the guy in the vest showed me how to hold the fish up in profile, close to my smiling face, so it would look even bigger than it was. His friend took another photo then, and we waited for them to develop. When they were ready, I marveled not at the fish, but at my own disheveled appearance. I had not shaved in three days, I had a scruffy baseball cap on my head, a bandanna wrapped around my forehead, and my vest and pants were stained with water, scales, and dirt. I was a real mess, and I was happy.

"Did we see you on the river yesterday?" one of the guys asked.

"Yeah," I said. "You caught a good-looking fish yourself."

When the guy offered to show me the photograph, I could hardly say no. We were comparing the relative size of the two fish when I noticed one of the guys look up in the direction I had come. There was another fisherman approaching, and he too had a sizable steelhead on a stringer.

"Christ, Mike, look at that," the hat said.

"We gotta get on the water."

"No kidding."

When the fourth man joined us, he and I held up our fish side by side and guessed their weights. His face was creased by many years of smiling and squinting. He too congratulated me on my first fly fish, and we had some more conversation about lures and conditions. He had gone upstream past the fallen log, he said, because he was "too old for that kind of thing."

The rest of us laughed and protested, which made the old guy smile and squint more than ever. Finally he and I were ready to head down river while the other two headed up.

"I'd wish you good luck," I said to them, "but luck has damn little to do with it, right?"

"Damn straight," said the guy in the hat.

"Superior intelligence," said the guy in the vest.

"I don't know," the old guy said. "I always figured it was patience, patience, and more patience."

The other two guys laughed and started walking off, but one of them called back over his shoulder. "If I see any patients out here, I'll send 'em your way, Doc!"

# NINE

"DOCTOR CLARK?"

"That's right. Have we met before?"

"No, we haven't. But I've heard people talk about you."

"Well, all right. Call me Jim."

"I'm Rye. Pleased to meet you."

"Rye," he said, sounding it in the wet air. "That's an unusual name."

So began our conversation. I had heard the remark about my "unusual name" from every doctor I went to as a child. There weren't that many of them, but they all said it. I guess it was the first thing that occurred to them when it was time to put a nervous child at ease. The child would invariably tell them about the right knee of Orion, the big hunter made of stars in the night sky. In the present situation, I figured I could dispense with the astronomical etiology.

We walked along, talking about fishing and related matters, until I gently guided the conversation to the natural beauty of Pomo Bluff and the surrounding area. Doctor Clark soon warmed to the subject.

"I've lived here as man and boy," he said, "and never gotten tired of it. Some people say the mountains are majestic, but I'll take the majesty of the Pacific any time."

"You must have left to go to medical school," I said.

"Oh, sure," he replied. "Went to UC in San Francisco, and stayed on in the city for my residency. But when I was ready to set up my own practice, I knew where I wanted to be."

"Speaking of the city," I said, "I happened to be at St. Horace when they found that guy from San Francisco."

Doc Clark squinted at me. "You were staying there?"

"I was visiting Sarah Gordon. You know her?"

"Yes, I do. Did she find him?"

"It was a housekeeper that spotted him. Sarah and I went in the room together."

"I see."

We walked along in silence for a moment, our fish swinging forward and back with our strides.

"I had a chance to talk with Fred Stone about it later," I said lightly. "He said you figure the guy died from something he ate."

The doctor squinted more narrowly. He was not smiling now. "Could be," he said. "But I didn't say that."

"Well, you know, I figured that, just based on the evidence at the scene—"

He shot me a look. "What evidence?"

I took my time now. "I'm no policeman," I said, "but it seemed unlikely that the guy died from something he ate without trying to get help or anything. That's why I wondered about…what you found."

"I didn't find much," the doctor snapped.

"They did seem to be moving things right along, didn't they?" I suggested.

This shot hit the mark. The doctor came to a full stop and stared off to the west. We were on a low knoll that gave a view forward to the ocean bluffs and back toward the creek gorge. A few broad rays of sun cut through a heavy sky, splashing pale yellow light on wild-grass meadows dotted with oaks.

"Your questions," he said, "betray some personal interest."

"I didn't know the guy," I shrugged. "I'm just curious what happened to him. He was from San Francisco, I'm from San Francisco."

"And you'll go back to San Francisco, probably in a day or two," the doctor said. "Those of us who live here will still be here, dealing with each other."

"You know," I said, "Sheriff Stone said something similar. As if small towns have a different set of laws for the locals than you do for everyone else."

"It has to do with who that man is, and something he did years before," Dr. Clark said sternly. "I gather you know that."

I nodded. "I understand," I said. "But you must have done your best to determine the actual cause of death—even if Stone doesn't care what it was."

"Of course I did. I examined that man from head to foot."

"And you were given some facts, I imagine, that fit a finding of death from anaphylactic shock." Clark said nothing, but his lips set a little tighter. "You must have some observations of your own."

Dr. Clark stared off to the west again. He still had a clear eye and erect posture, but age and gravity were taking their inevitable toll. I was sorry that he had become involved in Dick Shammey's messy end. "The facts *were* consistent with fatality from anaphylaxis," he said at last, still squinting toward the silvery horizon. "The deceased was apparently alone, or at least unaided, and in unfamiliar circumstances, when he ingested a toxic substance that caused fairly sudden cessation of respiratory activity." He was talking to himself now, as if dictating the report he never got to file.

"What substance?" I prompted.

"Unknown."

"Drugs? Some kind of injection?"

"No puncture marks were visible on the epidermis or in the mucus membranes. No evidence of drug use."

"Something he ate, then."

"Regurgitated food was found in his mouth and throat, suggesting recent or incomplete digestion."

"Something he was allergic to, you think?"

"Unknown. The effects were rapid, however. It appears that some sort of energetic physical exercise distributed the allergen, or toxin, throughout his body in a comparatively short time. Coma or complete respiratory failure ensued."

My forearms flashed with goose bumps as I remembered my unfortunate remark to Sarah about Shammey's appearance lying in bed, naked.

"What about the time of death?"

Clark looked down at the heavy fish hanging from the stringer in his hand. He let it swing back and forth, like a pendulum in a clock.

"I'm no coroner," he said at last, "and I didn't do an autopsy. But we country doctors do a little bit of everything over the years." I waited. Doc Clark looked up from his fish toward the western horizon. "I would say that man was dead by the morning," he said quietly. "I didn't see him until four o'clock that afternoon, and it looked like he'd been dead, or in a coma preceding death, for at least twelve hours."

WHEN WE ARRIVED BACK at our cars, the doctor gave me a plastic bag for my fish. Otherwise, we had little conversation. I wanted to let him know, though, that I didn't think he had done anything wrong. He was just another bit player in the drama, used by Larkin and Stone to bring down the final curtain on Dick Shammey as quickly and smoothly as possible.

"Tell me," I said. "Do you know Ben? Under the bridge?"

The doctor looked up at me from the trunk of his car, where he was pulling off his waders. "For a visitor," he said, "you seem to know a good many of our local people."

"It's been interesting," I agreed. "I was wondering, is that his real name?"

"It's the only name he uses."

"Any idea how old he is?"

"Yes." I waited, but Dr. Clark concentrated on a buckle that appeared to be stuck.

"Why can't you tell me?"

"Dead bodies are one thing," he replied, "but living patients are another. It's a simple matter of confidentiality."

"Would your standards of confidentiality allow you to speculate on Ben's diet?" I asked. Dr. Clark looked quizzical. "I just wondered," I continued, "if he eats fresh fish."

"I believe he does," the doctor said. He was squinting at me, and it seemed that he was smiling again.

I smiled back. "Good."

"In fact," the doctor allowed, "I believe Ben would appreciate such an addition to his nutritional resources."

"Thanks," I said. "It's been great talking with you."

"You're a persuasive young man."

"Curious, that's all."

"You know what they say about curiosity and the cat."

"Yeah. That's why cats have nine lives."

The doctor drove off as I got into my car. I did not follow him. Instead I opened my briefcase and carefully pressed the two photographs between the pages of my journal. Neither was sharply focused, but they both offered indisputable evidence of my catch. I put the journal away and got out my notebook. At the top of a fresh page, I wrote "Time of death: by 4:00 AM." Then I looked out the window and waited for the consequences to gather and rise. It did not take long.

The most obvious corollary of what Dr. Clark had told me was that no breakfast muffin delivered at 8:00 AM. could have killed Dick Shammey, because he was dead before morning. So how did the basket get into the cottage with him?

I closed my eyes and pictured Rachel stepping outside in a flowered dressing gown and plucking the basket off the porch. This little flight of imagination, though, collided with what I had imagined the day Shammey was found in the cottage. Then I had "seen" Carl Larkin coming down to the cottage from the woods above. At the time I felt tired and confused, and thought I was imagining backwards. Now it seemed like I might have been right all along. Had Carl Larkin come after breakfast was delivered? Had he arranged the scene to look like an accidental death?

I opened my eyes and looked down at the top of the page, and wondered again what had actually killed Dick Shammey. The bracelet he wore, the one that warned of his dangerous allergy, had made the cause of death seem so obvious. Looked at another way, though, the bracelet was a sign that Shammey would not eat anything that was dangerous to him. A man with a deathly allergy to nuts would be especially cautious with cakes, breads, and muffins. Maybe the bracelet didn't mean that he had died from allergic shock: maybe it meant he *hadn't*.

If Shammey was poisoned, it must have worked fast. He did not arrive in the room until after 11:00 o'clock at night, and was dead by four the next morning, at the latest. It was possible that Shammey was poisoned earlier, before he even got to St. Horace, and that he died at the inn from poison administered somewhere else. That would have been risky, however, if Rachel was riding in a car that Shammey was driving. It was more likely that the killers set up the room in anticipation of Shammey's arrival.

I closed my eyes and tried to remember the living room in the Hillhouse cottage. Eventually my inner eye lighted on the decanter and the two glasses—the ones that had no fingerprints on them after Stone left the scene and took Shammey's body with him. I opened my eyes and watched a squall of rain blow down onto the meadow around me. I could still see rays of sunshine in other directions. I looked back down at the notebook and let the two facts, time and cause of death, conjoin and procreate. For a while, though, nothing occurred to me. Shammey arrived, drank some poisoned wine, and died. Not much of a story. I watched the squall blow itself out.

I closed my eyes again and looked for the details I had not yet noticed. Many times in my early days on the paper my editor would say to me that "facts are not enough." She meant I needed a story to wrap the facts in, a way to make the facts come alive for the reader. So I would sit back and close my eyes and imagine the spaces between the facts. A surprising amount of the time, the details I imagined turned out to be true—or at least close enough to take me to the next step in my research.

The part of the story I needed to understand took place the morning after I arrived. I revisualized Carl Larkin coming down to the cottage from the woods and arranging the scene to look like an allergic attack. I saw him pick up a glass with some dregs in it and wash it out in the sink. My eyes flew open. Sherry was something you drank at night, not in the morning. You would not poison someone with an evening drink, and then try to make it look like death was caused by a breakfast food, unless you had a poison that took effect slowly, perhaps even eight or ten hours after ingestion.

But Shammey was dead by morning. The poison must have worked on him more quickly. I recalled what Rachel had said in the bar, when I asked her if she was with Shammey when he died. She said it was the loneliest night she had ever spent. Despite the official story that Shammey died in the morning, Rachel automatically connected his death to the night before.

Because she was there.

Now I remembered the bruises and scratches on her wrists and neck, and what the doctor had said about "energetic physical exercise" accelerating the toxic effects of the fatal substance. Had Shammey tanked up on the free sherry and then forced himself on Rachel, perhaps in a premature celebration of his control over her? I shuddered to think of Rachel pinned down on the bed, impaled by a rough passion, while her poisoned lover convulsed, collapsed on her breast, and died.

Even if she knew what was happening, even if she wanted Shammey dead, it was hard to contemplate. Not even Sheriff Stone could have meant it to happen that way. He and Larkin must have planned for Shammey to die in the morning, so that Rachel could call innocently for help, or go out for a walk and let the housekeepers find him alone in the room. But somehow it had gone wrong. Rachel saw Shammey die, and then she was stuck with him for hours afterward. No wonder she was so distraught, and no wonder Sarah was afraid her mind was playing tricks on her.

I left C Ranch Creek and drove back toward Pomo Bluff. The breaks in the western sky were sealing themselves up, creating a dark gray curtain that hung on the horizon. The ocean seemed restless, uncertain. The sun still illuminated a gray sky overhead, but it was clear that the weekend storm had not yet played itself out. I slowed down as I crested the last rise south of the Pomo River, and coasted down to the spot I had turned off and parked once before. Again I parked and got out. Carefully I clambered about halfway down to the anchorage, then stopped and got my balance. The fish was curled almost double in the clear plastic bag I held in one hand.

"Ben?" I called. "It's Rigel. I've got something for you."

There was no answer, and I descended to the edge of Ben's workshop. At first I saw no one. Then, with a start, I realized that someone was standing there, half into the hollow of the massive concrete structure. For an instant I had thought he was someone else, someone I did not want to see. Then I realized it had to be Ben. I let the flush of fear fade away before I spoke up.

"Hello, Ben. I brought you something."

"It's a fish," he said.

"Steelhead. I caught it in C Ranch Creek."

"It's big."

"Not too big," I said, holding it up. "If you cook it, it'll last longer."

"Smoke it," he said.

"Even better," I agreed, and laid the fish on one of

Ben's "tables." I moved away from it and turned to look up the river. I could see at least eight fishermen waist deep in the water, their lines all in parallel. Another wave of satisfaction rolled through me. When I turned around, the fish was gone and so was Ben. I realized I would not see the fish again, and a wave of regret coursed through me. At least I had pictures. I had proof.

When Ben returned, it was with two mugs of sugared tea. Then he sat down, his back to the open slope behind him. I could hardly discern the features of his face in the dim light. "It's heavy," he said, meaning the fish.

"I had to get wet to get him."

"Why did you give it to me?"

"I wanted you to have it."

"Why?"

"I've got to drive real far, and I can't keep it. I wanted to give it to someone who would appreciate it as much as I did."

"I'll keep the scales," he said. "You can have them back if you want."

"That's okay. You use 'em."

We were silent awhile, and then a quiet rain began to float down on either side of the bridge. The air grew slowly thicker, wetter, and colder.

"Would you tell me your last name, Ben?"

He became still. His answer did not come for a long time, and then I had to strain to hear it. "I lost it."

"Where?"

"It's gone."

"Do you remember what it was?"

He started to shake his head, then stopped. The whites of his eyes held still, and I could feel his attention on me. But he did not speak.

"I wonder if something happened to you, Ben, that made you forget."

Ben put down his mug and folded his hands in his lap. His lower lip was curled back between his teeth. I waited. I had learned while covering the homeless for the paper that schizophrenia didn't mean a person was stupid, or slow. It meant they had to process twice as much information when feelings or memories were involved. Finally he spoke. "I was supposed to go with him."

"Where?"

"By her house. Melissa's house. That's where it happened."

The hairs on my neck got itchy. Gibbie McPhail was shot dead a few blocks from Melissa Larkin's apartment.

"Who were you supposed to go with?"

"I was supposed to go with him. I was supposed to watch. There was this girl I went to see first. Then I went there. I found him."

"You got there late?" Ben nodded. "And you found Gibbie?"

There was no sound or motion in response. I waited. Finally Ben reached down, picked up his mug, and held it out in front of him. Slowly he turned it over. A few drops of tea slid out, hung on the lip, then dropped onto the stone below. He put the mug back down.

"I was supposed to watch," he said again. His voice had taken on a younger quality, less gruff and more vulnerable. "Then I found him, and then the trouble started."

For the first time, I got the idea that Ben had not always been like this. I had assumed, when he told me about helping Carl Larkin with the harvest in years past, that he was already a derelict. But of course someone who had survived in the drug business as long as Larkin would not hire help he could not trust. Ben must have been whole then. He must have been whole if he was involved in the deal between Gibbie McPhail and Dick Shammey near Melissa's apartment. Was it finding McPhail dead in the alley that pushed Ben into his current state? Or something else?

"There was a lot of trouble," I said. "Not just for Melissa, but also for you."

"Because of me," he said. His voice was bitter now. "No, Ben."

"I was supposed to watch. It was because of me."

"We can't stop things from happening."

"Oh yes we can! Oh yes we can!" Suddenly Ben was standing, pointing with a long arm and threatening finger at an imaginary person seated on the stone in front of him. The transformation was startling. His voice was hard-edged, authoritative—and eerily familiar. "You had one small job to do and you messed it up! Now he's dead, and you weren't even there! You as good as let him die!"

"I didn't mean to be late," I said softly, as if I were the one getting the lecture. I knew it wasn't fair to lead him on, but I had to figure out why this new Ben reminded me of someone else.

He swung his angry arm up from the stone and pointed it at me. His eyes blazed with cold fire. "I've got to clean up your mess for you, like always. What are you good for? Nothing! You make me sick. I can't stand to look at you!"

"I'm sorry," I said. "I got there as soon as I could."

"You're worse than a worm! You should go crawl in the ground and disappear!" He reached down, picked up the mug, and hurled it down on the stone. The pieces flew in all directions, but I ignored them. Before my eyes,

Ben was melting back into the frail man I had first met. The fire went out of him, the anger evaporated, and he looked stunned by what had happened. He knelt down in front of the stone and picked up two shards of the mug and held them together sorrowfully, as if they were the broken pieces of a favorite toy.

Suddenly I knew where I had heard angry words about "cleaning up a mess" before. I knew why the tone and tension were familiar. And I could see now the physical resemblance that had made me think Ben was someone else when I arrived under the bridge. It was bizarre, but somehow all of a piece with everything else.

"You know the sheriff's name, don't you, Ben?" He froze, but he did not look up or speak. I waited, then continued. "The sheriff's name is Stone. You used to have the same name as him, didn't you?"

Ben still did not look up, but he shook his head, no.

"Are you sure, Ben?"

He looked up at me then, like a boy who had lost something and wanted it back. "Freddie," he said. "His name was Freddie."

# TEN

I LEFT BEN with serious misgivings. He seemed calm, or at least quiet, but reconnecting with his part in the murder of Gibbie McPhail had shaken him. The fact that his own brother had condemned him for it afterward could not add much charm to the recollection. And I was the one who stirred it all up. I had seen my share of people break down while I interviewed them, or become hysterical with guilt and denial, and it was never pleasant. You tell yourself it comes with the territory, it's part of the job, and you go on. But Ben Stone was not some bureaucratic functionary or corrupt politician trying to preserve a false authority. He was at the mercy of the authorities, his life twisted almost beyond recognition.

I now understood why, according to Liz, Sheriff Stone would "just as soon kill Ben as do something nice for him"—but still make sure he was fed and clothed. Ben was a living reminder of the tragedy involving Gibbie and Melissa, and he was partly responsible, if in only a very small way. The fact that Ben was also his brother must have deeply gored the sheriff's pride.

I couldn't tell if Ben had a psychotic break at the time of the original murder, or if being outcast by the entire town of Pomo Bluff had driven him slowly to his present state. In a way, it didn't matter. Fred Stone was responsible for Ben both personally and professionally, no matter how much he might have wanted him to disappear from the face of the earth.

Ruminating on the two of them, I realized why their

relationship had escaped my notice at first. For one thing, I had been seeing Ben as the kind of homeless person I saw on the streets of the city countless times. Those people did not have brothers who were county sheriffs. In a similar way, I had been so busy standing up to Fred Stone the sheriff that I had forgotten about Fred Stone the man. The sheriff had power, prestige, and a moral certainty that he was right on all counts. The outcast had no power, no status, and a conviction that he was to blame for a murder most foul. It was sobering to realize how these intangible differences between the brothers had overwhelmed the physical similarities they once shared.

At that moment a California Highway Patrol cruiser rolled slowly by me, and the young buck in his dark glasses looked me over before continuing across the bridge and up the hill toward Pomo Bluff. The CHP, as we call them, have no official link with local law enforcement, but to a reporter, cops are cops. You treat them all as suspect until proven safe. Also, my appearance didn't help. I started up my engine and pulled onto the highway. The black and white patrol car continued through town and on up the highway. I turned off at the hotel and parked next to the phone booth. By now I knew its smoky plastic windows, its dilapidated phone directory, and its distinctive smell. There was one question the morning had raised but not resolved, and a phone call might get me an answer.

"Hi, Melodie? It's Rigel again."

"Well, what do you know? We missed you in church this morning."

I laughed. "How was the sermon?"

"It's not that kind of church," she said merrily. "We pretty much all get to say something, although some of us are more interesting than others."

"Is it Unitarian?"

"I think so, but I don't read the sign on the way in. I go with Eleanor and Stacy, because their husbands play golf. Although I'm wondering lately if the men don't have a better idea of how to commune with the Infinite on Sunday morning."

"They say some people see the Lord in a drive down the middle of the fairway."

"I'll tell you, Rigel, these days I see the Lord in a parking space by the beauty parlor!"

It was a relief to laugh.

"So what can I do for you, Rigel? Are you going to try out another story idea? Or do you want the name of the guy who grows the pears in the bottles?"

"It's a little different this time. I remember you said once that you read a lot of murder mysteries."

"You're not going to kill someone, are you? Not on Sunday? There's got to be a better story idea than that!"

"No, Melodie, this is serious. I need to know if there's a commercially available poison that would not show up or harm the person for, say, eight to ten hours. Something you could put in an after-dinner drink and then the person would die the next morning."

"Yuck! That is serious."

"It's hypothetical right now, but it may help explain some things that aren't clear."

"This is for some magazine or something?"

"Yeah," I fibbed.

"Well, let's see. Barium is very popular just now, but that's probably not what you're looking for."

"What's barium?"

"It's one of your bivalent metallics from the alkaline earth group," she said blithely. "Only works in combination, but it's totally toxic."

"It's commercially available?"

"Well, you can't just go to the grocery store. You have to go to scientific research places or someplace like that. Or just have the character steal it from the laboratory where they work. That's what most of the writers do."

"I'm out in the country, Melodie, and I don't think they have any laboratories or research facilities up here."

"Right. And anyway, it works too fast."

"The working hypothesis is poison mushrooms," I said.

"You really turned against that mushroom guy in a hurry, Rigel," Melodie observed. "And all because he wasn't cute and hunky? I shouldn't have said anything."

I ignored her joke this time. "The question is, can a posionous mushroom produce a delayed reaction?"

"Most toxins that occur in nature can be modulated by drying them out," Melodie informed me, serious again. "The trick is, you've got to feed someone a whole plate of poison if it was dried out first. That's what the Greeks did, you know. They'd make some wine, or go get it from Bacchus or whatever they did, and then they would mix dried poisons into it."

"To kill someone?"

"No, for a party!" Melodie exclaimed. "They didn't sit around smoking marijuana—they sat around drinking wine with just enough poison in it to knock them on their butts for a few hours. It's like that fish they eat in Japan, where the cooks have to have a license to prepare it."

"Blowfish."

"Right. Eat the right amount, it's better than drugs. Eat too much, you're gone. Adds new meaning to the idea of a 'destination restaurant,' doesn't it?"

"No kidding. So anyway, back to mushrooms."

"I'd say if they're potent enough to kill, they would

kill pretty fast,'' Melodie said thoughtfully. "Plus it's hard to hide mushrooms in other food, or in a drink. They smell too much. And if you dry them out so you can't taste them, then they're not strong enough to do the dirty deed.''

"So I'm back to square one."

"Well, why did you think of mushrooms? Because of that guy you wanted to write about?"

"I'm up in Mendocino County. There's a restaurant that sells a lot of dishes with wild mushrooms, stuff like that.''

"Well," she said, "there are plenty of poisonous things beside mushrooms that grow up there." Something about what she said struck me as odd, and I asked her to repeat it. The second time, I knew why it was odd: Carl Larkin had said the same thing to me the day I had visited his house.

"What kind of things do you mean?" I asked her.

"Well, let's see," she said. "There's oleander, that's really bad for you. I'm always telling my clients that but they don't seem to care. And Irish yew trees are bad, too. But I think the worst one is hemlock—specifically water hemlock. It's as bad as *amanita*.''

"Which is?"

"That's the scientific name of the most poisonous mushroom. It was real big with the mystery writers for a few years. Before they found out about barium.''

"Hemlock is what they used to kill Socrates, right?"

"Right. They also used it for euthanasia, and, like I was saying before, as a party drug.''

"People can use hemlock in different ways, to get different effects?"

"Right. But remember, the Greeks had lots of practice, because the senators got to kill people and stuff like that all the time," Melodie pointed out. "As private citizens in contemporary society, we just don't have the opportunities we need to practice these things anymore." I got out my notebook as Melodie continued merrily along. "Plus you don't know in advance how much of a concealed substance a person will consume," she said, "or if he's got any extra susceptibility to the particular poison."

"So the idea is, it's hard to be precise with poison."

"Exactly. If you're an amateur and you're going to kill one person one time using poison, there's a high chance you'll screw it up somehow. Especially if you're using hemlock, because there's more than one kind."

"Hang on," I said. "I've got to write this down."

"There are probably two ways to go," she said, pausing for my benefit. "If you want to make sure no one knows you're trying to kill a person, then you'd probably use spotted hemlock because it takes more time. That way there's plenty of separation from the time you poisoned the person 'til the time he kicked the bucket. And if you don't kill him, at least he'd get a really bad bellyache."

"That's one," I said, scribbling furiously. "What's the other?"

"If you want to make sure you kill the person no matter what, you'd use water hemlock instead. You squeeze the alkaloid—that's the poison—out of the roots of the plant and put it in some wine or something and get the person to drink it. He'd die right away. You just have to have a really good alibi if you're the killer."

In my mind's eye I saw Sheriff Stone. An instant later, a bombshell of understanding exploded in my brain.

"Rigel? Are you still there?"

"Yes, I was making a connection. Listen, Melodie,

I've got one more question. It's kind of off the wall and you don't have to answer it if you don't want to."

"Is it about sex?"

"How did you know?"

"My whole life people have been trying to protect me from sex. I tell them that after forty years and three husbands, there's not much left to hide!"

I smiled and closed my notebook. "The question is, would sex tend to make something like hemlock work faster?"

"You mean, after you poison the person, or before?"

"Come on, Melodie, I'm serious."

"Well, good sex does increase the circulation, and that's what carries the poison."

"That's what I figured, too."

"Boy, what a way to go!"

I STILL COULDN'T PROVE anything, but I was pretty sure I could paint the whole picture now. In a way, it meant I didn't have to think about it any more. I could be plain old Rigel Lynx, get a cup of coffee somewhere, and work on my fishing story until it was time to go say goodbye to Sarah. In fact, it was a delicious sensation to have the pump primed with two stories, both of which I could now sit down and write. I felt like a house painter who had nothing left to do but pull off the masking tape and admire his handiwork. Parting with Sarah would be hard, but I comforted myself by imagining her visiting me in the city.

I walked over to the bookstore where I had sat with Liz the night before, but it was full of people from the city being fussy about their cappucino. I turned around and walked up the highway toward the diner. It was closed for the afternoon, and I found myself looking across the highway toward the hotel. Its shabbiness was now a comfort to me, its plank porch a place I would always remember. The sun was out again, and the afternoon was still. Slowly I strolled across the highway, my briefcase in my hand, and pushed through the door into the bar.

This time, a few people glanced up from their drinks, but that was it. The room was mostly empty, the jukebox silent, the light soft through the yellowed glass in the front. I swung up onto a stool at the bar, which was empty except for a sturdy guy in a work shirt at one end and a pair of youngish women at the other. The guy was reading the paper, and the women were talking to each other in hushed tones punctuated with peals of laughter. The bartender, a burly woman with a prodigious bosom, greeted me and slapped down a paper napkin. I asked for black coffee. She picked up the glass pot, took a look at the dregs in the bottom, and poured them dramatically into the sink. I smiled and she went down the bar to make a fresh pot.

In the meantime I looked around. The first sight that caught my eye was myself in a mirror. Unshaven, hat and bandanna on my head, dirty shirt and sweater under my vest. I looked down at my jeans, which were dry now but stained brown up to my thighs. My grimy hands completed the picture. "Jeez," I said to the bartender, "I'm a mess. I'll be right back." I went into the bathroom and ran the water to wash my hands and face. Another guy came in a moment later. To my surprise, he spoke right up.

"Any luck?" he asked, craning his head around toward me.

"What, fishing?"

"Yeah. You looked like you been out all morning."

"Long enough to hook two and land one," I said.

"Yeah?"

"Got pictures," I smiled. He smiled back, crooked teeth and all.

"You know Andy Tate, works up at Buildertown? He got one at the North Fork Hole this morning, went seven, eight pounds. No picture, though."

"Don't know him," I said. "I was on the creek in the ranch."

"I heard Doc Clark got one down there today."

"Yeah, I met him coming back. Good-lookin' fish."

"Ain't many coming upriver this year," the guy said, shaking his head sadly. "There's a damn sight more fishermen than fish."

We laughed, he left, and I dried my hands and face. When I came out, there was a steaming cup of coffee on the bar. In the corner, the guy I had been talking to was sitting with a couple other guys. They all looked up at me when I came out of the bathroom, and one of them nodded. I nodded back and sat down at the bar aglow with the respect of my peers. I opened my notebook, took out the photos, and looked at them a while. Maybe it was my imagination, but they seemed to be more sharply focused now, and the fish seemed a little bigger, too. At last I laid the photos aside, found my place in the notebook, and began making notes about the morning's fishing.

After a while, I looked up, yawned, and stretched. Down at the end of the bar, where I had been sitting the night before, the guy was still reading. I watched him awhile. It appeared he was reading the entire Sunday paper from cover to cover, and each article from beginning to end. In my heart, I sent him a wave of appreciation on behalf of every reporter whose hard-earned story had ended up on page 17 next to the unfinished furniture ads. When the bartender came along and looked at the photos next to my coffee, she nodded in appreciation.

"You could feed your whole family with one of those," she said.

"If I had a family," I replied.

"Hell, I'm single," she announced, laughing heartily. I smiled and kept writing. The next time she came to refill my coffee cup, I looked up.

"Is the restaurant serving lunch?" I asked.

"For another half-hour," she said. "You want to order something?"

"What, in here?"

"Sure. They got a lamb steak, potatoes, and green beans for ten ninety-five, and I can just about guarantee you won't need dinner later."

"Sounds good," I said. She nodded and went down to the end of the bar to squeeze out and go through a back door into the restaurant. As I watched her go, one of the two women sitting at the bar looked full at me. I looked down at my coffee, but out of the corner of my eye I could see she was still looking at me. A moment later she materialized on the stool next to mine. I glanced quickly down the bar, where her purse still sat by her stool. Her friend's purse was there too, but the friend had vanished.

"Are you a writer?" she asked.

"As a matter of fact," I said, "I am." She looked about my age, or maybe a little younger. I would not have called her pretty by city standards, but up here I figured she got as much interest as she could handle.

"I dated a writer once, he was from New York City. He came out here and got himself a house and he was going to write a book. Maybe you know him." She told me his name but I didn't recognize it. "Then they had that damn war and he up and went over there instead," she continued. "What're you writin'?"

"Um, it's an article for a magazine."

"That's why he went over there to that war. Damn magazine."

"The Gulf War didn't last that long."

"Yeah, well, he didn't come back, if that's what you mean."

"Was he...?"

"No, I meant he didn't come back *here.*"

"Too bad."

"I read the article when it came out. Had to go all the way to Santa Rosa to find the damn magazine. Wasn't even about the war at all. Just about the women in that country, what was it?"

"Kuwait?" I guessed. I was beginning to wish her friend would reappear.

"That's it, Kuwait." She fingered the pages of my notebook. "You ever write a book?"

"No, I never did."

"You got a place up here?"

"No, just doing a little research."

"Research? You're doin' research about this little po-dunk town?"

"About the fishing, actually."

"Oh!" she said, as if a light was coming on. "Look at you, I shoulda seen it!"

"I guess I should have changed."

"Hell, nobody cares how you look around here," she said, gesturing around the room. "Everybody looks like hell half the time. *You* look like you been fishing. And here you are with your little prize!" She seized on one of the photos and examined it closely. I closed the notebook and put my pen aside.

"Well," she said at last, "it's you and a fish. Who took the picture?"

"Couple of guys, just happened along. One of them had a camera."

"You went fishin' by yourself?"

"Yes."

"You ain't got any friends up here?"

"No, I came alone."

"Hunh," she said. "When *he* came up here, he had a woman with him, but she only lasted the winter. Rained all the time that year. Then she was gone. That's when he started coming to town."

The bathroom door opened and the other woman emerged. The woman next to me saw me look over, and she lowered her voice.

"Her husband left her before Christmas," she said. "You can't tell to look at her, but she's a wreck inside."

"It's a tough time to be alone."

The woman looked up in surprise. "It sure is," she said, "but I never heard anyone good-lookin' say it before."

"Doesn't matter how you look," I said. "Pain hurts."

"Amen, brother. Well, I gotta get back to Shirleen. She's the one hurtin' now. And good luck with your book."

I opened my mouth to correct her, but instead just said "thanks." When the bartender brought in my lunch and set it down on the bar in front of me, I pulled some money out of my wallet.

"You don't have to pay now," she said.

"I want to buy a round for the ladies down the bar," I said. "And for the guy there with the newspaper. And what the hell, a beer for me, too." She nodded and set to work. I gazed in consternation at the heaping trencher before me, then dug in and ate until I could eat no more. When the recipients of the free drinks called out their thanks, I nodded and smiled and kept eating.

As I pushed the plate away at last, a yawn that made my jaws hurt pushed its way out of my mouth. For the first time in days I was relaxed enough to realize that I was tired. In fact, I was exhausted. It wasn't just that I had spent the last three days hiking, fishing, writing, and keeping my car from being run off the highway. I had also slept in three different places three nights running— a car, a couch, and a dead man's bed. I was bushed.

"How about dessert?" the bartender asked, and then laughed uproariously. I managed a weak laugh of my own, and asked her for the check. When I slipped off my stool and headed for the door a few minutes later, my hip ached where I had fallen on the log. My back was also a little stiff, and another wave of tiredness was rolling through me. I began to wonder if I could make it home without stopping for a nap somewhere.

I WENT OVER TO the gas station to fill up the car and change clothes in the men's room. To my relief, it was large, clean, and well lighted. When I was finished I was at least presentable, wearing the same clothes I'd driven up in. I motored up the highway in a kind of trance, thinking of what I would say to Sarah. It was easier to think of Liz, who would be getting off work just about the time I arrived at St. Horace. She had been both friendly and generous, like Sarah, and I wanted to thank her and say goodbye in person.

When I got to the inn and went into the lobby, I was surprised to find Sarah behind the bar. She finished checking out an elderly couple, then smiled and came out from behind the bar. Instead of saying anything she crossed the lobby and opened a door that was built into the wall so cleverly I'd never noticed it before. It led out onto a small balcony that overlooked the driveway, the trees on the other side of the highway, and a silvery-gray ocean preparing for a brilliant, broken-storm sunset.

"This is fantastic," I observed.

"One of the perks," she smiled. "Before you say anything, I want to tell you that Liz says goodbye. She and I traded some hours today so I could get off early, but she wanted you to know she missed saying goodbye to you."

"I wanted to say the same," I said. "But it was nice of her to make the sacrifice."

"Well," Sarah said, "when she offered, I could hardly refuse."

"I'm glad to hear that," I said. She smiled briefly and turned again to look to the west. I stood next to her feeling nervous, excited, and exhausted.

"I don't like to say goodbye to people," she said at last. "Too many times I didn't see them again."

"You'll see me again."

"Really?"

"If you want to," I said.

"I'd like that," she said, turning to face me. "I like you."

I studied her face. "I like you, too." She laughed, and I could see she was nervous, too. I decided to make it easier for her. "Why don't you give me your number, so I can call you when I get home," I said. She nodded, and slipped off the balcony into the lobby. She went to the bar to get a slip of paper, and I went out to the parking lot to get Liz's sleeping bag. When I came back inside I stopped in my tracks. Sarah was standing in the open door to the balcony, her face to the western sun. When she turned toward me, the golden light silhouetted her lithe figure from the side and behind. I wanted this to be the way I would always remember her.

"I'll give the sleeping bag to Liz when she comes in," she said, stepping into the room.

"I have to check out."

"It's all ready." She walked into the bar and I followed. We concluded our financial arrangements without speaking. Finally we were facing each other across the top of the bar.

"I have an idea," she said. She reached down below the bar and picked up a slip of paper with a phone number written on it. In the other hand she held a key. "Why don't you go to my house and take a nap? I'll make you dinner."

"I don't know," I said slowly. "It *is* a mighty long drive in the dark, and I *am* pretty tired."

"Then you could stay until morning," she said, "when it's light." I just looked at her. Slowly Sarah's cheeks colored and a smile of shy defiance bloomed on her face. "Don't you think it's a good idea?"

"I don't know," I said. "But I expect we'll find out."

"You know how to get up there?"

"I'm pretty sure I can find it."

"Good. I'll be home about seven-thirty."

She took the sleeping bag and put it behind the bar. She handed me the slip of paper and the key, then leaned over the bar. Her kiss was aimed at my cheek but I caught her jaw gently and steered her lips to mine. It was brief, but electric. Then I heard steps coming down the stairs above us, and had to let her go. Our eyes locked for a moment, before I stepped away from the bar toward the door. As I went out I glanced back. She was greeting her departing guests with intimate kindness, as if no one mattered more.

When I got to Sarah's house in the forest, I decided to leave everything in the car and lock it tight in the trunk. I slid my notebooks into a space I had made years before on the underside of the trunk floor. Then I walked into the house, let myself in, and got reoriented. In afternoon daylight, it looked different from the dark night and gray morning I remembered. Slowly I placed everything, remembered everything, saw myself in each place, and then looked over at the bed. I figured the couch was more appropriate, and I already knew it was comfortable enough to sleep on. I had a brief impulse to walk around, see how Sarah organized her domestic existence, but decided against that, too.

It wasn't until I got comfortable on the couch, with a blanket drawn up over my legs, that I got a good look at the painting I had noticed on my previous visit. I realized now it was a soft, somewhat expressionist portrait of Sarah. It favored her quiet beauty in a way that I liked immediately, but there was something about it that was not quite right. I wriggled around to get a little more comfortable and gazed at the painting again. It was something about her manner, something about her face... It had a little of Rachel in it, but that was not exactly right, either. I closed my eyes to see if the answer would come to me. As it happened, sleep was waiting for just such an opportunity...

I FLOATED UP toward wakefulness hours later. I heard Sarah come in and close the door. I started to get up and turn on a light or something, but I heard water running in the bathroom and then I was out again. When I woke the next time, there was soft music playing, the wood stove was crackling and popping, and Sarah was sitting on the edge of the couch gazing down at me. I smiled sleepily.

"Shall I make dinner?" she asked gently. "Or just put you to bed?"

"I'll get up," I said. I meant it this time.

When I woke the third time, Sarah was in the kitchen, opening a bottle of wine. I was disoriented and had lost track of time. I had been dreaming of Rachel as a homeless person in San Francisco, freezing in an alley as police cars drove by, one after another. Now I was in a cozy winter cottage with a lovely woman who offered food, a bed, perhaps more. This dream scarcely seemed more real than the previous one, and I forced myself to stand up and stretch. My hip complained, and I moved around a bit to warm it up again.

"That was some nap," Sarah said.

"I was dreaming of Rachel," I said.

Sarah's face fell. I understood for the first time that she must have heard that phrase, or variations on it, her whole life.

"It was not that kind of dream," I said.

"Could we talk about her later?" Sarah asked. "I just want to be together without all that other stuff, okay? Just for a little while?"

"Sure," I said, and stumbled into the bathroom. When I came out, Sarah was sitting on the couch, with her bare feet tucked under her. Two glasses of wine stood side by side on a table in front of her. I sat down on the couch, we touched the two glasses together, and sipped the wine. It was delicious. There was also a scent in the air, something musky that emanated from Sarah's direction. She seemed softer, too, and I glanced up at the painting on the wall behind her. Was that the difference?

"I want to hear about your fishing," she said. "Something tells me it was good."

"No," I said, smiling at her proudly, "it was great."

"Tell me," she smiled back, and I obliged. It was surprisingly fun to spin the story, and I realized why Doug was always so quick to tell his friends about every fish he had caught on his latest trip. It brought the whole experience back to life, so you could not only savor it again but add in all your thoughts, all your ups and downs, and all your excitement. For her part, Sarah was a great listener. When she got up to refill our glasses, I remembered that she had caught her share of fish, and that she knew exactly how much fun I was having telling her my story.

When I got to the part about meeting Doc Clark, something told me to leave out his identity and my conversation with him. I too wanted to enjoy some time with Sarah that was free of tumult or trouble. "So then I went to the hotel," I concluded, "had a huge lunch, and worked on the story."

"What did you do with the fish?"

"I gave it to the guy who lives under the bridge."

"You gave it to Ben?"

"Yeah. You think that's okay?"

"I think it's totally sweet."

"I suppose I could have brought it here, if I'd known I was coming."

"Are you hungry?"

"Well, what I'd really like is a little more of whatever it is I can smell right now," I said, and drew one of her wrists up to my nose. It was amber, a pungent mix of spice and earth, and I inhaled it deeply.

"Here's some more," Sarah said, "right here." She drew aside the collar of her plaid shirt to expose her collarbone. "But you'll have to get right up close." From the hollow at the base of her neck it was not far to the soft skin below her ears, and from there only a slight turn of the head to her lips. When the kiss began, we were fully clothed and sitting on the couch. When it ended, clothing had become an impediment and the couch a constraint.

"Time for bed," Sarah breathed in my ear, and slid from my grasp. I followed her to the bed, but stopped on the near side. She stood on the far side, and cast aside her shirt. I dropped mine. She wriggled out of her blue jeans and slid under the bedclothes. When I joined her a moment later, her skin met mine in long shiver of pleasure. Soon we were entwined together, alternating gentle caresses with fierce embraces, long kisses with quiet moments gazing into each other's eyes.

"You feel wonderful," I whispered.

"Incredible," she whispered back.

"I've wanted to do this ever since the night I met you."

"Come on."

"It's true. When I saw you running that bath…"

She laughed, a sound of pure delight, and I buried my face in her neck. Soon our heat made the quilts and blanket unnecessary. She flung them aside, and pulled me closer, and then there was no more need for talk.

Some time later, Sarah slid from the bed and went into the bathroom. I got up and tossed a couple of logs into the stove. When Sarah emerged, she was wrapped in the bathrobe I remembered from the first night. As she reached the bed, however, she slipped out of it and into my arms. Somehow making love with her had not discharged my passion. If anything, it had aroused my sensitivity. My skin against hers tingled with excitement and I pressed her close to maintain the sensation as long as possible.

"It's fantastic, isn't it?" she asked.

"Unbelievable," I said. "I guess I can't ever leave."

"If you do, you'll just have to come back."

"I'm serious," I said. "I think I'll just stay here forever. We'll have to call the inn and have Rachel bring us some food."

I felt Sarah stiffen, and I scrambled to undo the error. "I meant *Liz*," I said. "I don't know why I said Rachel. I meant that we could call *Liz* at the inn."

But it was no good. She was already rolling onto her back, out of my embrace. She looked sad more than angry, which hurt all the more.

"Sarah, I'm sorry."

"It seems you can't get her out of your mind."

"There's a reason for that," I said. "And it has nothing to do with you and me."

"What reason?"

"I'm not sure you want me to tell you this."

"I'm not sure I do either, but I think you better. Otherwise I'm going to feel something I don't want to feel."

"Sarah, please," I pleaded, and moved to kiss her. She did not pull away, but she didn't respond with passion, either.

"Just tell me," she said.

"Okay," I said. "But don't take it the wrong way. I'm here with you because there's no where else I'd rather be." She frowned but inclined her head like she was willing to listen. I took a moment to gather my thoughts. Then I gave Sarah an abbreviated account of Rachel's visit to the bar and subsequent retrieval by Carl Larkin.

I stopped short of describing my encounter with Sheriff Stone.

"So Rachel told you about what happened to Melissa," Sarah said when I finished. "It's a sad story, isn't it?"

"Yeah, but I think the whole time she was really telling me about what's happening to *her,*" I said. "It was like a kind of code, where she wants me to understand something she's afraid to say."

"What?"

"I think Carl Larkin and the sheriff are using her to get even with Dick Shammey for what he did to Gibbie McPhail."

"Wait a second," she said, confused. "Rachel told you that Carl and Fred…?"

"Some things she told, some I inferred."

"But you said—"

"It's complicated, I know. But it makes sense. It all starts with Gibbie McPhail." In the half-light she turned her head away on the pillow, as if thinking back. I waited until she turned back to face me.

"Rachel told you that guy killed him?"

"Not in so many words," I said. "But that's what happened, isn't it? Or at least it's what people up here *think* happened. It's what they're basing their actions on."

"Who? Carl and Fred?"

"Exactly. You see, Fred's involved not just as the sheriff. It turns out that his brother Ben was with Gibbie the night he was killed." Sarah's jaw dropped a little. "You knew Ben was the sheriff's brother, didn't you?" I asked. She nodded.

"I knew. I'm just surprised Rachel would tell you—"

"She didn't tell me that. I worked that one out myself."

"So how was Ben involved?"

"He was supposed to be with Gibbie, but he missed the appointment. When he showed up late, Gibbie was dead, presumably shot dead by Dick Shammey. So that gets Fred involved in Shammey's death up here twice: once as the sheriff of record and once as Ben's big brother."

"And Carl?"

"It was Carl's sister who took the rap for the murder, right? He still misses her. He says she'll be back, but she's doing hard time for another dozen years at least. And even then getting out early depends on the make-up of the parole board. They could make an example of her like they did at the trial. She could stay up there for the full thirty years or so." Sarah blanched. "So it appears that your pals Carl and Fred are getting revenge on Dick Shammey for what he did to Gibbie, Melissa, and Ben."

Sarah looked deeply concerned. "I still don't see why Rachel is involved in this," she said finally.

"She's the bait," I said. "They got her to bring Shammey up here somehow, and then had her give him something to drink. Something with poison in it."

"But you said he died from eating the muffin that had the walnut oil in it."

"Red herring," I snapped. "But that's not the issue. What those two guys are doing with their little vigilante action is not just illegal. It's also perverse. They're doing exactly what Shammey did. They're using a woman to do their dirty work."

"But Shammey didn't just *use* Melissa," Sarah objected, "he put her in jail for murder."

I hesitated to play my last card, but I had already put

everything else on the table. Sarah had to know the worst. "I know these guys are your friends," I said, "but you have to consider the possibility that they're planning to pin the murder on Rachel if anyone finds out. So it would be virtually the same thing."

Sarah's jaw went slack as understanding came into her eyes. It was a lot to swallow, and I let her work on it a moment. In the meantime I guided a stray lock of hair from her forehead and pulled the quilt up a little higher. Suddenly she flung it aside, got out of bed and into her robe, and began pacing around the room like a cat.

"So what you're saying," she said, running a hand through her hair, "is that Carl and Fred wanted to get even with that guy, and they used Rachel to do it."

"She must have told Carl that she was having an affair with Shammey, or something," I said. "I haven't quite figured that part out yet."

"And now that they've done it," Sarah reasoned, "Rachel is the only one who was with him when he died, the only one who had a relationship with him."

"Yup."

"So if anything happens to expose the situation, they could... They could say that..."

She couldn't bring herself to say it, but I knew she understood. I watched her pace around some more. Even in an old robe, with tousled hair and a face furrowed in concentration, she was beautiful to look at.

"Who knows about this?" she asked.

"You mean, besides them and you and me?"

"Yes. Who else?"

"No one. Sheriff Stone arranged for a fast cremation, so it would be hard to prove the guy was poisoned. I think even his deputy is in the dark."

"Wow."

"You're getting the picture."

She nodded distractedly, still pacing. "You said you found some of Rachel's hair in Hillhouse. What about that?"

"Stone took it," I told her. "That's why they searched my room. They had to get it back."

"But that would get her off the hook, wouldn't it?"

"Well, evidence is evidence," I pointed out. "The sheriff can use it to place Rachel at the scene just as well as I can."

"Okay, I see. And you think it was Fred that hit you on the highway?"

"Actually, I think it was the deputy."

"But you said—"

"I don't think the guy has a clue, really, but he knows damn well Stone wants me out of town. I'm sure it only takes a wink and a nod from the sheriff for him to saddle up his four-wheel drive and ride the bad guy out of town."

Sarah shook her head, like she had done in the diner that morning. "This is really hard to fit with my picture of Fred Stone," she said. "He is so committed to the true spirit of the law…"

"I think in his mind, that's exactly what he's doing. He's executing Dick Shammey to correct an injustice, and he thinks I'm interfering."

"But how can you help being curious? That's your job."

"Curiosity killed the cat."

"Well, he's not going to hurt you," Sarah said defiantly. "I won't let him."

"I'm not worried for myself; I'm worried for Rachel. Which is why we're even talking about this, if you remember."

She stopped pacing and looked at me with an apologetic half-smile. "I'm sorry I reacted that way," she said. "It's just that my whole life I've always either been bailing her out of trouble or losing a boyfriend because of her."

"You're in no danger of losing me," I told her. "This one's a bail-out."

"Right." She paced around some more, then came to the foot of the bed. "So let me see if I understand this: Dick Shammey finally gets what's coming to him after destroying a bunch of people's lives. Fred and Carl do most of the work, but they get Rachel involved because they need her to get Shammey up here. But because Fred is involved, too, there won't be any investigation or anything."

"Well, that's where it gets sticky."

"Why?"

"Because of me," I said. "They didn't count on me being around."

"Well," she said with a sly smile, "neither did I and look what it got me."

"I'm serious," I protested, but she had already crawled up onto the bed. Her bathrobe fell open as she rose up and pulled the covers away from my body.

"Now I've got you," she said with relish. "What are you going to do about it?"

"Wait," I said. "What are we going to do?"

"Decide tomorrow."

"But I wanted to ask you about Gibbie and Melissa."

"Too late," she said, her voice husky and her body gleaming in the firelight.

"You knew him, right? You knew Gibbie? Just tell me that."

"Everyone knew Gibbie," she said, and lowered herself to me.

# ELEVEN

THE NEXT MORNING dawned clear and bright, a sparkling winter day among the California redwoods. Sarah was awake when I opened my eyes. We embraced each other with shy tenderness and uttered the small phrases new lovers use. At length she slipped out of bed and into the bathroom, and I laid back in the bed and let myself remember the night before. The recollection became a rush of sensation when Sarah came back to bed.

"I'm glad I stayed," I said.

She smiled. "Stay for breakfast?"

"Afraid not. I've really got a lot to do."

"It won't take long."

"No matter how long I stay, it won't be long enough," I reasoned. "We just have to promise we'll see each other again."

She pulled back so she could look at me. "Promise? No matter what else happens?"

She wasn't kidding around now. I remembered what she had said about people saying goodbye to her: too often, they didn't come back. I knew she meant her mother and father, and there were no doubt others. Friends who moved. Pets that grew old and died. Men who left.

"I promise," I said. "I'm not leaving the planet, just going home to work for a while."

She got up, put on her bathrobe, and went to the stove to put on a kettle of water. I waited a moment, but she went on to other tasks. I understood then that she wasn't cutting me off, just practicing being alone again while we were still together. I gathered my clothes on my way into the bathroom. I looked at myself in the mirror, saw a four-day growth, and rubbed the hair on my jaw.

As I came out of the bathroom, Sarah was blowing up a fire out of the embers of the previous night. When it was blazing, we sat together on the couch and gazed into the flames. It was cold in the room, and I pulled her close. She seemed smaller somehow, as I tucked her under one arm and felt her nestle beside me. We sat like that for a while, until she raised her head. We kissed, and then she cleared her throat.

"You have to go and I don't want to keep you, but..."

"But what?"

"I know you have to do what you think is right, but I wanted to put in a word for Rachel. I was awake last night for a while thinking about it—"

"Why didn't you wake me?"

"I didn't want to disturb you. You had a smile on your face."

"I was happy."

"Me, too. So listen." She wriggled a little closer and tucked her feet under her. When she was still again, she continued. "I know it's bad what they did, if they did it. It's bad. But that guy was bad, too. He took advantage of everyone he met up here, and what he did to them, especially to Melissa, was cruel."

"That's how it looks," I agreed.

"No one should have to die for their sins, but once they're gone there's no way to bring them back."

"Shammey, you mean?"

"I meant anyone, but yes, him, too. So in a way, it cancels out: a bad person comes to a bad end. The only bad thing left is that Melissa is still in prison."

"And something could still happen to Rachel."

"If she's involved."

"Right."

"That's why I'm saying this. I don't want anything to happen to my sister. She's the only family I have, and she's already been through so much."

"I guess if they were planning to frame her they wouldn't have let her loose to find me in the bar."

"Or destroyed the evidence she left lying around."

"So if Stone gets away with the cover-up," I concluded, "Rachel's probably in the clear."

"Will he? Will he get away with it?"

This was not a question I had considered before. There had never been any question of Stone getting away with something, because I knew what was going on and I was a member of the press. In the past, I had never hesitated to tell what I had seen or found—once I could verify the facts, I put them into a newspaper story and went on to the next thing. It was not a choice, it was just the way it had to be done. Now there was a different possibility: that I could know about something unjust, and turn away without doing anything at all. It was a strange sensation.

At the newspaper we used to say, "Let the public judge." The idea was that the paper would report the facts and let the chips fall where they may. Those of us who took this notion seriously prided ourselves on remaining above such relative considerations as appropriate punishment—unless, of course, a public debate on the question became news. This often happened with sentencing laws for violent crimes, like the one that got Melissa Larkin an especially harsh sentence.

Now I had a choice: I could judge that even though laws had been broken, some kind of ultimate balance had been restored. I could decide that the acts of a few men and women, wrong as they were, effectively canceled each other out and needed no further examination in a court of law. The strangeness of it was almost physical, like being off balance or out of breath. No matter what you tell your brain, your body is still off-kilter.

"It really comes down to me, then," I acknowledged.

"You have to do what you feel is best," Sarah urged.

"I feel sorry for Rachel."

"Me, too. And I love her."

I squeezed Sarah tighter with one hand and caressed her cheek with the other. "Will she go back to her husband?" I asked.

"That's a hard one," Sarah sighed. "She needs someone to anchor her, but I'm not sure he's the one. They fight; he cheats on her; it's a mess."

"Would she move back here, where you could look after her?"

"I don't know. I'm not sure that's the best thing, either."

"I think she loved that guy, Shammey. At least that's how it came across when she talked about him."

"You see what I mean about what she's been through?"

"You mean tearing myself away from you isn't the worst thing that can happen to a person?"

"Oh, but it's very, very hard," she teased, turning to kneel on the couch next to me. "You deserve a medal!"

I held her close to me for a long time before she opened the door and I stepped out into the crisp, clear morning. I felt light and clear myself as I walked down the driveway to my car. I knew then that I had decided not to decide. I did not have to delve any further into a dark history that would now be closed. I did not have to upset anyone's life any more. It was not a completely noble result, but it freed me to go on with my own life.

WHEN I REACHED the highway and cruised along with the ocean on my right, though, the reality of my destination began to sink in. I was headed south now, toward the hard gray city, a cold apartment, an empty wallet. To cheer myself up, I replayed the events of the previous night and morning over again in my head. It worked. Soon I was blushing from the memories and basking in a glow of reportorial pride. I was almost looking forward to getting home and getting to work.

As I approached the outskirts of town, I decided to stop at the bookstore and treat myself to a warm roll and hot coffee for the road. I was joined in line by a stout woman with ruddy cheeks and lively eyes, wearing sweat clothes. It was someone I had seen in the town at some point, and I smiled at her with the expanded affection of someone whose heart is full.

"Beautiful morning, huh?"

"Yeah, great," she said. She pointed to my sweatshirt. "That's Shakespeare, right?"

"Right."

"You had that on the other night," she said. "In the bar." For a moment I was confused, because I had not worn the Shakespeare shirt since my first night in Pomo Bluff. "So did you get a room up there at St. Horace?" the woman asked.

The fog cleared. This was the woman who had been tending bar the night I arrived in town. I laughed. "I didn't recognize you without your bar," I joked.

"Yeah," she said, "I called up there after you left the hotel, to let her know you were coming."

"Thanks," I said, and turned to take my coffee. As I

waited for my roll to come out of the oven, the woman's last remark rang again in my head. I wondered if I had heard her right. I turned back to her. "You called St. Horace?"

"Sure," she said. "You looked dead beat."

"I was. When did you call? Right away?"

"I didn't think of it for a minute or two. But then, yeah, I called up there."

It had taken me less than ten minutes to get up the highway to the inn. "Did someone answer?" I asked.

"Like I said, I told her you were coming."

"Who? Who did you talk to?"

The woman shrugged. "It was the gal who minds the place, she works late on Thursdays, same night I do."

"Sarah."

"Yeah, that's her. Wasn't she up there waitin' for ya?"

"Yeah," I said. "She was there."

I SAT IN MY CAR and stared out the windshield, but I wasn't seeing anything. Instead I was puzzling over Sarah's behavior the night I arrived. If she knew I was coming, why was she getting into her car to leave? The obvious answer was that she didn't have any rooms available and didn't want to deal with a stranger that late at night. But another possibility also occurred to me: that she wanted it to *look* as if she didn't know I was coming. That way whatever she did afterwards would appear to be completely spontaneous.

When Melodie said that amateur poisoners needed to have a really good alibi, I had understood for the first time that Stone had carefully scheduled the murder to coincide with his monthly overnight arrest of Ben. That way he had an alibi for those crucial hours. If Sarah needed an alibi of her own, what could be better than taking in a stranger who just showed up, without a reservation?

I remembered going into Sarah's house, taking a bath, falling asleep. I remembered, with as much detail as I could muster, the lovely morning I had spent with her having breakfast and going fishing. Sarah could not possibly have planned something like that, or anticipated someone like me. I told myself firmly that there was absolutely nothing to indicate that she was using me to cover herself.

Then I remembered the phone call I answered the morning of the murder. The caller had said nothing, then hung up in consternation. Sarah's explanation was perfectly reasonable: people didn't expect a man to answer her phone. Or it could have been a wrong number. I began to go over my conversations with Sarah about Rachel and Fred Stone and Carl Larkin, the conversations that had begun the night before in her bed. There was nothing out of place, nothing to make me think she was hiding anything. Nothing at all.

My brain was suddenly on full alert. Sarah had said something about the evidence linking Rachel to Shammey. I struggled to remember it. I knew I had told her about the hair from the bathtub, and about Stone stealing it back, but I didn't think I had mentioned anything about the cup with the lipstick stain in Shammey's car. Then I remembered her exact words: "the evidence Rachel left lying around." That description hardly applied to hair in the drain of a bathtub. But it was particularly accurate for a coffee cup discarded in the back seat of a car.

The alarm in my head kept ringing. I remembered now that Sarah had been talking about Stone, not Rachel. She said that if Stone was planning to frame Rachel, he would not have "destroyed the evidence." But I had not said anything about anyone destroying evidence. In fact, I was guessing that Stone was keeping whatever evidence he needed to clear himself if necessary. But Sarah seemed so sure that there was no longer any physical evidence linking her sister with a murder.

Now my heart was boiling with a bitter mixture of love and dread. The dark history was reopened, and I had to confront the two questions I had not yet answered regarding the death of Dick Shammey: When did Rachel leave Hillhouse, and where did she go? I felt strongly that she was already gone from the cottage by the time Liz saw Carl Larkin in the woods. Rachel had bolted from the cottage ahead of schedule, because Shammey had died ahead of schedule. Even if Larkin had come to fetch her, it didn't make sense to do it on foot.

But if she had gone off on her own, where had she gone? Someplace safe, where she would not be seen by anyone who knew her. Larkin's house was the obvious choice, but it was almost twenty miles up the highway and Rachel had no car. Fred Stone's house was another possibility, but I didn't know where Fred Stone lived. The only other address I knew in Pomo Bluff was the address I had just left: Sarah's.

I pulled out the maps and examined them. It took a while to get my bearings and locate the points I wanted, but eventually I saw that the local coastline wrapped around a pair of intersecting ridges. St. Horace was on one ridge, and Sarah's house on the other. By way of the coast highway, it was a fairly long drive from St. Horace to Sarah. By traversing the ridges, however, that long drive became a surprisingly short walk.

I quickly calculated how long it would take to cover the distance on foot, accounting for topography. If Rachel·

left Hillhouse at first light, around six o'clock, it would have taken her nearly three hours. That would put her at Sarah's house around nine that morning...while I was on the stream, fishing. I thought back to Larkin's remark that there were plenty of trails near St. Horace, if you knew where they were. In other words, you had to be a local resident or the friend of a local mushroom gatherer. Rachel qualified on both counts.

I looked out the window, up the highway, toward the hotel. The bright sun made everything a little too sharp, and I closed my eyes. In my mind I heard the woman in the bookstore saying, "Wasn't she up there, waiting for you?" It was too unbelievable, too bitterly unfair to have Sarah mixed up in the murder of Dick Shammey. It had to be wrong. It had to be. I opened my eyes and looked past the hotel toward the bridge, C Ranch, and home. I imagined myself driving home for the next few hours, tormented by doubt. I started my engine and pulled out to the highway. I had to know for sure that I was wrong. I had to. I turned left and headed north.

As I passed St. Horace, its red roofs were catching their first rays of direct sunlight. I glanced up at the ridge behind the inn, where the sun was just peeking through the treetops along the ridgeline. I tried to imagine the trails that must weave among the trees, and a tormented young woman deep in cold woods still wet with the night. The image was surprisingly clear, and on impulse I turned right at the first road I came to that went up the hill.

As soon as I was up high enough to get a broad view of the trees and ocean below, I parked the car and studied the maps again. One of them had a few ridgeline trails marked in, but there were no landmarks to help me locate them. The only thing I knew for sure was that a trail that connected the inn and Sarah's property would have to cross this road. I got out of the car and walked up and down the road looking off into the forest on both sides. My mind churned with arguments for and against Sarah's involvement in the murder. I could also feel my heart wrestling with love and betrayal, and I had no choice but to let that struggle continue, too.

As I walked back down toward the car, I remembered the compass I found in the trunk after the county deputies had searched my stuff. Evidently Doug kept the compass with the fishing gear, but I had not noticed it before. I spread the maps on the trunk of the car, oriented the compass, and tried to figure out where the trail should be. I realized almost immediately that the trail had to be much higher up. I brought the maps and compass into the front seat and drove on up the hill.

The trees were thicker up here, and it became harder to distinguish things in the dimmer light. I was sure I had gone too far and was about to turn around when a large bird whooshed out of the trees on one side of the road and into the trees on the other side. It was not a bird I had ever seen flying before, and I guessed from the broad wings and stubby body that it was an owl. I pulled up the road and stopped even with the owl's flight path. To the right, it was possible to see deeply into the forest along a narrow alley between the trees. To the left the trees closed quickly together…or was there a trail that turned up the hill after crossing the road?

I parked the car, changed into my hiking boots, zipped my vest up tight, and slipped the compass and maps into my back pocket. Only a little ways into the woods I had to stop and let my eyes adjust to the light. After that it took some probing, but there was unquestionably a trail leading through the trees. Not a trail, really, but a continuous clear space that kept opening ahead of me. The forest floor was covered with pine needles, redwood bark, and seed cones. It was cold and wet and a little eery, and beautiful for all that. Occasionally a shaft of sunlight would penetrate the forest and I would see a brightly colored fungus or curious bird, otherwise, I was alone.

After an hour of steady climbing, the woods opened into a shallow ravine covered with thick, willowy green underbrush and splashed with sunlight. As I approached, I saw that the ravine was a natural drainage, and that the trail crossed right over it. Up the slope, the ravine became much steeper. Below, it was a rockslide. Both offered good opportunities to twist an ankle, or worse. I remembered hurtling down the highway with the deputy's truck behind me, almost out of control. This time the scenery was different, but I was still alone, on their turf, courting danger. I swallowed, looked across the ravine, and plunged into the brush.

The ground was alternately muddy and rocky, and it was necessary to look down at my feet when I wasn't looking up to push the brush away from my waist. Halfway across the ravine, the ground fell away. Soon the brush was at my chest, but I forged on. Finally I could not see ahead of me and had to duck under the gray-green brush. As I was straightening up again, something near my head caught my eye. Perhaps it was the eye-sharpening time I had spent tying knots with incredibly thin, nearly transparent fishing line, perhaps it was a lucky shot of sunlight, perhaps it was fate, but there was no question about the thing itself: a long strand of red-gold hair, tangled in a twig.

The trail continued on the other side of the ravine. An hour later, I came to an intersection where another trail crossed the one I was on. I went up the crossing trail about a hundred feet, where I could see out to the ocean and employ the compass. It turned out I didn't need it, because I had been this way before. I recognized the angle of the ridge, the slant of the sun, the orientation of the coast. I struck down the intersecting trail which descended, then leveled, then rose up out of thick brush onto the driveway halfway between the road and Sarah's house.

Sarah's car was gone, and I walked up the driveway to the house. I listened outside, but heard nothing, and went into the house. My heart tumbled sharply in my chest as I entered and looked around. It was hard to think that my earnest affection for Sarah had been repaid with cynical manipulation, but fortunately I had seen the same and worse during my months in the state capitol. My heart could hurt about it, but my mind was clear. I turned and gazed at the painting of Sarah hanging next to the door. From my new perspective, it was no longer a cipher.

I was sitting on the couch, facing the painting and the door, when Sarah returned a half an hour later. She paused on her own doorstep and looked in through the window. When she came inside and closed the door, I stood up. Neither of us spoke for a moment. With a sharp pain I realized that only a few hours before we had kissed each other goodbye in virtually the same spot.

"You were younger then," I said, indicating the painting.

"And more impressionable," she responded.

I looked at the artist's signature. The night I arrived, it was an opaque scrawl of paint. Now that I knew what I was looking for, it was not that hard to make out.

"He was good," I observed.

"He was."

"Everyone in town knew Gibbie," I said, echoing Sarah's comment from the night before as I turned to face her. "But you knew him best."

She shrugged. "He painted lots of people up here."

"I don't know that much about art, but I know something about men. I'd bet the few dollars I've got left that the guy who painted this picture was in love with you. And I think you were in love with him. That's why you've been alone ever since he was killed, and why the guy who killed him was killed at your inn. By your sister. And your friends."

Sarah turned into the room, took off her jacket, and threw it on the couch. "I thought we agreed," she said slowly, "that there was no need to raise any more ghosts. There's been enough pain and suffering already."

"The last time I withheld something I should have reported it cost me my job," I said, my voice rising. "I had a perfectly good reason at the time, but it blew up in my face. I don't want to make the same mistake twice."

"You have nothing to lose," Sarah replied, an edge of bitterness in her voice. "Rachel could lose everything."

"Aren't you the one who put her in that position?"

"The world is not black and white, Rigel. Maybe newspapers are, and maybe you have to see the world that way to work for them, but real life is shades of gray."

"Murder is murder, no matter what color it is."

Sarah frowned, then picked up her jacket and hung it on a peg. She was still lovely to watch when she moved, but I didn't feel quite the same way about what I was watching. Finally she turned to me. "What are you going to do?" she asked.

"About the murder? Or how I feel inside, knowing that what happened last night was just the final piece of the cover-up?"

"What happened last night was real."

"A real act, you mean."

"It *was* real, for me!"

I saw something in her I had missed before, more dimensions than I had allowed her in my mind. She was a human being, no more and no less, capable of the sweetness of love or the fury of hell. It didn't scare me exactly, but it made me see that she was more than capable of involvement in Shammey's murder: she might in fact be the brains behind it. She wasn't trying to protect Rachel because Rachel was innocent; she was protecting Rachel because Rachel was one of the pawns in her plot. I felt my own anger focusing, my own edges getting sharper.

Outside, there were footsteps on the gravel. I spun around and looked out a window across the room in time to see Carl Larkin approaching the house with Rachel. I turned to Sarah with a question on my lips, but the look on her face froze me still: it was the same imploring look I had seen from Rachel on the porch of the hotel.

"Please," was all she said.

I forced myself to turn away from her. "Sorry," I muttered, my heart in my throat. I turned away, to face Carl and Rachel coming in the door.

Rachel glanced at me once, then went to a window to fold her arms and stare outside. She looked terrible. Larkin looked like an honorable man caught in a dishonest business; he was going to brave it out, no matter how much it cost him. I nodded to him briefly, knowing that under other circumstances I could have liked him, learned from him. He nodded back, warily, then frowned at Sarah. It seemed she was angry at them, perhaps for screwing up. Finally Larkin spoke up. He addressed Sarah, but he was looking at me.

"I brought Rachel around to say goodbye before I drive her down home," he said carefully. "But if we're interrupting anything…"

"I was on my way home, too," I said. "But something Sarah said made me come back." Carl shot Sarah a glance, but again she betrayed no reaction. I turned to Sarah. "I never told you Stone destroyed any evidence, only that he took the hairs I found in the bathtub. You knew he destroyed the cup she left in the car, because he told you so himself."

Sarah said nothing. Rachel turned around and looked across the room at me, her eyes wide. "That's why they let you come to the bar and talk to me," I told her. "I found some of your hair in the drain of the tub at Hill-house. They had to get you near me in public somewhere so they could claim that was how I really got it." Rachel looked at Larkin, then at her sister. "What did they tell you?" I continued. "That you should come and tell me how innocent you were?"

"I wanted you to know what happened to Melissa," she said. "That's all."

"What happened in the past is never justification for murder," I replied. "Particularly premeditated murder."

"You don't know what happened," Larkin said. I could hear the emotion contained beneath his reserve, and feel the moral force that generated it. "You have no idea how that man wrecked the lives of people in this community. He killed one person, he put another in jail—"

"And turned another four into killers," I finished.

There was another silence, with Sarah frowning and Larkin exhaling deeply. For all their murderous rage at Dick Shammey, they were not hardened criminals. Finally Larkin turned to me. "Why did you come to my house?" he asked. He sounded more upset than curious.

"I'm sorry about what happened to your sister," I told him. "But it doesn't change the law, or allow people to take the law into their own hands."

"But why are you trying to hurt us?" he demanded. "We never did anything to you. Sarah here can't say enough good things about you, but you seem dead set on opening up the gates of hell for her and her family."

"She used me," I said, "just like she used the two of you." Again Rachel looked at me, her jaw slack. Larkin, too, looked surprised.

Behind me I heard Sarah's voice. "Be careful," she said. I saw Larkin close his mouth. Could she hear his thoughts, too, before he uttered them?

I turned to her. "It doesn't matter if they admit what they did. I think I've pretty much got the whole story figured out."

She met my gaze and held it. "I feel hurt, too," she said. "I thought you cared about me."

"That's quite a poker face," I told her bitterly. "You'd make a hell of a card player."

"But I don't like games," she said.

"Me either," Larkin said. "What are you after?"

"The truth."

"Truth is hard to know," Larkin said.

"Not always," I told him. "It starts with what Shammey did to Gibbie and your sister. Then there's a long wait for the right opportunity. When Rachel meets Shammey in San Francisco, the rest of you put together a plan using her as bait for a trap. You sprung the trap last Thursday night, after Rachel brought Shammey up to St. Horace. Of course, the innkeeper had made sure they were in the most secluded cottage on the grounds." I looked at Rachel, who had slowly come forward, toward the couch. "What was it you promised him? An introduction to a local dope grower? Or something more personal?"

"That's not necessary," Sarah said.

But I saw Rachel and Larkin exchange glances, and I continued. "What did you have to do to make sure you arrived late, after the restaurant was closed?" I asked Rachel. "Take a long time to pack? Pretend to lose your wallet? Or just make him stop for a cup of coffee?"

"Please, Rigel," Sarah said, as she went to her sister and guided her around to sit on the couch.

"He goes inside to check in, you stay in the car. Then you go up to the cottage. The sherry is already there, spiked with poison." I turned to Larkin, then back to Sarah. "Which one of you had that pleasant task on your list?" Neither of them responded. "It doesn't matter, because Rachel had the hardest task of all: making sure Shammey drinks the sherry and dies from it."

Rachel looked at me with wide eyes, as if she were hanging on my every word. I looked down at her. "You knew you had to do it," I said softly. "But you didn't want him to die, did you?" Her eyes filled with tears and her lower lip trembled. Sarah sat next to her and held her by the shoulders. Rachel stared at me a moment, then broke down and sobbed. I spoke to the others.

"While she takes a bath, Shammey drinks the sherry. He's finally alone with her, far from her husband and the city, and when she comes out of the bathroom he doesn't hesitate. She's confused, she doesn't know what she should do. He forces the issue, she's too scared to scream and not strong enough to stop him, and some time after that, he dies. Or, as the doctor suggested, he slipped into a coma he never came out of. She had to spend the entire night alone in that cottage with a man she loved, a man she helped to kill.''

The room was still. I turned to Larkin. "Did you forget that part?" I asked him. "Or was it intentional?"

"What are you talking about?" Larkin demanded, his face dark.

"Were you punishing Rachel, too, because she left you for someone else?"

Larkin looked grim, then looked away. Rachel cried quietly on the couch. Sarah slowly raised her eyes from the floor and looked at me. For the first time, I realized that I could turn her in for first-degree murder, give evidence at her trial, and perhaps even write about it. I thought I had known heartbreak before, but nothing in my past prepared me for what I was feeling now.

"Why?" I asked her, blinking hard to keep my eyes clear. "And why me?"

I never got an answer. Instead we heard the sound of more footsteps outside. I felt the hairs on my neck stiffen, saw Rachel look up with wide eyes, and turned to the door to see County Sheriff Fred Stone looking in the window. As he opened the door, he set his jaw and narrowed his eyes.

"You might as well come in," I said. "It wouldn't be a conspiracy without the conspirators."

Stone hitched up his belt, laden with the tools of his trade. He looked at the others, but none of them spoke. They were all looking at him. He blinked and looked at me.

"I thought you left town," he said.

"Sarah invited me to stay another night."

He looked at her, but she avoided his glance. "So you were just leaving, then."

"Just about," I said. "Only a few questions left."

"About what?"

"Well, how about what you did with the cup Rachel left in Shammey's car and the hair she left in the room?"

Stone blinked, then swallowed. "You got no evidence for the existence of those items," he said quietly.

I laughed scornfully. "I *saw* them, remember?"

"You're speculating," Stone said quickly. "You didn't see anything, or hear anything, and you don't have any evidence."

"I saw Shammey's body, and I've heard all of you talk about it ever since I've been here," I reminded him. "I've talked to some other people, too. Like the poor guy in the kitchen who Sarah set up as the unwitting poisoner."

Sarah looked up at me. For the first time, I saw surprise come into her eye. "You waited until everyone was gone, then went into the kitchen and made sure the walnut oil bottle was full. Then later we had your little charade about how the muffins were made." I looked at Rachel, her cheeks streaked with mascara tears. "At dawn you left the cottage and came here the same way I did, through the woods. I found more of your hair in the bushes, at the ravine."

"You got that hair in the bar," Stone said quickly. "We saw you."

I ignored him. "You arrived here while I was fishing. Sarah cleaned you up and called Carl to come and get you." I turned to Larkin. "It was you, wasn't it? You had to come get Rachel before I got back from the stream, and then you had to go to the inn and set up the room so it would look like Shammey died from his allergy to nuts." I turned to Sarah. "You figured someone might spot the sheriff and get curious, so you sent the mushroom man instead. The only problem is, when Liz saw him she recognized him."

"Liz hasn't lived here that long," Sarah said. "I wouldn't count on her word as gospel, especially in something this serious."

She was a cool customer, I had to give her that. Oddly, I felt just as cool now, my feelings cut off from what was happening in a kind of slow motion around me. "After you sent Carl to the inn, you came down to the river to freshen up your alibi," I said to her. "It was pretty gutsy, considering that I could have come back to the house by then. But I guess that wouldn't have mattered. Everything would have gone off according to plan if I hadn't come to the inn that afternoon to give you flowers."

"It was sweet," Sarah said.

"And it seemed kind of you to take me in the night before. But you did it for the alibi, not the kindness."

"You don't have to think of it that way."

I turned to Larkin. "You called about eleven-thirty that morning to report that everything was set up, but I answered the phone. You should have just asked for Sarah."

Larkin looked mystified. Rachel spoke up. "It was me," she said. "I was scared. I didn't want to be alone."

"Don't talk to him," Stone barked at her. "That's what he wants."

"I can already piece the whole story together," I informed him. "With the help of Doctor James Clark." The good doctor's name hung in the air like an executioner's axe.

"Who told you about Doc Clark?" Larkin asked at last.

"He did," I said, pointing at Stone. "The doctor just filled in the details."

Sarah and Larkin looked at Stone gravely. "I didn't say anything!" Stone defended himself. "I had Deputy Sheriff Anderson read his report, that's all!"

"I'm afraid we're going to have to drag Deputy Sheriff Anderson in as an accessory to murder after the fact," I pointed out. This, at least, was something that would not hurt too much.

"No jury would convict on all this conjecture," Stone announced. "It would never even go to trial."

My disgust at the deputy suddenly transferred itself to the sheriff. "Hell, your career is over no matter what happens," I informed him. "Covering up a murder is bad enough without conspiring to commit it in the first place. Attempted vehicular manslaughter is another good one. Your career is over."

"You don't know what you're talking about," he stammered.

Sarah cut him off. "What are you going to do?"

I turned to her in disbelief. "You think I can just walk away from this like it never happened?"

"You don't really want to go back to work for the newspaper," she said, as if we were having a supportive chat over coffee. "You would rather do something on your own. You said so."

"I can write this story on my own," I said. "With or without a trial."

"He deserved to die," Larkin said forcefully. "He killed one man and wrecked the lives of three other people."

"That doesn't suspend the rules."

"The rules put my sister in prison for what he did!"

Larkin thundered. "The rules let a killer go free to rape the woman I love! *God damn the rules!*"

Rachel began sobbing again.

"I'm sorry you all got yourselves into this mess," I said quietly, "and that I had to be the one to see it." I took a step toward the door, but Sheriff Stone did not move aside. Instead he had one hand on the butt of his service revolver. The gun was still in its holster, but the security strap on the holster was undone. I looked around at Larkin and Sarah, who seemed frozen. I turned to face Stone.

"You planning to kill me, too?" I asked, mockingly.

"I can't let you leave." His eyes shifted from me to the others in the room.

"Sorry," I said. "I've really got to run." I took a step toward him, but he put out his hand to stop me. "Get out of my way," I rasped, my hands balled into fists.

"I'm afraid not," Stone said, and fixed his eyes on mine. "I'm placing you under arrest for the murder of Richard G. Shammey of San Francisco." He spoke quietly at first, then with more force. "You have the right to remain silent. You have the right to have an attorney present during questioning and anything you say can and will be used against you in a court of law."

# TWELVE

For reporters, hearing a law enforcement officer read someone his rights is a natural high: it means your hard work paid off and you were at the scene for the climactic arrest. You learn to relish it, because of what happens afterward: the case, and your stories about it, grind to a tangled halt of motions, pleas, and other things only lawyers can love.

Hearing my rights read to me was a different experience. It didn't matter that I was innocent and Stone was grasping at straws. At the moment of arrest, the American laws of jurisprudence seem to be suddenly reversed: you're guilty until proven otherwise, because if you weren't guilty they wouldn't be arresting you.

"Carl, get Deputy Sheriff Anderson on the phone, will you?" Sheriff Stone was speaking with more confidence now.

"Wait," Sarah said.

"This is a police matter," Stone said to Sarah. "You'd best let me take him out of here and do things by the book."

"Fred, I think we can convince him to let this whole thing blow over."

"You tried your way," he told her. "This is mine."

I finally found my voice. "Let him arrest me," I said. "We'll run the whole thing down in open court. I'll invite every reporter I know, provide them all the leads they need, and watch you get slaughtered by the best lawyers the newspaper can buy."

"Don't be so sure," Stone said. "My version of events will make a lot more sense to a jury than yours. I've got a suspect with means, motive, and opportunity, and an established history of bad judgment where ethics are concerned."

This stung. I looked at Sarah. "What did you tell him?"

"She didn't tell me anything," Stone said. "I tried to tell you this was an accidental death that should just be left alone, but you keep pushing the homicide angle. So I did a little digging of my own."

I kept looking at Sarah, who betrayed no reaction to this sudden turn of events. "It appears you followed the victim to Pomo Bluff and poisoned him in his room," Stone continued. "You obviously don't know squat about fishing, so that whole magazine thing's just a cover."

I stared at him. "Would you like to talk to my editor, Stone?"

"I'm sure you went to the trouble to set something up," he said. "Just like you set up Shammey. Once you got him up here and in the room alone, you gave him a drink with poison in it."

I exploded. "This is ridiculous!"

"A jury will have to decide on the evidence," Stone said. "You and Shammey show up at the same place on the same night. First time any of us lay eyes on you, you're in the parking lot shortly after he registers. We've got your registration card—in your own handwriting, by the way—which indicates premeditation."

"I took that room after he was already dead, you know that. I filled that card out after the fact."

Stone blinked and swallowed. "Well, that's not what the date says on there," he said, patting his breast pocket.

I spun around and stared at Sarah. She was studying Stone, as if weighing whether or not he could make his arrest stick. "I'm sure it says whatever you want it to say," I said, with as much disgust as I could muster.

"You showed up at the murder scene just as the body was discovered," Stone continued. "You provided that phony story about the allergy to throw us off the scent, then you conned a brand-new housekeeper into letting you move back into the room so you could cover up the evidence."

"You're the one who took the evidence."

"Now, the doctor, he had a little trouble figuring things out. But once I talk to him he'll agree that Shammey didn't die from some allergy. He was poisoned, plain and simple. And you know what we found? Someone poured a big bunch of sherry on the ground behind the cottage where the guy was killed. I guess you city folks don't know that the ground up here doesn't absorb much liquid this time of year. We picked up a little sample, and you know what? That sherry had a whole bunch of bad stuff in it."

"You put the poison in the decanter," I said accusingly.

"Well, we have that particular article in the county's possession," Stone said, "and you know what? It has your fingerprints all over it. No one else's. Just yours."

I felt the same furious frustration I had when Stone and his deputy had pulled their trick with Rachel's hair on the porch of the hotel. Only this time, Stone wasn't trying to get me out of town. He was trying to put me behind bars. It was my turn to swallow hard and blink.

"I was with Sarah the night he died," I declared. "I slept in her living room."

"But the next morning, you go off by yourself for three whole hours. No one knows where you were."

"Sarah came down to the stream. We fished together."

"That's afterward."

"It doesn't even matter if I have an alibi for that morning," I sneered. "The doctor said Shammey was dead before morning."

"Ain't got no coroner's report, ain't got no autopsy. It's your word against a respected member of the medical profession. And that's one face-off you're going to lose, because you already got yourself a reputation, remember? Lied about your information up there in the state capitol, covered up all kinds of nasty business. Got fired for it and everything."

I couldn't believe that nothing I said slowed Stone down. But now I was sure I could shut him up. "I had no reason to kill Shammey," I pointed out. "I never even knew him."

"Well, my lawyer friends tell me it's hard to prove we never met a person, never had any business with 'em, that sort of thing. Very hard to prove. But we do know that you lost your job and you're mighty upset about it. We do know that Mr. Shammey had friends in the state government, and that some of them were put out of their jobs by things you wrote about 'em. We also know that Shammey had friends at the newspaper you used to work for. If he had a hand in getting you kicked out of your job, you got even the only way you could."

"That's the longest stretch yet," I said. "I can see the jury shaking their heads."

"They'll probably pay attention when we tell them about the newspaper stories you were carrying around with you, the ones about Shammey especially. Seems you were obsessed with the guy."

I realized with a cold shot of fear that I hadn't seen my faxes from the morgue since I had been chased out of St. Horace on Saturday night. Stone's deputy must have taken them. I covered as best I could.

"There's one thing you overlooked," I said. "On Friday afternoon I put a few strands of Rachel's hair into the mail, addressed to a friend of mine at the paper."

It was Stone's turn for sarcasm. "So what?" he said.

"The postmark on that letter will prove that she was in that cottage well before the time you all say she arrived on Saturday. It will prove she was there, and that you've all been lying to cover up your conspiracy to commit murder."

"You're bluffing," Stone said. "You never went in the post office."

"Raise me and find out."

Stone ran his tongue along his upper lip as he thought it over. "Of course Rachel was in that room," he said at last. "She arranged a ride up to the country with Shammey, and she told you about it before she left. That's how you knew where he would be, and that's why you took off after him. You knew it was your best shot at killing him someplace far from the city, where no one would know—or if they did, they'd be just as happy to have him dead. It was all part of your plot. Rachel saw what you did, then she came to her friends."

I laughed. "You keep making up relationships that don't exist. I never saw Rachel before I came up here."

"Like I say, that kind of thing is hard to prove," Stone said slowly. Then he smiled. "In fact, I've got a dozen witnesses saw the two of you in that bar together, looking mighty friendly. I'll just bet she was begging you to come forward and admit what you did to her friend."

"Why didn't she just go to the police?"

"She did," Stone said, as if he had just been given some good news. "Here I am. And you're under arrest, for murder in the first degree!" He stuck his thumbs in his belt and rocked back on his heels.

"I've had enough of this garbage," I said disgustedly. "I just want to say that hanging a false murder conviction on me would be the same thing Shammey did to Melissa. Really classy company you keep."

Stone's face flushed red. "You don't even *know* Melissa!" he snarled.

"Speaking of that, I'm not sure you got *any* company for this little jaunt of yours," I advised him. "Everybody in this room would have to lie, and keep lying, to support your story." Stone blinked and narrowed his eyes.

"They've been lying to you all along," he said. "They're lying to you now. What makes you think they won't go right on doing whatever they have to?"

I looked from Sarah to Rachel to Larkin. None of them met my gaze. I felt claustrophobic. No one thing Stone had said was enough to really endanger me, but his cumulative insistence on setting me up as a murderer was having an effect. I wanted to neutralize him once and for all so I could get out of Sarah's house with my hide, if not my pride. But I could not think of anything, and Stone barked out an order.

"Carl, please get Deputy Anderson on the phone."

I turned and watched Carl Larkin struggle with himself. Finally he stepped grimly to the telephone. He was about to dial when I raised my arm and pointed to Rachel.

"You know I'm going to fight this," I told him. "And you know my defense will be based on destroying Rachel as a witness and implicating her in a murder. Is that what you want?" The color drained from Larkin's face, and he put the phone down.

"I said call him. *Now!*" Stone commanded. His voice broke, making him sound younger and afraid. I turned back to him, my confidence returning.

"It's over," I said. "Get out of my way." Stone remained between me and the door, but his eyes were on Carl Larkin. His face was red and his eyes were a little wild.

"Carl, this is a direct order," he warned. "You call Deputy Sheriff Anderson and tell him we have captured a suspect that is presumed to be armed and dangerous." Larkin still hesitated. Sarah spoke up softly.

"Fred, listen—"

Stone turned to her. "You tell him: tell him to call Deputy Anderson!"

"Get out of my way," I said again, and took a half step toward the door.

"*Call him!*" Stone yelled.

I turned to look at Larkin, who frowned and then, after a long pause, stepped back from the phone. Behind me I heard Stone's belt rattle, and I spun around. He had drawn his service revolver and was pointing it directly at me. I felt my body flooding with adrenaline, my face flushing hot with fear.

"You're out of your mind!"

"Put the gun away, Fred," Sarah said.

"We can't let him leave," Stone said.

"There's no need for that," Larkin said. He advanced slowly toward Stone, who waved the gun toward the phone.

"Carl," Stone said, and swallowed hard. "You understand. Everything we worked for. All the trouble we went to—"

"I know," Larkin said. "But using the gun will only bring it down for certain." He seemed bigger somehow, like something in him had taken all the ugliness it could stand and was swelling up to stop it.

"Put the gun away, Fred, please," Sarah said.

"We can't let him leave," he insisted. "We can't."

"But we can't kill him, either."

"There's four of us, and only one of him," he said, spreading his hands in a gesture of pleading. "It's better this way. Otherwise...we lose everything."

The fact that the gun was no longer pointed at me emboldened me to add my voice to the dissenting chorus. "Is this your idea of law and order?" I asked Stone. "Kill whoever doesn't do things your way, or drive them out of town to live under a bridge?"

Stone's eyes widened and focused on me. Slowly he raised the gun until he was holding it level with my heart. At this range, even with his shaking hand and blinking eyes, he could not miss the center of my chest. In the silence, we could all hear the click of the safety catch before he spoke.

"You want to talk about Ben, is that it?"

My mind was suddenly blank, my tongue dry. For the first time I felt the final chasm open beneath my feet. I saw my hand out in front of me, but I didn't remember putting it there. Stone was still talking. I forced myself to hear what he was saying.

"...so screwed up now he don't know who he is anymore. He ain't been this bad since this whole thing started, and you're responsible! *You!* You messed him up worse than I ever seen him!"

"Put the gun down!" Sarah insisted. "Put it down."

"Fred, listen to her," Larkin argued.

"Hell, no!" Stone argued back. "We should have run his butt off the highway when we had the chance."

"Put it down!" Sarah said, louder. "Just put it down!"

Larkin approached Stone gingerly with one hand out in front of him. "It's gone far enough," he said.

"Outside," Stone snapped at me. "Let's go."

For another long moment, no one said anything. We were all breathing heavily. Rachel's muffled sobs sounded from Sarah's lap, where she had buried her head.

"What happened to Ben?" I asked.

"Don't you ask me that!" Stone barked. "You know damn well what you done!"

"I asked him some questions," I said. "I didn't mean to upset him."

"Don't act innocent now, it's way too late. You upset him like you upset everyone you come in contact with."

"I'm serious," I argued. "I like Ben. I didn't want to hurt him. I went there to give him a fish I caught. I only asked him what his name was."

"You're lying!" Stone shouted. "I ought to shoot you right now!"

"No," I insisted, "I swear it. He didn't seem that bad when I left him."

"What do you know about it, city boy?" Stone asked sarcastically. "He's so bad I don't know what to do with him."

"How about bringing him in from under that bridge?"

"Don't play shrink with me," Stone hissed. "He likes it there. He don't want to come back."

"Maybe he would want to come back, Fred. Now that it's all over."

This was Sarah talking, in that soothing tone she used with guests at the inn. I wanted to look at her, study her face, but I couldn't take my eyes off Stone. He looked confused, then suspicious. "You don't know what you're talking about," he said.

"She's right," a small voice said. We all turned toward Rachel, who had raised her head to address Stone. Her face was a mess, but her voice was low and clear. "It's not fair. Ben didn't do anything, really. We were all just so upset. We didn't know how it would affect him."

"Keep her quiet," Stone said to Sarah. "This ain't about Ben."

Rachel's courage kindled something inside of me. "But it could be," I said.

"No sir," Stone warned me, eyeing me over the top of his gun. "You done enough to him already. We're going outside, that's all you and me got to look forward to."

"Wait," I said, and turned to the others. "You want this to be over. But it's not, not as long as Ben is left out of it."

Again there was a silence. I could feel eyes shifting from one face to another, Stone fighting his own confusion, and my own heart beating in my chest.

"Would it change things," Sarah asked quietly, carefully, "if we brought him back? Took him in again?"

I realized she was talking to me, not Stone. "It would change things for Ben," I said.

Then I realized she meant something else. Slowly the strange sensation stole back over me, the off-balance feeling from earlier that morning. Again my mind filled with the possibility of walking away from the whole thing without exposing it to the world. Only now there was a chance for a better result.

I glanced at Larkin and saw that he too understood Sarah's meaning. Rachel looked up at me from the couch, her face stained with tears. Even she had understanding in her eyes, or maybe it was hope. Stone cocked his head like he was trying to spy out a trick. It was Carl Larkin that spoke up. "We could make a trade," he said.

No one spoke. Stone lowered his gun a few inches. "What trade?" he asked. "What are you talking about?"

"He needs you," Sarah said. "More than anything in the world."

Stone's eyes narrowed, and he blinked twice before lowering the gun a bit farther. Sarah stood up and looked at me, eye to eye, and I met her gaze. This was a negotiation conducted without words, yet without ambiguity.

"Would that end it?" she asked at last.

"Maybe," I said. It was a slim chance, but given the circumstances it seemed worth taking. I would have to have assurances, though. I would have to know that the trade Carl and Sarah were proposing would stick. I turned to Sarah, but before I could speak she put a hand up.

"I'm an innkeeper, remember?" she reminded me. "I take care of people."

"This is different."

"Not so different," she said. I looked for a moment at Rachel. Again I saw the hope in her eyes, a wish that a path would open before her and lead her from the thick woods she was lost in. I turned again and my eyes found Sarah's face.

"It's not just Ben," I said to her. There were, after all, a loaded gun and a murder charge still pointed in my direction. Sarah nodded once, and turned to face Stone. I turned to face him, too.

"You have to promise, too," Sarah said to the sheriff. "We can end it right here."

"What promise?" he growled.

All eyes were on me. "You bring Ben back in, I go home," I said. "Like Carl said, a trade."

"We ain't got no guarantee," Stone growled.

"I'll help you, Fred," she said. "You won't have to do it alone."

"We can all help," Larkin said.

"I don't mean Ben," Stone argued. "He could sell the story to any damn newspaper any damn time."

"But he won't," Sarah said, with more certainty than I felt.

"He gets a little short of money, all of a sudden we're his meal ticket."

Sarah faced Stone squarely. "You have to take the chance," she said to him. He looked at her, then at Larkin, who nodded encouragement. Slowly Stone lowered the gun until it hung at his side.

"I didn't mean to make Ben upset," I told him.

"You don't know the half of it," Stone said accusingly, but his fury was spent. He sounded more worried now, like an upset parent.

"I know it looks like Ben's split into two different people sometimes," I said. "But I think he's half of one person. You're the other half. He needs you. That's the only way he can get whole again."

Stone's eyes narrowed again, and no one spoke. At length he looked down at the gun in his hand. He slipped it back into his holster and mechanically snapped it in place. Without looking up he spoke half to himself, half to the rest of us in the room.

"We're all a little goofed up," he said. "We just want things to go back to normal."

WHEN LARKIN ushered Stone outside a few minutes later, Sarah straightened up the room, then went to the couch and sat beside Rachel. I went to the kitchen sink and drank a glass of water while the sisters spoke to each other in hushed tones. Larkin came back in, this time for Rachel. The two of them said goodbye to Sarah, and then we were alone. I leaned back against the sink as she turned around and leaned against the door. We stayed that way for a while, and I imagine she was thinking along the same lines I was.

"Well," I said, "I told you I would come back."

She smiled wryly. "I figured I would have a little more time to miss you first."

"Will he let me out of town in one piece?"

"I think so," she said. "But I wouldn't hang around if I were you. It'll only rile him up."

We regarded each other a moment. In the silence I felt my heart beating more slowly, felt my breath returning to normal. "So whose idea was it?" I asked finally.

Sarah looked away, then back at me. "I never saw evil like what that man did to Gibbie and Melissa. You see things in movies or on television, and you know it's bad, but it's different when it happens to someone you love."

"Someone like…Gibbie McPhail?"

She nodded. "It just didn't seem right to let something like that pass on through the universe. I had to rebuke it somehow. When the opportunity came, the others went along."

"Just went along?"

Sarah tossed her head and looked out the window. She seemed to grow heavier before my eyes, as if filling with some invisible weight. "Carl and I were living together when Rachel moved here," she said quietly. "After that he decided he wanted to be with her, instead. At first it was hard, but then I found Gibbie."

"Carl left you for your sister." Sarah nodded. "And then Carl's sister Melissa gets your new lover shot dead."

"It wasn't like that exactly, but...I did feel burned."

"So Carl and Rachel, they owed you."

She shrugged. "They went along."

"And Stone?"

"Poor Fred," she sighed. "He really needs someone to love."

"Maybe Ben will be a start."

She nodded introspectively. "Maybe."

I put down my glass. Sarah looked at me across the room, then came around the wood stove to the arm of the couch.

"Are you still mad at me?"

I didn't know how to answer that question, so I asked one of my own. "Why did you take me in that first night? I know it was for the alibi, but you couldn't have known someone would just show up."

She looked down at her hands, a sad smile playing at the corners of her mouth. "Gibbie was always walking into unknown situations and counting on the kindness of strangers," she said, looking up. "I used to tell him that sooner or later he would make a mistake, but he always did it anyway."

"Until the last time."

"Yes. But I liked that quality in him, and I liked it in you." She looked down at her hands again, then up at me. "Plus you look like him a little. I guess I thought you were my reward for ridding the earth of Dick Shammey."

"Some reward," I said.

"I'm proud of you," she protested. "For all of it."

I had no more questions, and no stomach for another gut-wrenching parting. I sighed, picturing my car sitting by the side of a small ridge road.

"You want a ride to your car?" she asked. It was like

the first night all over again, me thinking something and her saying it.

"That's okay," I said. "I'll hitch a ride down on the highway."

She met me at the door with her hand on the knob, but she did not pull open the door. Instead she looked into my face with questioning eyes.

"Remember your promise? To come back and see me, no matter what?" she asked. "Is it still good?"

I looked at her and wished I knew the answer, but I didn't. When she leaned forward and came up on her toes to kiss me, I gently turned my head, letting her lips meet my cheek. When she stood down, I pulled the door open myself.

"You know," she said, wiping something from her eye, "the women keep getting the worst of this whole thing. It's the one part of it I haven't figured out how to fix."

"WHAT'LL IT BE?" the barman asked.

"Scotch and soda, no ice," I said, and dropped a few bills on the bar. It was just after five in the afternoon on Friday. The place was not far from Union Square, and it was starting to fill up with men in suits, women carrying briefcases, and androgynous types from the galleries, boutiques, and advertising agencies that ringed the area. Soon Doug and Marcy would come in, and a couple of my friends from the paper, and maybe Hollis from the morgue, too.

I had also invited my editor from the magazine, but he had a previous engagement and couldn't make it. He liked the story, though, and was going to forward it on to London without requiring any changes. He had also reimbursed me for my expenses, and promised payment for the story as soon as I made any final changes that came from his superiors. For now, I could settle back and reward myself for making a good impression on my first client.

The barman set down the drink. I tasted it and looked around. I was more comfortable in the bars south of Market Street, near the editorial offices of the newspaper, but I had made a conscious choice to investigate some new haunts in other parts of town. If I was going to be a lifestyle writer, I reasoned, I had to sample some other lifestyles besides my own. I focused on the people around me, their attitudes and their interests, but it wasn't long before my mind wandered back to where it had been most of the week. I could see the ocean, the trees, the silvery light in the western sky, a chrome-bright fish leaping from the water...and Sarah, slipping out of her robe and into bed beside me.

I shook that image out of my mind and gulped down some whiskey. I had gone back and forth all week about my deal with her and her friends, wondering if it was the right thing to do and whether there was any way to renegotiate it. All week I kept coming back to the beginning and starting all over again. Now I felt it was time to put an end to the matter once and for all. I thought about Ben, and the healing I hoped he was finding with his brother and the other people in the town. That made me felt better, and it occurred to me that it would not have happened if I had not been able to solve the murder of Dick Shammey.

This was an appealing new perspective, and I felt a small glow of pride begin to spread in my chest. It was true that the killers had not gone to jail following my brilliant investigation, but it was also true that justice, in its own way, had been done. Ben would, perhaps, get better. Rachel would, perhaps, return to Pomo Bluff. Things would, on balance, improve.

In a way, I reflected, it was like catching and releasing a fish. Once you landed it, you could make the fish pay the ultimate price for its mistake in taking your fly. But you also had the choice to literally let the fish off the hook, so it could live to become an even smarter fish. Other fishermen still had a chance to hunt the fish, and the fish had more experience to elude the hunters. It was an overall improvement, provided you made the right choice.

I liked this way of looking at things, and turned it over in my mind for a while. The glow of satisfaction from solving the case remained with me, and for an idle moment I imagined taking my career in a new direction. Instead of changing from an investigative reporter to a lifestyle reporter, I could change from a newspaper investigator to a private investigator. I laughed to myself. If nothing else, I thought, at least I would have plenty of time to fish.

It was just about time for another drink when Doug and Marcy came in. She gave me a friendly kiss and hopped up on the stool next to me. I greeted Doug and pulled out my wallet. Before he could say anything, I handed him a sheaf of bills.

"This is two hundred dollars," he said, looking up expectantly.

I slipped the photos out of my jacket pocket and handed one to him, one to Marcy.

"All right!" she said, and patted me on the back.

"I guess you had great fishing," Doug said.

I couldn't help beaming. "It was just fine."

"I don't think you ever caught a steelhead that big, did you, Doug?" Marcy asked, and winked at me.

He shot her the kind of look husbands shoot wives after that kind of remark. "No, but I caught a wife with a big mouth," he said.

She giggled. "The better to tease you with," she said.

"I've got the gear outside in the car," I said.

"Well, I'm glad you mentioned that," Doug responded. "I just bought a new rod and some reels, so..."

"So what?"

"Why don't you keep that one, so we can go fishing together?"

I got a small lump in my throat that made it impossible to speak. I was saved by the arrival of a couple of my buddies from the paper. Soon everyone was crowding around the photos, laughing and pointing. Marcy in particular was very complimentary of my unkempt appearance. Finally the bartender came and everyone turned to order their drinks. As I put the photos away, Doug took one last look.

"You know," he said, "that really is a pretty big fish."

"You're not going to believe this," I said, "but you should have seen the ones that got away."

# HARVEST OF BONES
## A VERMONT MYSTERY

## NANCY MEANS WRIGHT

Ruth Willmarth, busy working to keep her rural Vermont
dairy farm in a manageable state, is plunged into a mystery. It
starts with a finger bone, and leads to a skeleton.

New neighbor Fay Hubbard has just opened a farmhouse
B&B and finds her home invaded by its original owner, a
gutsy septuagenarian who announces the dead body is that of
her husband—whom she murdered twenty years ago.

The bizarre discovery puts Ruth and Fay in the middle of a
twisted history of hatred, blackmail and murder, as deep and
dark as the rich Vermont soil.

*Available October 1999 at your favorite retail outlet.*

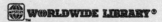

**WORLDWIDE LIBRARY®**

Visit us at www.worldwidemystery.com          WNMW325

# Take 2 books and a surprise gift FREE!

---

## SPECIAL LIMITED-TIME OFFER

---

**Mail to:  The Mystery Library™**
**3010 Walden Ave.**
**P.O. Box 1867**
**Buffalo, N.Y. 14240-1867**

**YES!** Please send me **2 free books** from the Mystery Library™ and my free surprise gift. Then send me 3 mystery books, first time in paperback, every month. Bill me only $4.19 per book plus 25¢ delivery and applicable sales tax, if any*. There is no minimum number of books I must purchase. I can always return a shipment at your expense and cancel my subscription. Even if I never buy another book from the Mystery Library™, **the 2 free books and surprise gift are mine to keep forever.**

415 WEN CJQN

| | | |
|---|---|---|
| Name | (PLEASE PRINT) | |
| Address | | Apt. No. |
| City | State | Zip |

MYS98

It's

**NOW OR NEVER**

## For three women who find themselves in danger...because of the men they love.

Award-winning author

**ANNE STUART**

brings you three heart-stopping stories about intrigue, danger and the mysteries of falling in love.

**Now or Never** by Anne Stuart, coming to a bookstore near you in November 1999.

Available wherever Harlequin and Silhouette books are sold.

**HARLEQUIN®**
*Makes any time special* ™

Visit us at www.romance.net

PSBR31199